She'd been tracking him a long time.

She still rode out to the Tunstall ranch virtually every day hoping to get her rifle on Billy. Her life had no other meaning. She ate to stay alive so she could kill Billy. She took no pleasure in whiskey or romance or sex. She had tried all of them from time to time but they gave her no solace whatsoever. Her sleep was restless and rarely fulfilling.

Billy did not appear.

Once, she mistook another man for Billy and she felt an almost orgasmic excitement. At last, the moment was here. At last.

But it was not Billy, and she felt foolish. She should have better control over her feelings than to fancy that another man was Billy. That was her only ambition: to stay in control of herself so that when the time came . . .

STORM RIDERS

ED GORMAN

BERKLEY BOOKS, NEW YORK

STORM RIDERS

A Berkley Book / published by arrangement with
the author

PRINTING HISTORY
Berkley edition / November 1999

ISBN: 0-425-17192-2

BERKLEY®
Berkley Books are published by The Berkley Publishing Group,
a division of Penguin Putnam Inc.,
375 Hudson Street, New York, New York 10014.
BERKLEY and the "B" logo
are trademarks belonging to Penguin Putnam Inc.

PRINTED IN THE UNITED STATES OF AMERICA

10 9 8 7 6 5 4 3 2 1

Note to the Reader

As you'll soon see, this is my version of the Billy the Kid story. I took liberties with time and place by using fictional names and places, but I did try to present a realistic portrait of Billy. At least as I see him In writing this book, and doing all the research, I came to form a coherent picture of Billy. The myth had little to do with the reality.

—EG

To some of the good ones along the way:
Ed and Sylvia Popelka, Bob Gibson, Mike Kane,
Gerry Rayman, Dick Weltz, Tom Owen, and Irv Janey.

Historian Nancy Hamilton helped me considerably with this book, as did Sue Reider and Ron Adkins.

STORM
RIDERS

Part One

Part One

1

A LOT OF town boys had crushes on Mae Roberts. This was in Keokuk, Iowa, in the spring of 1870.

Mae lived by the creek on the edge of town, in a tiny place that was more shack than house. She was sixteen and an orphan, her father, a drummer, having been killed in a stagecoach robbery in Texas. He'd sold dental appliances, and his company had asked him to visit Texas to establish a territory there. She got a telegram from the high sheriff of Waco explaining what had happened. She never forgot the name of the man who the high sheriff said had killed her father and then escaped capture.

Until that time, Mae had been pretty much an average girl. She and her father grew most of what they ate, so when she wasn't in school, at least in the warm months, she worked in the garden. Her mother had died of consumption two years earlier but had shown Mae how to work the earth.

After the murder of her father, Mae changed. She no longer attended school. She no longer joined other girls in games or gossip. She no longer found time to flirt back with the town boys who rode out on their bicycles to visit her.

About the only time she was seen, in fact, was hauling glass bottles and cans back from town. She set them up as targets down by the creek and spent two or three hours a day shooting at them with an old Colt she'd found in one of her father's drawers. A lone woman named Cecily showed her how to shoot.

Cecily had been in the war as a nurse in a field hospital and had participated in a locally famous battle with rebs on the Missouri side of the Des Moines River, in a slave trade town called Athens.

During this time, Mae's looks suffered, too. Oh, she was still the prettiest girl in the valley. But there was a hardness—even a craziness—in those blue eyes that made most folks uncomfortable. When she did stop to talk to people, the subject was always the same: the man who'd killed her father. According to *The Police Gazette* and various dime novels, he was just about the most feared gunnie of them all. And he was getting more feared all the time.

The year she was eighteen, a backhander—that being a man who apprentices to a blacksmith—came to town with his fine fancy mustache and his beguiling Irish tenor. He became the topic of many a dinner conversation, the women inevitably for him, the men inevitably against him, though they couldn't quite say why. They were jealous was why. He was a decent young man of twenty-two. He married Mae three months after meeting her. The town noticed right away how he changed her. She didn't spend all her time killing cans and bottles. And there was something like humor and kindness in her eyes again, the way there had once been, and she was pleasant to be around. A year-and-a-half into their marriage, the local doc told her she was pregnant. Mae and her husband glowed with true happiness and contentment. Four months into her pregnancy, on a buggy trip back from a nearby town, a cold and rainy night in spring, a buggy neck yoke snapped, spooking the horse and sending the buggy down into a steep ravine where it smashed against a shallow and rocky creek bed. Mae's husband, Bob, was killed when his head cracked against a small boulder. Mae lost the baby nine hours later in the doc's office.

The town saw the old Mae again. The old, cold, distracted Mae, her eyes turned inward, witnessing some terrible kind of spiritual struggle.

Three weeks after the buggy accident, Mae bought a train ticket and left town. She understood now that she was part of some unfathomable cosmic drama. Her father's role had been to be murdered; and it was Mae's role to avenge that murder. Her one attempt at happiness, her husband and her child, had been slapped away from her by the dark gods, who wanted her to get on with her true calling.

She was twenty-one years old that sweet, warm June afternoon, the day she left Keokuk, and nobody in that town was ever to see her or hear from her again.

2

EARLE CONLON WAS just finishing up with his saddle-bags when somebody started knocking frantically on the door of the small hotel room.

"Hurry up, Marshal! It's me! Deputy Glencoe!"

Larry Glencoe was a "nephew." There were a lot of nephews in law enforcement these days. Man takes a job as a sheriff, as Stievers had, he can put two, three of his nephews to work as deputies. Glencoe was actually a little bit better than the average nephew. He wasn't mean or gun-happy. In fact, there was a sweet-natured side to him that was appealing in a sort of dopey way.

Conlon, a tall, slender man with graying hair and a trail-dusty blue suit, went to the door and opened it.

Glencoe looked pale and jumpy, his extra thirty pounds jiggling beneath the somewhat theatrical western shirt he wore. He'd ordered himself a special badge from Kansas City, an outsize one every bit as theatrical as his fancy shirt. Nephews were inclined to such things.

"It's Uncle Henry," young Glencoe said breathlessly.

"What about him?"

"His heart. You know how bad it is. We was talkin' in the office, just talkin', and he just fell down. Grabbed his chest and rolled his eyes and fell right down on the floor. I had to have Lester go get Doc Talbot." He sounded young and on the verge of tears. His uncle was a decent man.

Lester was a black man who worked ten hours a week at the jail. He'd gotten into some minor trouble but couldn't pay the fine, so he was working it off.

"Where is he now?"

"Doc Talbot has got him over at the office. You better come quick, Marshal. My uncle wants to talk to you real bad."

Conlon knew what the sheriff wanted to say to him and resented it. He'd been telling Henry Stievers for two years to get himself an heir apparent and start training him. Stievers had had a bad heart for years. No way was his nephew ready to become sheriff.

Conlon looked around the room. Too many rooms like this the last eight years of his life, ever since coming west from a nice, easy life as a police lieutenant in New York City.

But then a new mayor had been elected, one who'd run a campaign of cleaning up the police department. Conlon hadn't been any more crooked than any other

cop of similar status—he mostly covered up crimes
for rich people—but he decided to resign before the
reformers worked their way down the line to him. He
came west the day of his thirty-second birthday. He
had a cousin who was a congressman and who had
something on somebody in the Justice Department.
Following a routine signature by President Hayes, he
became a U.S. Marshal, assigned to working with
sheriff's offices in Texas and New Mexico. He hadn't
accepted a dime in pay-offs or covered up a single
crime. Life was easier that way, and he didn't hate
himself quite so much for ruining a good marriage by
devil rum and women no better than he was. He still
wrote to his two daughters, but they never seemed
enthusiastic about hearing from him. They liked their
stepfather very much and talked about him constantly
in the few letters they wrote back. He was a New
York police lieutenant, too, but an honest one, one
who always remembered birthdays and never cheated
on his wife.

"I got to get back now," Glencoe said. "I'll tell my
uncle you're on the way."

Conlon nodded and went back to finishing up with
his carpetbag. He'd hoped to be out of this sleepy,
little, Mexican-style town by one o'clock this afternoon. That looked doubtful now.

3

HE WALKED ALONG the dusty main street, passing between crowded board sidewalks that fronted a variety of false-fronted stores. In the shade of a building, a man with a good tenor voice sang a melancholy song in Spanish, while a half-dozen Mexican children played ring-around-the-rosie in the baking sunlight. Sombreros seemed to be on most male heads. The Mexican culture had taken some getting used to over the years, but now Conlon liked it and understood it better. Except for the machismo. He got tired of angry young men with something to prove.

He was halfway to the doc's office when a shay, one of those two-seater carriages, pulled up alongside him and a stout, bearded man said, "Little warm for a suit, isn't it, Conlon?"

Conlon smiled. "I might ask the same of you."

Governor Lew Adair returned his smile. He was wearing a vested suit as well. Adair was known in New Mexico as the man sent here to stop the range wars, particularly the one known as the Furner County War. In the east, he was better known as the author of a best-selling novel called *God's Tears*. He was now writing something called *God's Triumph*. That was all anybody knew so far. The title. Over brandy at his sprawling house, he'd tell you that he planned to have it finished in the spring.

Adair said, "You heard about Henry?"

"I heard. I'm on my way there now."

"He was supposed to come over to my place this afternoon."

The horse harnessed to the shay dropped a big jade-colored road apple that instantly attracted a half-dozen noisy flies.

"That's too bad," Conlon said.

"Too bad for you, you mean," Adair said. "Now you'll have to come over."

"I'm leaving town."

Adair shook his head. "Not any more you're not, my friend. I've got territorial business, and, as a U.S. Marshal, you've been sworn to help me."

Conlon sighed. He knew there was no use arguing. Adair was right. U.S. Marshals, who doubled as county sheriffs, were at the disposal of territorial governors.

Conlon said, "Any words for Henry?"

Adair shook his head. "You know I didn't like him."

Conlon nodded.

"Law officers swear an oath to uphold the law. He's like Brady was when Brady was sheriff—just a messenger boy for Barcroft and his cronies." John Barcroft was a cattle baron fighting against an equally ruthless batch of would-be cattle barons headed by a man named Tunstall. Neither Adair nor Conlon liked either side. Adair sighed. "He's probably not going to make it, is he?"

"Doesn't sound like it."

"Then give him my best."

Conlon laughed. "That's what I was going to do anyway. Wouldn't do for the governor to be cursing men on their death beds."

"I suppose it *would* be a little unseemly, wouldn't it?"

Conlon took off his black Stetson and wiped a finger around the sweaty leather band inside.

"My place at three o'clock."

"I'll be there."

Adair snapped the reins, and the shay drove off.

4

THE DOC WAS young and from the East, and that meant he'd likely gotten in some trouble back there.

Young docs who were any good stayed in the civilization of the eastern seaboard. The ones with low grades, the ones who'd killed a patient or two too many in surgery, or the ones who'd elected to have sex with their prettier patients—they were generally the ones who came west.

And they were generally the best docs out here. The indigenous ones still practiced a brand of medicine that incorporated Indian medicine, granny medicine, and anything else they'd been able to cadge from the medical tomes they'd scanned in their spare time. Most of these men and women had no degree of any kind.

So the eastern docs, despite their background, were welcomed out here. They were gradually replacing the older kind of docs, and, as a result, western medicine was getting better all the time.

Sheriff Henry Stievers lay on a cot in Dr. Talbot's back office. An Indian blanket had been laid over him. Only his neck and face were uncovered. The red blanket rose and fell with his massive belly. He resembled a corpse except for two things: the occasional whistle when he exhaled and a minor tic in his right eyelid.

"Maybe we should let him sleep," Conlon whispered as they peeked in on Glencoe.

"He said he wanted to talk to you," Talbot said, "that it was urgent. Just go over and say his name a few times. He'll wake up."

Conlon was uncomfortable around dying people. He knew that soon enough he'd be one of them. It was bad luck to see them. A regular sheriff, he saw a lot of dying. A U.S. Marshal was more of an administrator than anything else.

Henry Glencoe smelled of sleep and spittle and sweat. He had a lot of liver spots on his big hands that lay on his stomach the way they would when he was in his coffin.

Conlon reached down and touched Stievers's shoulder. "Henry."

Henry shuddered. Not a dramatic shudder, just a small one, like an afterthought, and Conlon knew he was dead.

"Sonofabitch," Conlon said. Then, "Doc, you better get in here."

The young doctor came into the room. He had a pipe stuck in the corner of his mouth and a stethoscope coiled snakelike around his neck. He looked almost hopelessly young, an impression increased when he stumbled across the threshold on his way in, knocking ashes from his pipe. "Good thing I never went for ballet," Talbot said, smiling at his own clumsiness. He toed pipe ash into the wooden floor. "What's wrong?"

"What's wrong is he's dead."

"But he was alive just a few minutes ago."

It seemed a silly thing for a doctor to say.

"Check him for yourself," Conlon said.

Talbot went over and took a look. "I'll be damned. He *is* dead."

"He tell you anything?"

Talbot looked back at him. "About what?"

"About anything that sounded important."

"He told me about his grandkids. One of them fell off a horse recently and sprained his ankle."

"Anything about the sheriff's office, I mean."

Talbot looked back down at the dead man. "No. Nothing like that." He checked pulse zones for the next few minutes and then slipped the blanket from beneath the arms and hands. He drew the blanket over everything now, including the face.

"Guess I'd better go find his missus."

"I'll tell her," Conlon said.

"You'd be doing me a favor if you would. She's an emotional woman."

"You sure he didn't tell you anything?"

Talbot shook his head. "Nothing about the sheriff's department." He let his gaze narrow, fixed on Conlon's face. "You don't sound real broken up about this."

"I didn't know him very well."

"You've been here three weeks."

"That doesn't mean we were friends or anything. What the hell're you hinting at?"

Talbot said, "A lot of people say you were pretty hard on Henry."

"I just wanted him to do his job was all."

"His wife told me he wasn't able to sleep or eat very well since you came to town."

Conlon stared at him. "So you're saying I killed him?"

"No, but I'm saying you could show a little sympathy for a man you may have pushed a little too hard."

Conlon sighed. He wasn't good at expressing himself, and this kind of conversation always made him self-conscious. "As lawmen went, he was pretty damned good. But he was in Barcroft's pocket, and that was a real big problem for both the town and him. I was just doing my job, pushing him to try to resolve this damned range war of yours. I'm sorry if I made him sicker than he was."

"I hope you'll be a little bit nicer about him to his widow. You don't have to say he was in Barcroft's pocket."

Conlon smiled coldly. "Any other advice for me, doc?"

5

HE WAS HALFWAY up the street when he saw Mae, and he started feeling things he didn't want to feel.

Mae was this solitary prairie woman, no more than twenty-three, who'd been Stievers's assistant. The sheriff had shown good sense there. His three nephews were worthless. Mae had quickly organized the office and read all the new books on crime detection and the orderly way to assemble clues on the spot where a murder had taken place. Back east, this kind of detection was pretty much taken for granted. Out here, it was scoffed at by the pot-bellied lawmen who still believed that most crimes could be solved by pistol-whipping confessions out of Mexicans in the back room of the jailhouse.

Mae stood on the stoop of the Furner County

Courthouse, which held the Murphy-Dolan store downstairs, and the courtroom and jail upstairs. A lot of the so-called Furner County War was fought right here in the courtroom, with each side filing endless legal petitions to punish the other. An area of rich grass like this—which three irrigation systems had made even more fertile—was perfect for raising cattle. And for raising greed. The Barcroft faction of the war owned the Murphy-Dolan store, meaning that the Barcroft folks had lunch every day with the same judge who ruled on all their petitions. The judge had been long ago bought and paid for.

Mae was talking to a small crowd. No doubt about the topic—the health of Sheriff Glencoe. Mae was a slender young woman who usually wore a blue workshirt and cords. Even in a homely outfit like this, her quiet beauty had an almost mesmerizing effect on Conlon. He'd whored himself out several years back. Now he was looking for a woman of his own. Mae had never paid much attention to him.

He walked to the head of the crowd, pushing a little harder than he needed to. Crowds had always scared him. He'd once stood helplessly by in New York as a crowd of drunken whites lynched a Jamaican. He'd tried to save the man but the crowd turned on him, beating him severely, taking his gun away. All he'd been able to do was watch. He'd never understood the dynamics or the dark soul of crowds before. Ever since, he'd understood crowds all too well.

He stepped up on the stoop next to Mae. He said to the crowd, "Sheriff Stievers just died. Funeral arrangements'll be announced a little later. If you want to be a help, you can take some food to the widow. You all know where she lives. In the meantime, I'll be in charge here until the city council figures out a new man."

"Whose side you gonna be on, Marshal?" a man asked. "The Barcroft side or Pecos's?"

"Neither side," Conlon said. "I'm on the side of the law." What a fine and noble thought that was. In his cop days, he always laughed at law enforcement officers who offered such bouquets of flowery sentiments. But now he found it a natural thing to say because it was the truth. He didn't plan to cotton to either side in this damned senseless range war.

"You gonna keep on Stievers's nephews?" somebody else asked.

"That'll be the decision of the man who takes Stievers's place. I'm just filling in for a few days."

"You gonna work with Governor Adair?" a woman asked. "Glencoe didn't seem to like him much."

"I've got a lot of respect for Governor Adair," Conlon said. "So, yes, I plan to work with him." He looked over at Mae. "We've got work to do now, in the office. We need to break this up."

The crowd had learned what it needed to. Glencoe was dead; there'd be a permanent replacement soon.

"You handle people well," Mae said, watching the crowd split up.

"They scare me."

"Are you serious?"

He told her about New York.

"I don't think most people are like that."

"That's what scares me," he said. "I think we're all like that. The right time, the right place, our better instincts get away from us."

She watched him a moment. He saw real curiosity in her eyes, as if she'd just now realized that the man she'd been working next to for the past few weeks was a living, breathing being. "I can't imagine you involved in anything like that, Marshal. You seem like a really honorable man."

He thought of New York. Covering up the crimes

of the wealthy. Hanging out on the edges of that society and destroying his marriage in the process. Oh,
yes, he was an honorable sonofabitch, all right.

"C'mon," he said, "we've got work to do."

They walked down to the sheriff's office.

6

AN HOUR AFTER finishing up with Conlon, Mae rode
out to the Tunstall ranch. The idea was simple. With
the help of her field glasses, she'd get a good, clear
look at Billy. He'd be out riding alone for some reason. And then she'd take the Winchester from its
scabbard and kill him.

She'd been tracking him a long time. Twice, when
he was still called Billy Dodge and spent most of his
time rustling cattle, she'd come close to assassinating
him. One night he'd stood buck naked in a whore-
house window. She'd had her Winchester all ready to
go when a whore wandered by and saw her and
screamed. Billy disappeared instantly from the window and began pumping rounds in Mae's direction.
A second time she'd been about to shoot him from a
tree. He'd been riding fence, only the fence didn't
belong to him. He was checking it out for some rustling he planned for later. But sunlight glinted off her
rifle and he saw her and spurred away fast. Both these
missed opportunities had been in Silver City.

She followed him to Arizona, where he killed four
more men and was once again part of a gang of rus-

tlers. He seemed to like the life: a little rustling, a little killing. It was clear he enjoyed his reputation. By this time, he was known to lawmen and dime novel hacks alike as Billy Pecos. Almost as legendary as his prowess with guns was his prowess with women. He had the boyish good looks of a scamp, the naughty but not fatal persona that evoked the maternal in many women. They wanted to smother and protect him with their love. Which was fine with Billy. Who could say no to so many women? Mae couldn't be objective about his looks. She hated him too much.

Eventually, Arizona got too full of law for Billy. The West was becoming more or less civilized. Hell, Washington even had certain segments of the U.S. Army riding down outlaws. Word was New Mexico was a better place for folk like Billy.

Billy settled in Furner County, on the ranch of an Englishman named Tunstall. It was often said that the only people Billy was loyal to were certain older men in his life, substitute fathers, really. While Tunstall wasn't that much older than Billy, Billy liked the man's polish and education and determination to make his way in this new world. The Furner County War was pretty simple when you boiled it down— rich John Barcroft controlled most of the dry goods sold in the county by virtue of the Mason-Dolan store in Furner. He also controlled 95 percent of all beef contracted to the U.S. Army. He had all the judges and lawmen in the area bribed and blackmailed. They had no choice but to go along with him. Tunstall and his group wanted to open a competing general store in Furner, and they wanted the opportunity to sell beef at a lower price to the Army. Barcroft saw to it that they didn't succeed on either count.

Tunstall and a few other ranchers decided to challenge Barcroft, and that was how the range war started. Both sides had hired gunnies. Blood stained the grazing lands and seeped into the river. There was no one in Furner County who had not been affected by the war in some respect. The turning point came nine weeks before when Barcroft's friend Sheriff Brady—or one of his deputies—killed Tunstall in cold blood. Billy was so enraged that he killed Brady, and Brady's first deputy Glencoe took over, replete with nephews. Federal authorities brought in war hero and lawyer Lew Adair, a bright, stern but fair-minded man to settle the dispute as quickly as possible.

None of this deterred Mae. She still rode out here virtually every day hoping to get her rifle on Billy. Her life had no other meaning. She ate to stay alive so she could kill Billy. She took no pleasure in whiskey or romance or sex. She had tried all of them from time to time but they gave her no solace whatsoever. She ate only enough to stay alive. Her sleep was restless and rarely fulfilling.

Billy did not appear.

Once, she mistook another man for Billy and she felt an almost orgasmic excitement. At last, the moment was here. At last.

But it was not Billy, and she felt foolish. She should have better control over her feelings than to fancy that another man was Billy. That was her only ambition—to stay in control of herself so that when the time came . . .

She waited an hour and a half and then rode back to town.

7

GOVERNOR ADAIR WAS staying in a house on the edge of Furner, a two-story white house with an abundance of neatly kept lawn and an even greater abundance of shade trees. A golden Labrador lazed in the shade, with two white kittens doing the same nearby. If only humans could abide each other so well.

Conlon had walked out here. Bad food and lack of exercise were starting to flesh out his belly. Graying hair was enough. He didn't want a pot to go along with it.

A timid Mexican woman greeted him at the door and led him inside to a study. The house was at least ten degrees cooler than the outside. Drapes were drawn. Sunlight was a demon to be repelled.

The study smelled of brandy and cigars. It was small but neat, everything mahogany and leather. A large globe stood on a five-shelf bookcase. The walls were decorated with a variety of Mexican artifacts, the most imposing of which was an Aztec-era rendering of a god who was also a gladiator of some kind. The crude drawing radiated with violence.

Adair came in a few minutes later. He shook hands, got them both whiskeys, and then sat across the desk from Conlon. Adair looked uncomfortable, shifting around in his chair. "Hemorrhoids."

"Mine flare up sometimes, too. They're no fun."

Adair positioned himself in the chair again and said, "You're not going to like what I have to say, Marshal."

"I appreciate the warning."

"It's going to strike you as naive. And maybe even a little bit crazy."

Conlon smiled. "I can't wait to hear it."

Adair squirmed in his chair, getting comfortable. With his full beard and gleaming blue eyes, he had the visage of an Old Testament prophet. "I'm going to declare an amnesty for everybody involved in the range war."

Conlon said, "Even the killers?"

"That's where you'll think I'm naive. But yes." He paused. "It's worked in other territories."

And so it had. Amnesties had brought at least temporary peace to a number of violent spots in the Midwest and West. The key word was "temporary." Most of the truces were of relatively short duration. Some men needed to be imprisoned or killed. There was no way around it.

"I take it you're including Billy?"

"Of course."

"He killed a lawman."

"A lawman who was basically a part of the Barcroft operation. I don't think he deserved the term lawman, if you want me to be honest."

Conlon wondered what an honorable man like Adair would make of Conlon's years on the Metropolitan Police Force in New York City, where bribes were coin of the realm and Conlon had done more than all right for himself. Conlon said, "You're going to piss off a lot of lawmen letting Billy go free. Sheriff Brady had a lot of friends, even if he was involved with Barcroft."

"I'm also going to piss off the esteemed county attorney of Furner," Adair said, "another man who is in the pocket of Barcroft and his cronies. Bill Stockton's going to fight me on this."

"What if Billy won't do it?"

Adair smiled. "That's where you come in, my friend."

"Me?"

Adair nodded. "I'm going to be very honest with you. I need more time to finish this book I'm working on. So I have two reasons for wanting to get this range war settled. One, I hate bloodshed. I had plenty of that in the war." Adair had been a much-decorated Union Army officer. "And two, I want to be able to spend more time on my novel—which means getting back home and not living here in somebody else's house."

"I still don't see how I can help."

"Very simple," Adair said. "Right now, Billy can't do anything. He's pinned down at the ranch. There's a $15,000 bounty on his head. Any direction he moves, there'll be lawmen and bounty hunters gunning for him. I can't believe he wants to live that way. So you ride out there and tell him that I'm going to give him amnesty if he rides in and gives himself up. He won't even have to stay in jail. I've arranged for a house he can live in here until we get everything set down on paper and agreed to by all parties."

"What about the county attorney?"

Adair shrugged. "He wants to be the next governor. How'll it look if I go around telling everybody how he stopped me from stopping the Furner County War? He won't like granting Billy amnesty, but he won't have any choice."

"You sound pretty confident."

"I am."

"Are you also confident that I'm not going to get my ass shot off when I ride out to Billy's ranch?"

"You're a professional lawman."

"That doesn't mean I'm invincible."

"No, but a U.S. Marshal's badge is going to impress Billy. Especially when you show him the letter I've written him."

Conlon sighed. "You make it sound real easy."

"Billy won't be able to turn it down. He's young. He wants a life. And being a gunnie's no life at all."

"When am I supposed to do all this?"

"I was thinking tomorrow morning. Bright and early."

Conlon smiled. "Well, that'll at least give me time to buy my burial plot. I don't want to spend time worrying about it—maybe I'll head out there today."

"You like another drink?"

"No, thanks."

"I'm told you broke the news to Stievers's widow."

"I was supposed to. But her nephew beat me to it."

"He's something, isn't he?" Adair said. Then he made a sour face. "Small town lawmen and their relatives. It's enough to make you root for the outlaws."

Conlon laughed as he stood up, lifting his Stetson from the governor's desk. "Little town on the Rio Grande where a sheriff has a cousin of his as his number-three deputy. His cousin's blind."

Adair stood up, grinning. "That's the best one I've heard yet. Too bad he isn't deaf, too."

Conlon clinched his hat on. "By the way, I read your novel last month and really enjoyed it. What's the new one about?"

"About Jesus," Adair said. "I call it *God's Triumph*. But that's all I'll say. Bad luck to talk about books in progress."

Adair walked Conlon to the door. "I'll wait to hear from you tomorrow."

"Me," Conlon said, "or the undertaker."

8

CONLON HAD A clean, orderly desk waiting for him. He sat down and looked at the sheet of white paper lying on the freshly polished desk. It listed four items that he, as acting sheriff, had to attend to in the next few days.

1. Council meeting 8 A.M. tomorrow

2. Schoolhouse appearance—meet kids 1 P.M.

3. Horse auction 2 P.M.

4. Wake for Sheriff Glencoe tomorrow at 7:30 P.M., Monahan Funeral Home

All this was written in an easy and attractively feminine hand. Glencoe had said that Mae was indispensable, and he obviously hadn't been exaggerating. Conlon poured himself a cup of coffee. He wondered where she was. It had been a while since he'd found himself missing a particular woman. But after a few hours of being around her, he'd taken every opportunity to be around her again.

He knew he should be leaving for the Tunstall ranch to make his pitch to Billy, but he was in no hurry. He wasn't old enough to do something this dangerous. Nobody ever is.

He went upstairs and looked at the prisoners. They were a sorry lot, two white drifters, young, smelly, sullen. They'd beaten up and robbed a Mexican who'd been full of payday beer. To Glencoe's credit, he hadn't made any distinction in skin color. You beat up a man, you paid the price. Period. Unless, of course, you belonged to Barcroft. That was a different matter. But there was no way Conlon could feel morally superior to that, now was there? Not after accepting all the rich-boy bribes he had back in New York.

When he went back up front, Mae was there, washing the windows.

She didn't seem to hear him come in at first, giving him a moment to admire her backside. Over the years, Conlon had perceived that there were many kinds of backsides—sexy ones, arrogant ones, even angry ones. Mae's, fittingly, was somehow quiet and sweet, and Conlon liked it a whole hell of a lot, especially now that she was standing on her tiptoes and her faded Levi's had shaped themselves perfectly to her bottom.

"Hi," he said.

She turned. "Oh, hi."

"You sure work hard."

She smiled. "That's what they pay me for. Sorry I missed you. I had to run down the street and get some more cleaner."

He went to his desk and sat down. "Thanks for the list."

"I thought it might help. Since you're going to be here for a few days."

"If I'm alive," he said, and he tried to make it sound like a joke, but the anxiety was clear in his tone.

"If you're alive? Did something happen?"

She walked away from the window, came over, and stood in front of his desk.

"Governor Adair wants to give Billy Pecos amnesty."

"Are you joking?" She seemed astonished, even angry. "He's a killer."

"That's what I said. But Adair argues that both the Barcroft and the Tunstall sides have killed people, so that the only way to end the range war is to give them amnesty."

"I just can't believe that he'd let Billy go free."

He was watching her carefully. She was doing her best to contain real rage. It was understandable enough that she wouldn't agree with Adair's position. But she seemed to be taking this almost personally.

"Are you all right?" he asked.

She nodded, obviously making a conscious effort to calm herself. "I guess I was just a little surprised is all." Then, "I take it Adair wants you to go see Billy."

"That's the general idea. He thinks Billy's going to be very impressed with my U.S. Marshal's badge."

"And you're scared?"

He laughed. "You don't mince words, do you?"

"Nothing to be ashamed of, Marshal. You don't know what you're riding into out there. Billy's very moody. Very moody. Who wouldn't be scared?"

He studied her again. "You seem to have some kind of personal stake in this, the way you reacted and all."

She clearly took her time answering. "No personal stake. It's just that I know what a snake he is. He killed Sheriff Brady. Not to mention at least twenty other people."

"That's probably an exaggerated number."

"Close enough for me," she said.

He paused. "I get the feeling that there's a lot about you I don't know."

"That's funny."

"Oh?"

"I get the same feeling about you."

He leaned forward, the swivel chair squeaking. "Maybe we could have supper tonight."

"You really think that's a good idea?"

"Why not?"

"I just don't want you to get any wrong ideas. I'm not what you'd call available, Marshal."

"You have a boyfriend?"

"No."

"Fiancé?"

"No."

"Husband?"

She giggled like a little girl he was teasing. He loved the sound of her giggle. "Not hardly. I just mean I'm not available—in here." She touched her heart.

"I see."

"I don't have time for it."

"It's pretty nasty stuff."

She grinned. She had a kid grin, and it was every bit as fetching as her giggle. "Yes. Nasty stuff."

"I just figured maybe you'd want to help me celebrate getting back alive from Tunstall's place."

"I guess I hadn't thought of it that way."

"Help a weary old lawman feel good about still being alive."

"You're not *that* old."

"Now there's a compliment."

She giggled again. "All right. When I get done working for the day, I'll go home and clean up and then come back here and wait for you." Then, "You really going out there?"

He stood up. "I am."

"You could take one of the nephews."

"No offense, but I think I'd rather go alone."

"Yeah, I guess I know what you mean. I just can't believe you're going out there alone."

He walked over and grabbed himself a rifle from the case. "Like you say, that's what you pay me for."

He pulled on his hat and headed out the door.

9

THE EASIEST THING would be to kill him in his sleep.

Sam Bowen had, in fact, considered just such a move last night, while Billy had lain three cots away in the bunkhouse.

Sam was a nineteen-year-old from Tremaine, Nebraska, who'd come west to avoid a jail sentence for drunkenly smashing out store windows the night of his seventeenth birthday. An orphan raised by a minister, nobody had much wanted him around any more, certainly not the minister or his wife, and so the judge gave him his choice—stay in Tremaine in county lock-up, or high tail his shabby ass westward. Thus was the territory of New Mexico blessed with one more aimless hothead eager to convince people—as well as himself—that he was one real bad cowpoke.

There were two problems with Sam's daydreams of being respected and feared as a gunnie: one, he was half-blind in one eye; and two, he couldn't shoot for shit. Not even *three* eyes would have helped him. He just plain didn't have the knack.

So it was that when medium-tough gunnies wanted to push people around, the first one they grabbed was

Sam. During his eleven months on the Tunstall ranch, his cot had been set on fire, he had been de-pantsed on four occasions, and he had been forced to chew so much chewing tobacco that he couldn't quit vomiting (or shitting, given the strange effects of tobacco) for forty-eight hours. He got mad, of course, and plotted all sorts of vengeance. But somehow he never got around to acting on it.

But this situation was different.

Some of the Tunstall cowboys had met some gals in the adjoining county. This was the sixth time the gals had visited the ranch for a debauch that would have sent ministers shrieking from the pulpit. The second time the gals visited, Sam let it be known that he had given his heart to a full-figured strawberry blonde named Trudy. She had about the cutest dimples and the biggest tits the smitten Sam had ever seen. Sam had never been in love before, and he'd never even suspected that love could sometimes be as painful as it was pleasurable. He'd never known about missing someone, about being afraid of saying the wrong thing, or not saying the right thing. And he'd never known about jealousy, either. Oh, he was crazy jealous. He'd catch somebody even looking at her—especially at her tits—and something wild took him, something dark and barely controllable. He didn't want anybody else even glancing at her. Fortunately, the Tunstall boys were pretty good about respecting these kinds of property rights. A fella announced that a gal was his property, his wish was generally respected.

Except for that sonofabitch Billy.

Billy had two moods—real friendly, or real *not* friendly. It was his not-friendly mood that had won him his reputation. So what did Billy do last night at the party? He looked around and decided that the gal he wanted to take down by the creek—a favorite spot of Billy's when he was feeling randy—and put the pig to was none other than Sam's gal Trudy.

Sam was drunk enough to put up a fight. Billy was understanding about it for a while. He said, "Hell, in the mornin' you won't even remember it, Sam." He said, "I'm feelin' kinda low right now, Sam. All I wanna do is borrow her for an hour or so." He said, "Sam, if it'll make ya feel any better, next time I'm sweet on a gal, I'll let *you* take her down by the creek, how's that?"

Billy didn't like to be a bad guy. He liked people to like him. So when he was stealing your girl, he tried to sweet talk you just as much as he was trying to sweet talk *her*.

But there was no mistaking one thing: Billy was going to have his way. He'd buy you drinks, he'd slap your back, he'd flatter you, he might even promise to shoot a person or two for you. But he was going to take your gal, and you weren't going to stop him.

This was evident last night to everybody but Sam.

Sam kept bitching. Sam kept saying no. Sam kept saying she was *his* girl. Trudy herself didn't say anything. If she said she *didn't* want to go with Billy, he might shoot her. If she said she *did* want to go with him, Sam might shoot her. She kept silent.

And then it happened.

Here they were standing no more than three feet apart, and Billy whipped out his six-shooter and put it right on the tip of Sam's nose. Sam looked funny as hell, all cross-eyed looking at the barrel of the Colt pressed against his nose, but everybody knew enough not to laugh.

"I'm takin' her down to the creek, Sam," Billy said, "and it's as simple as that."

Sam started to go for his gun, but his friends grabbed him before he could complete that disastrous mistake.

They poured enough liquor down him to knock him out, and then they carried him to the bunkhouse and tossed him on his cot. Straight moonshine has that kind of effect on a man, any man.

He woke up in that sweaty, fearful land that only drunks know—having to piss, with a dry mouth, fighting a throbbing, stabbing headache, wondering where exactly he was, and wondering, even more, what the hell had happened.

And then it was there, all of it, Billy and Trudy, and so many feelings seized him then: rage and jealousy and humiliation. Three or four times during the night he'd slipped his gun from its holster and started up from bed. But something always happened to make him lie right back down again, somebody else getting up for a piss, or somebody in a nearby cot sounding like they were coming awake, or his own headache being so bad that he had no choice but to rest for a time, being so shaky and weak and sweaty.

Empty his six-shooter into Billy. That's what he wanted to do. Didn't care about it not being a fair fight, didn't care about Billy being asleep, didn't care what the others would say afterward. Hell, Sam, you didn't even give him no chance.

He slept.

And then it was dawn. And breakfast. And ranch duties. Yes, there was a range war going on, and yes, Tunstall himself was dead, but there were still ranch duties. Riding out to drive back scattered cattle. Branding calves. Castrating male calves. Or working in the barns. Or repairing some of the outbuildings. The Tunstall ranch kept a man busy.

Billy didn't work, of course.

He slept all morning, getting up just in time to have lunch with the real cowboys. There was a lot of tension at the long picnic table where the men ate in the shade of a big tree. They'd look to see how Sam was

doing. Sam was glowering was how Sam was doing.
Staring down the table at Billy and glowering his ass
off. Billy paid him no mind. He made a lot of jokes,
and everybody dutifully laughed. He only spoke to
Sam once and said, "Hey, Sammy, I hear you really
poured down the moonshine last night." Sammy went
for his gun; once again he was saved from suicide by
the quick hands of his friends. "You're one hot-
headed sonofabitch," Billy said, returning to his meal,
"you know that, Sammy?"

Sammy threw up twice, once when he was working
on some fence, the second time when he was washing
up for the day. He was scared. He knew he was going
to do it. He was going to kill Billy. It was the only
way he'd ever get these terrible pictures out of his
mind. He'd seen a deck of playing cards once (from
Paris, France, the gambler had insisted) where the
backs didn't have designs; they had photographs of
men and women screwing. Sam liked to think of other
people screwing. It got him hot. But when he thought
of his beloved Trudy with her big tits screwing Billy,
all he could do was throw up. All he could do once
and for all was make his mind up that he was going
to kill Billy.

And kill him very soon.

10

"SOME OF THE boys was talkin', Billy."

"Oh?"

"Yeah. And we—"

You could see Jimmy was scared. Jimmy was forty-six. There was a solemnity, a sadness about him that made you take him seriously. He was the peacemaker of the Tunstall group. He had a terrible scar on his right cheek from barbed wire. He'd gotten thrown from a horse and come right down on the wire, tearing skin from ear to jaw. But for all his fearsome looks, he was a gentle man who, in his cups, talked about the long-ago family he'd had back in Ohio. Influenza had killed them. He had been known to weep openly sometimes, and nobody thought him a lesser man for doing so. Jimmy, with his plaid shirt and soiled baggy Levi's and long bony arms and knobby Neanderthal hands, was a square shooter.

Billy sat under a tree playing with one of the ranch dogs, a sweet-faced border collie. Jimmy stood over him.

"We think you should apologize to Sam."

"To Sam?" Billy said. "Now why would I apologize to Sam?"

He wasn't going to make this easy, Jimmy now saw. Billy could have said yes or no. But he was going to tease, play coy. With his mussed blond hair, his brilliant grin, and his playful but wary eyes, Billy looked like the world's most dangerous teenager. You just never knew what he was going to do next.

"Well, you know, you takin' Trudy down by the creek last night."

"She told me she had a nice time."

"Oh?"

"She told me Sam doesn't really understand how to please a woman."

"I see."

"And you know what else she told me?"

"What?"

"She said I had just about the biggest one she'd ever seen."

Jimmy was blushing. He liked a dirty story as much as anybody, but this kind of personal talk embarrassed him.

"He loves her, Billy. He's like a sick animal since it happened."

"You see me take a gun to her?"

"Nope."

"A whip?"

"Nope."

"A knife?"

Jimmy sighed and watched a blue butterfly. It'd be nice to be a butterfly. Peaceful and free. None of the human sorrow all around you touching you in any way. "Nope, you didn't take a knife to her, either."

"She went of her own free accord. Is that right, Jimmy?"

"That's right." Hearing Billy was like listening to a trial lawyer standing in front of a jury.

"So why should I apologize to Sam?"

"Well, we was all drunk, Billy, and sometimes when you're drunk—"

"I wasn't drunk, Sammy. I was cold, clean sober."

"Oh."

"I saw her standin' there with those big tits of hers and I just had to try her out."

"The thing is, I guess Sam always considered his-self and you pretty good pals."

Billy smiled. "Then that's what you tell Sam, Jimmy. You go back to the bunkhouse and find him and tell him that I said all I wanted was a little taste. The rest of the meal's all his. And if them two kids want to get married, I'll be happy to be best man. You go tell him that, Jimmy."

Billy was having a high old time. Saying one thing, meaning quite another, daring Jimmy to speak up. But Jimmy was too scared, and Billy knew Jimmy was too scared, and that's what made this so much fun for Billy.

"You want me to go tell him, Jimmy?" Billy said. "I'll be happy to go tell him if you want me to."

Jimmy knew what this meant. Billy'd go talk to him all right and goad him into a gunfight. And Sam was so hurt and mad that he'd let himself be goaded.

Billy swatted away a fly. "You want me to go tell him?"

"No, that's all right."

"Because I'll be happy to."

"I'll tell him, Billy."

Billy smirked. "Yeah, it's probably a better idea if you do it. Sam might get mad at me. And we sure wouldn't want that to happen now, would we?"

Right before the dinner bell, Sam lay on his cot, exhausted from the day's chores, sweaty and dirty and needing to clean up at the well. The day was dying and with it, with Trudy on his mind, was Sam. Outside, he could hear the ranch hands laughing and telling stories. He'd never felt more alone.

Jimmy came in and sat down on the cot next to Sam's. He said, "Want you to give me your Colt, Sam."

"My Colt?"

"Yep."

"Why?"

"So you won't try nothin' at dinner tonight."

Sam didn't say anything. Then, "I knew she wasn't no virgin."

Jimmy just listened.

"I knew she wasn't no virgin and I got over it. But her goin' off with Billy, I'll never get over it, Jimmy. I just keep thinkin' of his hands all over her. I thought he was my friend."

"Billy don't give a shit about nobody but hisself, Sam. You know that."

"He spoiled her for me." Sam sounded as if he wanted to cry. "I couldn't ever touch her without thinkin' of Billy."

If there was ever a time for a gentle lie, it was now. Jimmy said, "She only went because she didn't want Billy to hurt you."

"Oh, bullshit."

"It's true."

"It's bullshit and you know it, Jimmy."

"I don't know it. It's the absolute hand-on-the-Bible truth."

"Bullshit."

They were quiet for a time. You could hear the men laughing as dinner was being served up on the big outdoor tables. You could hear the men and you could smell the food and you could see the red sun bleeding to death in the windows of the bunkhouse. It hurt like hell to be a human and to be alive. It hurt like hell, and Sam wished he were dead. He said, "You think so?"

"I think so what?"

"You think that's why Trudy done it? To protect me?"

"Sure that's why she done it. Why else would she do it? It's you she wants, Sam. You."

"That's what she told me."

"See. See, what I'm sayin'? And Trudy herself said it."

"I want to kill him, Sam. I want to kill the sonofabitch."

"Now you give me that Colt, Sam, and right now."

"You'd want to kill him, too, Jimmy, if you was in my place."

Jimmy snorted. "Sam, you're not thinkin' too clear."

"Huh?"

"All them murders the lawmen want him for. The law's gonna take care of him for you. The law, Sam. You won't have to worry about him much longer, not after he shot Sheriff Brady, you won't."

"I guess I never thought of it that way."

"Sure, and that's God's truth. It's one thing killin' other gunnies. You kill a lawman, though, and they'll hunt you down."

That would end it, Sam thought. See the sonofabitch dangling from the end of a rope. That would end it. Trudy would be his again, his completely, and he could forget all about Billy, knowing that she'd only given herself to him to protect Sam.

Trudy was a good woman. She sure was. And he shouldn't go blaming her.

And he shouldn't go fighting Billy. Like Jimmy said, the law was going to take care of Billy, and soon. Damned soon.

Sam sat up and swung his legs off the cot. He hadn't felt this good since before it had happened last night.

"I sure am glad you come in here," Sam said. "I sure am, Jimmy."

Jimmy felt good, too. Sam wasn't going to go picking a fight with Billy and getting himself killed. "Now we'll go down to the end of the table and we won't even look at Billy, and if he says anything, we'll just smile and nod. You understand? Just smile and nod. We won't let him go goadin' us. He wants to goad, we just let him go ahead and goad. And we eat and talk betwixt ourselves. Just betwixt ourselves. You got that now?"

"Oh, I got it, Jimmy, I got it all right," Sam said, feeling suddenly so happy he wanted to sing, now knowing in his heart that Trudy had only gone with Billy to protect him. "Oh, I got it just fine."

And then they went to have dinner.

11

THE TUNSTALL RANCH buildings were a painting in blacks and charcoals, with lights from the Spanish-style house and the barnlike bunkhouse painting the grass green and the outbuildings white.

Conlon sat his horse on a hill to the east of the ranch. Below him, several hundred head of cattle were settling down for the night.

His stomach was bad; it always got that way when he was angry or scared. When he was twenty, he'd always told himself that facing death wouldn't be so scary if he was thirty. And so on. Now, he was past forty-five, and he knew that death would be scary even if he lived to be ninety.

The thing was Billy's mood. That was the only constant story that ran through all the bullshit about him. If he was in a good mood, you could practically go up to him and slap him across the face and he wouldn't do anything. But if he was in a bad mood and felt even the slightest insult, he'd kill you. Without warning, without mercy, he'd kill you.

He was tempted to slide the Winchester from its scabbard. A rifle'd make him feel better if nothing else. But a rifle would also set Billy's guards on edge, so he left the rifle alone.

He started slowly down the hill so as not to spook Billy's guards and elicit gunfire. He figured he'd be spotted soon enough, assuming that Billy's guards were any good.

The coming night brought fireflies, glimmers in the gathering gloom.

He reached the road leading to the front of the ranch. He'd gone no more than a tenth of a mile when a disembodied voice from a big full oak ten yards ahead said, "Hold it right there, mister. Who are you?"

It was strange, the voice without a body.

"I'm U.S. Marshal Conlon."

"Adair's man, huh?"

Conlon had expected the accusation. He hadn't taken either side in this local dispute, so both sides figured he belonged to the other. A reasonable man was always suspect in the eyes of hotheads.

"How come you're out here?"

"How come you're sitting up in a tree?"

"Huh?"

"Skip it. I'm delivering a letter from Governor Adair to Billy."

"Just leave it in the road. I'll see he gets it."

"This one has to be delivered personally."

"Says who?"

"Says Governor Adair."

"Governor Adair don't make no never mind to me."

"Well, he makes a never mind to me," Conlon said, not sure exactly what the expression meant. "So if you'd take me to him, I'd appreciate it."

"Billy don't want no visitors."

"Just tell him I've got a letter from Governor Adair."

"Oh, sure, that'll get him all excited. He's Billy Pecos. Why would he give a shit about some governor?"

The man spoke the name "Billy" the way a Christian would say "Jesus Christ."

"Just go tell him, would you please?"

The man snickered. "A U.S. Marshal who says 'please.' Now that's a new one."

"I even say 'excuse me' after I fart."

The disembodied voice giggled. "You're one strange bird."

A barn owl hooted. Moonlight merged with shadow to lend the ranch buildings a real beauty. On both sides of the road were small gullies, at least one of which had to run with water because Conlon could hear frogs.

Conlon said, "Just go tell him what I told you." He didn't say 'please' this time.

The guy came down from the tree with the dexterity of a man. Limbs shook, bark was scraped with the soles of cowboy boots, and there was a heavy thump when the man landed on the ground. He was all hair and beard and hillbilly suspenders. All he needed was a moonshine jug and bare wiggly feet to complete the cartoon of a hillbilly, at least a hillbilly as perceived by the folks back east.

"Jeb! Tyler!" he called.

And up from either side of the road they came, from those shallow gullies. He hadn't even sensed them, let alone seen them, the two of them with the wild hair and wild beards of the tree-dweller. They had rifles and they had eyes gleaming with mean intent. They also smelled like shit.

"I gots to go talk to Billy," the tree-dweller said. "You hold this pecker here till I get back."

They said nothing. The two from the gullies just watched the tree-dweller run toward the ranch house, a shadow darting among other shadows.

Sounds of crickets, cows, horses, men. Smells of grass, minty bushes, roasted meat from dinner, wind.

"Nice night," Conlon said.

"We don't hold much with talkin'," the first man said. He wore a yellow flannel shirt and had hair turning gray.

"Yeah, Billy says ever time we open our mouths, we put our foot in it," the second man said. He wore a red flannel shirt and had blond hair.

"Billy says ever time somebody says somethin', they're tryin' to trick you into sayin' somethin' you shouldn't," the first man said.

"All I said was 'nice night,' " Conlon said.

"We don't got nuthin' to say, mister," the second man said.

"Yeah," said the first man, "you're just tryin' to trick us just like Billy says."

Gosh, it'd be fun to live out here on the ranch with guys like these, Conlon thought. Talk about a good time.

The tree-dweller came back in ten minutes. He ran. He was out of breath. He poked his carbine right up in Conlon's face and said, "I want all your hardware, includin' a knife if you got one."

"I don't have one."

"Then I want your rifle and your Colt."

"All right."

"And I want you to swing down from that horse just as soon as you give me your guns."

"What happens to my horse?"

"You don't worry about your horse."

"I don't want him hurt. He's been a damned good friend of mine." Conlon liked him because he took orders about 65 percent of the time, which was a hell of a lot more than he could say for any other horse he'd ever owned, and because he had one of those sweet-sad faces you see only on horses and dogs of a certain age.

The tree-dweller giggled. "A friend of yours. You surely are one strange sumbitch, you know that, mister? You surely are."

"Careful," the first one said, "he's just tryin' to trick you into sayin' somethin' you shouldn't."

And so it was, accompanied by three prairie geniuses, that U.S. Marshal Conlon got his chance to meet Billy Pecos.

12

"WHAT ARE YOU thinkin' about, Mae?"

"Oh, nothin' special, I guess."

"You're still thinkin' about that U.S. Marshal, aren't you?"

"No."

"Come on, Mae, you know I can read your mind."

The Excelsior Café, a rather extravagant name for a place that seated only thirty-seven, and that included the cockroaches, had been Mae's hangout since coming to Furner nine weeks ago. And her mother-confessor was Sienna, the half-Mexican grandmother who owned the place. Even with wrinkles, even with an excess thirty pounds, Sienna was still beautiful.

The evening rush was over. Mae and Sienna sat at a table, their faces flattered by the jumping light of the candle between them.

"He is very handsome."

"If you like the type."

Sienna smiled. "I have always preferred his type, myself. The handsome type."

"He didn't have to go and ask me to have dinner with him. It kind've made me mad, actually."

"You could have said no."

"I *did* say no."

"So he threw you on the ground and beat you until you said yes?" Sienna said, pulling her shawl tighter around her. Sienna was always cold, no matter what time of year it was. "I heard about it. The whole town was talking. How he beat you and then shot you in the head until you gave in."

Mae was laughing. She couldn't help it. "You forgot to add that he dragged me behind his horse."

"Oh, yes, that, too. Twenty miles he dragged you, wasn't it? He is a *muy* terrible man, this one."

Two men wanted to pay their bill. Sienna pushed herself up from the table and walked over to the counter. She spent several minutes joking with the men. She wasn't a great cook, but she was a great person, and it was that, as much as the cuisine, that kept the regulars regular. The atmosphere was nice, too. There were always clean red-and-white checked cloths on the tables and matching curtains on the windows. Any cowhand with excessive dung on his boots was asked to leave them outside.

Mae started thinking about Conlon again, resenting herself for doing so. The thing was to concentrate on Billy. That had been her sacred vow. She'd made this

vow to the Blessed Virgin, kneeling at the wooden
altar in the small dusty chapel of St. Michael's back
in Iowa. It had been a true vow, not anything made
lightly. A man would be nothing more than a distrac-
tion. And anyway, if he found out what her plans
were, he'd arrest her.

Sienna came back and sat down. "I have been
thinking, and I know what the problem is."

"What problem?"

"The problem you have with señor lawman."

"Oh, gosh, Sienna, can't we talk about something
else?"

"You are afraid he might guess your secret is what
you are afraid of, my little friend."

"Oh, no," Mae laughed, "both of my least favorite
topics at once—Conlon and my secret."

"You know, I know the gift."

"Yes. The gift. I believe you've mentioned that before."

"You mock me, but it's true. I can sense you have
a secret. A very deep secret. I can also sense that
you're afraid of señor lawman for this reason. That
he will learn your secret."

"Maybe I'll tell him about it on our wedding
night."

"You are mocking me again."

The door opened and two half-drunk cowboys
came in and looked around at the empty tables. "You
open?" one of them said.

"We are always open to such fine people as yourselves," Sienna said.

The cowboy laughed. "Nice to know you're just as
full of shit as we are, Sienna."

"You think about what I said," Sienna whispered
as she rose to serve the men. "You are afraid he'll
learn your secret."

13

THEY WORE THEIR histories on their faces.

For the cowboys, this meant broken noses, busted teeth, glass eyes, hands with three fingers.

For the gunnies it meant wary eyes, tiny tics of cheek and lip, and a constant reflexive touching of holster and gun.

The boys at the Tunstall ranch seemed to divide about half and half between cowhands and gunnies.

The tree-dweller led Conlon inside the ranch house. It was a fine house with expensive leather furnishings and Mexican motifs. Billy and four others were in the dining room, using the long table for poker.

Conlon was disappointed in him, the same way he'd been disappointed in the handful of other famous gunnies he'd met. The dime novels built these people up into myths, so much so that even otherwise sensible lawmen got taken in and started thinking of the gunnies as mythic, too.

Billy had dirty blond hair, some complexion problems, and a mouthful of teeth that a dentist could retire on. But he also had an impish look that no doubt appealed to women. He would have been the cutest boy in third grade and the toughest boy in fifth. But his school days were long behind him, as could be seen in the hard, quick wisdom of his blue eyes. Every town bigger than a watering hole had a Billy. Most of them died before they reached maturity, usually as a result of too much cheap liquor and too little judgment, gut-shot by a genuine gunnie weary of the whole business. But every once in a while a Billy made it just long enough to inspire the hacks back east. Conlon was looking at just such a Billy now.

Billy looked up from his cards and said, "Make it quick."

Conlon had been put in his place very quickly. He was a supplicant. He said, "We need to talk."

Billy had gone back to surveying his cards. "Then talk."

"Alone."

"I'm busy, and you're leaving." Billy still looked at his cards.

Conlon sighed, glanced around. The other players just watched and said nothing. This was Billy's call. The elegant room was wrong for a game as crude as poker. There was a gentle woman's touch on the appointments in this room—the china cabinet, the grandfather clock, the mullioned windows.

Just as Billy was about to say something else, Conlon went into a crouch, jerked a hidden six-shooter from his waistband, and began firing. A single rifle shot cracked through the window, piercing Conlon's Stetson. Every man at the table went for his own gun. But by then it was all over.

Shouts in the room; shouts from outside. Billy, a lot more shaken than he would probably admit to, pale, trembling, looking in complete bafflement at Conlon. Somebody calling through the window: "It was Sam, Billy. He had a rifle! He was gonna kill you, Billy!"

Billy said, "Our friend the county attorney ain't gonna like this one bit, Marshal."

"Oh?"

"You savin' my life this way."

"I s'pose not."

"He wants to hang me."

"A lot of people want to hang you, Billy."

Billy smiled. "Aren't you just a little bit afraid of me, Marshal?"

"I'm very afraid of you, Billy."

"But you're not afraid to talk?"

Conlon smiled back. "If I wasn't talkin', Billy, you'd hear my knees knocking."

14

JIMMY GOT TWO of the hands to help him carry Sam back to the bunkhouse. They laid a tarp on the bed so the blood wouldn't soak into the mattress.

Jimmy didn't say anything. He knew if he spoke he'd say something that would get back to Billy, and Billy would kill him.

Jimmy thought of how the Tunstall spread had been before Billy came. Yes, there were gunnies, but they weren't important ones like Billy. In fact, the regular hands looked down on them, had little to do with them. The hands were out working their asses off all day in the baking sun, and the gunnies were just lazing around oiling their guns and reading magazines and killing time. The place had been a good place to work.

But all that changed with Billy coming.

He humiliated people. That's how he'd established his dominance. He made all the key hands eat a one-pound bag of shit in front of the other hands, so that there'd be no mistake as to who was in charge. After Sheriff Brady killed Tunstall, it got even worse.

Worse to the point that Billy felt free to "borrow" another man's woman for the night.

"Poor crazy bastard," said one of the hands.

"Damn marshal," said another.

"Was Billy who killed him," Jimmy said. He couldn't control himself any more. "If he wouldn't've stolen Sam's gal the way he did, Sam'd be alive tonight."

The men looked at each other, and then one said, "Jimmy, you oughtn't to say stuff like that. If Billy ever hears you—"

Billy's spies were all over the ranch, men who wanted to curry favor by repeating things they heard. These two were trustworthy—at least Jimmy believed they were—but they were right. He had to be careful what he said.

"Let's say an Our Father," Jimmy said.

"Cliff here's a Jew," the one hand said.

"That's all right," Cliff said. "I'll just say my prayer silent."

They said their prayers. The smell was getting bad. He'd shit himself. There were flies.

They emptied his pockets. Jimmy took the sweated red kerchief off Sam's neck and put all the things in his pocket in the kerchief. Then he cinched it up. He'd mail it back to Sam's kin.

They took shovels and went out to a stand of trees where other hands had been buried from time to time. There were a lot of fireflies, and the light from the half moon made Sam look as if he wasn't dead, just sleeping, the way he was laid out on the grass, a sad old hound sniffing around him till the men ran him off. With three of them shoveling, it didn't take long. When they started pushing the dirt on Sam, Jimmy thought of his nightmares about being buried alive. Sometimes he'd wake up screaming like a little kid.

· · ·

Men were already going to bed for the night. The
bunk talk was all about Sam. Jimmy lay in shadow
at the far end of the bunkhouse, listening to them.
They wanted to tear into Billy, cuss him for the mean
prick asshole bastard he really was. But they were
scared to, not knowing which among them would
carry the words back to Billy.

Jimmy thought of all the ways he could kill Billy.
Backshooting him was likely the best way. But even
trying to backshoot Billy was dicey. He'd been
known to kill several men who'd tried to sneak up
behind him. Or at least that's how the stories ran.
With punks like Billy, it was hard to know what was
true. They spun yarns about themselves, and the yarns
got spun again by the dime novelists.

He fell asleep thinking of ways he was going to
pay Billy back.

15

"LOOKS LIKE A trap to me," Billy said.

"No trap," Conlon replied. He was two hours behind schedule, thanks to helping out an old man
whose buggy wheel had come off. The wheel had
been obstinate as hell, and the old man hadn't been
much help.

They were in the dining room of the Tunstall place.
A night breeze fluttered the candles, the breeze coming through the shot-out window frames. Conlon had
spent a few minutes talking about New York. They

had that in common—Conlon the detective, Billy the street gang member. But conning Billy wasn't easy. He saw how transparent Conlon's words were and changed the subject.

"No trap? I ride into town and he's got twenty deputies with rifles waiting for me?"

"You didn't read his letter very carefully, then."

"Oh, I read it carefully all right. Especially what was between the lines. Some dumb sonofabitch riding in there thinking he's going to get amnesty and he gets hisself shot to death."

"He's a decent man."

"That don't mean shit to me, Mr. Marshal. Lots of 'decent men' have gunned down people like me before in cold blood."

"Yeah," Conlon said, "we sure wouldn't want to have decent men acting like outlaws now, would we?"

"I never shot anybody in cold blood."

"Guess I'll have to take your word for that."

Billy smirked. "Meaning you don't believe me?"

"Meaning what I believe doesn't matter. We're talking amnesty here, Billy. A chance for you to start your life all over again."

"You'd make a good salesman."

"Adair wants you and the Barcroft crowd to settle this thing once and for all. That's his only interest here. If it takes letting gunnies go free, then so be it."

"You agree with that?"

"Like I said, Billy, my feelings don't matter."

Billy stared at him. "You don't like me much, do you?"

Conlon almost laughed. Pecos carried a load of vanity that would make a princess blush. "Billy, the reason I came out here was to persuade you to go see Governor Adair."

"Tunstall was like my father." He then plucked an

apple from the table—in these parts, apples made for a very special dessert—and then proceeded to carve off pieces with the six-inch blade of a bone-handled skinning knife he pulled from his pocket.

"He wasn't much older than you."

"Don't matter," Billy said, and the quicksilver rage was there. He swept everything off his end of the dining room table. Glasses smashed against the wall; silverware flew like delicate silver birds. "You understand me?"

His rage was suffocating to behold, a physical force holding Conlon down. He was scared and fascinated at the same time. Billy's face was an unholy red, his eyes almost comically protuberant. Spittle whipped from his lips as he screamed, "You understand me? He was like my father!"

Conlon said, "All right, Billy. I don't mean to rile you."

"That's why I shot Sheriff Brady. The only reason. Because he killed Tunstall." He was still shouting. "Now is that clear?"

Conlon decided this probably wasn't a real good time to point out that Billy had disarmed Sheriff Brady before shooting him. Probably he should wait till later to remind Billy of the circumstances.

Billy grew calmer by taking deep breaths. His face became one degree less red with each exhalation.

Conlon said, "A new life for you, Billy."

Billy said, "I want your ass out of here right now, Mr. Marshal man, because I can't stand looking at your ugly face any more and because I'm about ready to kill you. You understand?"

He said all this calmly.

A few minutes later, Conlon was on his way back to town.

16

MAE WAS JUST walking down the street, on her way to the sheriff's office, when it overtook her.

It was like a seizure.

Her heart started racing. Her palms started sweating. A tic appeared on the edge of her left eye. She felt dry-mouthed. Her stomach was sour. Her bowels were slithery and cold. And she felt such a combination of fear and sorrow that she just wanted to go somewhere dark and hide.

This could mean only one thing.

Mae was in love.

All the time Conlon had been in town, she'd had to fight the feeling, deny it, find other words for it. But there could be no more denying it because when he'd asked her to dinner, she'd seen it on him, too. Love.

Oh, God, it wasn't what she wanted or needed at all. And some big, shaggy U.S. Marshal yet on top of it.

She was going to fight it.

Burn it, shoot it, strangle it, drown it, stab it— whatever it took, she was going to get rid of being in love with Conlon.

She most devoutly was.

17

CONLON WAS HANGING his hat on a peg when the door leading from the back room opened and Mae came out carrying a broom.

"What're you doing here?" he asked.

"Couldn't sleep. Just decided to get some more paperwork done."

"Sorry I got back so late. About our dinner and all."

"Oh, that's right," she said, going over to cull through some of the older WANTED posters. "I forgot about that."

He walked over to her and took her by the shoulder and turned her gently around. "You really forgot about it?"

She looked right back at him. "Yeah."

He smiled. "What happens if I say I don't believe you?"

"That's up to you, I guess."

"I think you actually *wanted* to have dinner with me."

"You do, huh?"

"Yeah, I do."

"Well, like I said, that's up to you, what you want to believe."

"You're a hard one."

"Look who's talking."

The door opened and one of the nephews came in. This nephew was named Luke, and he was the youngest of the three. No fancy badges or cowboy duds for Luke. You could always tell what he'd had for dinner because it was on his shirt. And he'd worn the same baggy pair of soiled corduroys the whole time Conlon had been in town. He was desert-wandering skinny, slightly cross-eyed, and owned breath so bad he could drop you from ten paces away. He said, "I just jugged somebody up for the night."

Conlon said, "Anything you can't handle?"

"It's the preacher's son again."

"Is that somebody special?"

"Last time I jugged him, he tried to hang himself."

Mae said, "He shouldn't be jugged, Marshal."

"He was drunk and bothering people in the street."

"You did the right thing, then," Conlon said, not understanding what the tension was.

"Mae here, she chewed my ass out good the last time I jugged him," Luke said.

Mae said, "They put him away a couple of times."

"Away?" Conlon said.

"He thinks he's got devils inside him," Mae said, "so they put him in one of those places. For troubled people."

"Crazy is what she's trying to say," Luke said.

"Oh," Conlon said, starting to understand. "So if Luke doesn't jug him, what *does* he do with him?"

"Let me take him over to the nunnery," she said.

"The nunnery?"

"There's a sister there he likes," Luke said.

"You put him in a cell," Mae said, "and he'll try to kill himself again."

"Not if I strip him down to his underwear, he won't," Luke said.

"I knew of a prisoner who killed himself by banging his head against a cell wall," Conlon said.

"I'm s'posed to be makin' my rounds," Luke said, "checkin' up on stores 'n makin' sure they're locked

up. It's up to you, Marshal. I keep him jugged or
what?"

"Let me take him over to the nunnery," Mae said.
"I can handle him."

"He won't get violent?" Conlon said.

"He's sweet on Mae," Luke said, giving Conlon a
cheek-searing blast of bad breath. "She can calm him
down real good."

"You sure about this?" Conlon said.

Mae nodded.

"All right," Conlon said. "Why don't you stop back
when you're finished?"

Mae looked as if she was going to say no but then
said, "I guess I could do that."

18

RONNIE SAID, "I couldn't stop them, Miss Mae. They
was just too strong for me."

The night was quiet as Mae and Ronnie Pritchett
headed toward the nunnery on the edge of town. The
small houses looked snug. She remembered her married days and how good it had been to have her husband next to her in the middle of the night.
Everything seemed so settled and sane, so *knowable*
back then.

Ronnie said, "They just snuck up on me."

"Did your father beat you again?"

"He was just tryin' to help me, Miss Mae."

Ronnie was a fat boy inside the body of a fat man.

At twenty, he was already losing his hair and had a
heavy, dark beard. For all his power and violence—
both of which were overwhelming—he was one of
those big, dainty men people made fun of. His father,
a minister who taught pure hatred for anyone who
disagreed with him, whipped Ronnie with a belt
whenever he felt that demons had possessed the boy.
This had been going on since Ronnie was three. Long,
long ago he'd convinced the boy that he was demon-
driven. Ronnie now heard voices, demonic voices
telling him to pick fights with people, set fires to
buildings, and peek into windows trying to catch a
glimpse of naked women. He'd been in an institution
for insane people, but his father always managed to
get him out. His father missed having somebody to
beat. All the hatred in his soul had to be expressed
somehow. And he couldn't just go around beating
strangers. The law frowned upon that. So he beat his
son.

Ronnie said, "People just don't understand my pa.
He just tries to save them from goin' to hell is all,
Miss Mae. He wouldn't beat me if he didn't love me."

"You don't need any more beatings right now,
Ronnie." He'd shown her the lash marks on his back.
His father had expressed a good deal of love tonight.
The lashes needed tending to. The nuns would do a
good job.

"I like Sister Angelina. She gives me cookies."

"That's good."

"You know the kind of cookie she gave me last
time?"

"No, what kind of cookie?"

"With chocolate in it."

"That does sound good."

"She give me three of them."

"Great."

"And then you know what?"

"What?"

"She took me upstairs and put me to bed like my mom used to."

"I'll bet you enjoyed it."

"I even asked her to sing 'Bluebirds in the Maple Trees' like my mom did. She has a real nice voice. Except she said the 'Our Father' funny."

"Oh?"

"Yeah, Catholics, they don't say it right. That's what my dad always says. That they don't say it right. He always says Catholics are just one step up from Jews, anyway."

"I see."

"I mean, no offense, Miss Mae, I know you're a mackerel-snapper."

She smiled at the mild insult. "That's very nice of you, Ronnie. That you didn't mean any offense."

The nunnery was a two-story white house. A light shone in the windows in the back.

"I hope she'll sing 'Bluebirds in the Maple Trees,' " Ronnie said. "And give me some of them cookies with chocolate in 'em."

19

BILL STOCKTON AND his wife, Ellie, had had an argument on the way back from the Barcroft party earlier this evening. Bill, drunk, had led a toast to John Barcroft that had thoroughly sickened Ellie.

In the surrey on the way back she said, "He pays

off government officials, and he rustles other people's cattle, and he hires gunnies to kill people for him— and you lead a toast to him."

"It was his birthday."

"You're already his errand boy, Bill. Isn't that enough? Do you have to bow and scrape in public, too?"

"Well, thanks for the compliment."

"It's the truth and you know it."

"Where would we be without him, Ellie? You ever thought of that? Or did you like it when we were starving to death in Waco?"

"At least you were an honest man back then, Bill."

They rode along under the silent and indifferent stars, clop of horse hooves, bay of distant coyote, Bill skinnier than he'd ever been, Ellie heavier after their fourth child. Ellie was a very idealistic woman, one who believed that women should be given the right to vote and the right to hold public office, opinions that Bill was always begging her to keep to herself. Bill had been a sickly boy, never much sought after by other boys. He hadn't even had great brains to compensate for his sickliness. He'd been a mediocre student and had barely gotten through law school. In Waco, already the father of two, he'd worked for a small, struggling firm that mostly did land law. They had a bad spring and fired him. That's how Bill and Ellie ended up here, answering an ad for an attorney who was retiring. Bill earned even less money than he had in Waco. At the time, John Barcroft was on the lookout for a new county attorney, one he could put on the payroll. The old one was just that, old and arthritic and growing more useless by the day. He invited Bill and Ellie out to his enormous ranch and made the offer to Bill. How'd you like to be county attorney? Ellie could see the affect the proposal had on her husband. He looked as if he wanted to grin but knew better. For the very first time in his life, he had been accepted into the company of important men. And it was a heady moment. She loved her husband with a sensible mixture of tenderness and exasperation. Somehow, they had bumbled through their life together, but now she wondered. John Barcroft was the kind of man who used anybody he could . . . and then discarded them. Even if he asked her husband to commit an illegal act, there was no way Bill would have the courage to say no. That night, after they finished making love, she told him of her fears and reservations about him becoming Barcroft's handpicked county attorney.

Now, standing at the window of his parlor, he thought of all the arguments they'd had during the year and a half he'd been in office. She used to pity him, and that had been bad enough, but now she was openly scornful of him and the way he acted whenever Barcroft was around. He couldn't explain to her what it felt like after all these years to be accepted by powerful men. A woman simply couldn't understand. He felt tough and purposeful these days. People feared him. He could see it in their eyes and in the deference of their movements when he walked down the street. Important men asked him to do them favors and in turn saw to it that he and Ellie were invited to all the important social functions, though he feared that Ellie's sour disposition turned some of the women against her—and the influence of wives on important men was a fearful thing to contemplate. At these affairs he'd at least persuaded her not to talk about women voting.

Ellie had gone right to sleep after getting home. Stockton had tried to sleep but couldn't. The arguments were getting too bitter. He worried about his marriage. She was strong enough to walk away, and he knew it.

He was just glad that she hadn't asked him what he and Barcroft had talked about for an hour tonight in the privacy of Barcroft's den.

"Lew Adair wants to get back to his book," Barcroft had said, "and everybody knows it. That's why he wants this thing settled fast and why he's willing to give goddamn Billy amnesty." Barcroft had leaned forward and said, "Stockton, I want you to see to it that Billy doesn't get that amnesty. He killed two of my best men, and he's not going to get away with it. I don't care what you have to do. Billy doesn't get amnesty. And it has to happen fast, before he can sign any amnesty agreement."

"I understand, John." He was still uncomfortable calling Barcroft "John," but calling him "Mr. Barcroft" all the time sickened him. He could just hear Ellie scorning him about it.

So now he was up at 1 A.M., both his boss and his wife making his life hell.

Somehow he had to take care of Billy and make sure that Ellie, who wanted the amnesty, never found out about it.

If she did—

Well, he didn't want to think about it, if she did.

He went over to an armchair and sat down. He felt very old and very sad sitting there in the darkness.

He was just about to fall asleep when he felt silken hands on his shoulders. He looked up to see Ellie's face above his. She said, "I'm sorry we argued. I love you so much."

"I'm sorry we argued, too."

He felt uncomfortable with her massaging him this way.

"It's been a while, Bill."

"A while?" But of course he knew what she was talking about.

"Over two months now, we haven't made love."

"Oh."

"We're man and wife."

"I just have so much work—I'm just tired is all."

"I miss being with you. Not even the making love—just you holding me."

"Well, we'll try for the weekend. How's that?"

She hesitated. "Right now would be good, too."

"I'm just so tired . . ."

Sometimes he wondered if she knew about the woman he had on the side. Over the years he'd had several women on the side. They always made him feel more manly. There was no conquest in taking your wife or having her be in love with you. But with a new woman, a fresh one, there was a definite sense of conquest—and exhilaration. But this new woman was so complicated . . .

He wondered if Ellie ever suspected about these women.

"We'll get together this weekend," he said. "I promise. You go on back to bed now, honey. I've got some office things I need to think about."

"I love you, Bill."

"Me, too. Love you, too. I mean."

Then she was gone—gone from the room, gone from his mind. He started thinking about his new woman.

20

CONLON HAD JUST gotten back from the town council meeting and was smoking his pipe and going through some papers the sheriff had left behind when the front door opened and Mae came in. This was 10:30 on a bright, hot morning.

Conlon said, "Guess you didn't come back to the office last night after taking Ronnie to the nuns."

She just looked at him. "Guess I didn't."

She went over to her small, orderly desk and sat down and started sorting through her mail.

"Any particular reason?"

"Nope. No particular reason."

"I waited a couple of hours."

"Good for you."

She was doing it to him again. She'd been doing it to him since he'd met her. Giving him that dopey, helpless feeling. Liking her and disliking her at the same time. Making him think about her all the time even though he tried not to. And now being airy and even arrogant about not coming back to the office last night though she said she would. Or at least *hinted* she would. This had been his experience with women when he'd been a young man. They knew things and they knew they knew things and they knew that you would never know these things and boy that could make a man crazy sometimes.

"You're late," he said.

She just kept right on looking through her mail. "I told you, I had to help Judge Beams this morning."

"You told me?"

"Uh-huh. The day before yesterday."

"Oh."

"I even left a note on your desk."

He looked around his desk a moment. I'LL BE AT THE JUDGE'S THURSDAY MORNING. MAE. He held up the note. "This must be it."

"Must be," she said.

She didn't say anything else to him for the better part of an hour.

21

JUST BEFORE NOON, a big city man came into the sheriff's office and said, "I'm looking for Marshal Conlon."

"I'm Marshal Conlon."

The red-haired man with the green eyes came forward and extended his hand. He wore a fresh suit, a celluloid collar, and a bowler, which he now took off. He managed to look refined and tough at the same time. "Considine. I'm one of Governor Adair's assistants."

"Nice to meet you. This is Mae Roberts."

She nodded to Considine.

"The governor would like you to come to his place as soon as possible."

"Is everything all right?"

Considine nodded. "More than a little all right. Looks like your help with Billy paid off."

"Oh?"

"He rode up to the governor's door this morning and turned over his guns."

Mae said, "He's at the governor's?"

"For the time being," Considine said. "The governor's got some ideas about how this whole thing should be handled."

Conlon noticed how tense Mae had become. Why would the mention of Billy unsettle her this way? He said, "How about right after lunch."

"That would be fine."

He put his bowler back on his head, touched it in a little salute, and said, "Miss Roberts."

They nodded at each other and Considine left.

They sat there in silence for a moment, and then Conlon said, "You should've seen yourself when he mentioned Billy."

She was back to perusing her mail. "I can't really talk right now, Marshal. I've got too much work to do."

"How about having a bowl of soup with me?"

"I just had soup last night."

"Then some fried potatoes."

"I hate fried potatoes." Still reading her mail.

Conlon said, "You got some kind of connection to him?"

"Who?"

"Billy."

"What kind of connection would I have to him?"

He watched her. He liked watching her. He said, "Another thing."

She sighed. "And what would that be, Marshal?"

"You've been acting very strange since I asked you to have supper with me."

She said something he couldn't hear. "What?"

"Nothing."

"No. You said something. What was it?"

She kept scanning the letter in front of her. "I said I was doing both of us a favor."

"Oh?"

She finally turned her pretty head and looked at him. "One of us would get hurt, and I don't want it to be me."

"I just asked you to have supper."

"But that wasn't really what you were asking for, was it?"

He couldn't help himself. He blushed and then stammered, "No, I guess it wasn't."

Women knew things, dammit. Women knew things.

A few silent minutes later, he went over and took his Stetson down from the peg and went out and had a lonely lunch.

22

BILLY SAID, "WHAT happened was, Governor, he's a damned good talker. Conlon, I mean. He come out to the place last night and brought me the letter you wrote and started talkin' to me real, real good." Billy smiled. "And if that wasn't enough, the sumbitch broke down and saved my life."

"Saved your life?" Lew Adair said. "Is that true, Conlon?"

Conlon shrugged. "It wasn't as dramatic as it sounds. This Sam was standing outside the window with a rifle. He wasn't real hard to spot."

"Still," Governor Adair said. "That's something, saving Billy's life that way."

"I'm a regular hero, all right," Conlon said.

"Well, this is sure going into your federal file," Adair said. "I can guarantee you that."

They were sitting in his den. A middle-aged Negro man with three gold teeth had just served them some kind of sugary blueberry drink. Conlon didn't have much of a sweet tooth.

"I've got a house where Billy is going to stay," the governor said, "while we work out the details of the amnesty and everything."

"A house?" Conlon said. "What's wrong with the jail?"

"That's part of the deal, Conlon," Billy said. "No jail. I been in too many jails already in my life." He smiled. "And I'm barely twenty."

Conlon didn't like it. "How we going to make sure he doesn't get in any trouble?"

"Now that's a hell of a thing to say," Billy said. "I don't want no trouble. I just want my amnesty. And then I'm movin' to Missouri and gettin' a farm." He brushed the palm of a hand against the boiled white shirt he was wearing. He'd shaved since last night and slicked down his hair. He looked like a fifteen-year-old just slightly intimidated by his adult company.

Conlon said, "So where are you going to put him?"

"The Ryerson's house. Bob and Marsha Ryerson are friends of mine. They run the local paper, and they're good folks. Bob helped me a lot on my first book. Very religious folks."

"That doesn't mean he knows anything about keeping prisoners."

"I'm not a prisoner," Billy said. "Right, Governor?"

Adair glanced uncomfortably at Conlon. "I explained to Billy that just because he turned himself over doesn't mean he's a prisoner. He's just staying in town as my guest while I work out the details of the amnesty."

"He killed a lawman."

"He wasn't a lawman," Billy said, "he was one of Barcroft's gunnies."

"That should've been decided by a jury," Conlon said. "A lot of people around here aren't going to like any of this—giving Billy amnesty and letting him wander around free."

"You're turning into a real prick, Conlon," Billy said. "You know that?"

"Billy's going to help us convict some of the other men Tunstall hired," Adair said quietly.

Billy had been glaring at Conlon but now he looked away, embarrassed. There was a silence. So Billy was going to inform on some of the gunnies he'd ridden with. Conlon wondered how finking out like that would play into Billy's wild legend. Most people would probably choose not to believe it, say it was some kind of rumor started by the federals to discredit Billy.

"I see," Conlon said quietly.

"These are real bad folks, Marshal," Billy said. "The only reason I'm ratting them out is because they're a real menace to society."

Conlon almost laughed. Menace to society. Billy must read a lot of dime novels. The cliché had come so easily to him.

"And you're not?" Conlon said.

"You'd best watch that mouth of yours, Marshal," Billy said.

"Now, let's cut this out," Adair said. "We're here to set the amnesty in motion. Marshal, I invited you to let you know my plans."

"I appreciate that."

"I'm well aware that you don't agree with my strategy, Marshal, but I expect you to carry out my orders. I've asked Billy to stay away from town and from the saloons to avoid trouble. He's agreed to do that. For your part, I want you to give him help if he needs it."

"Help?" Conlon said.

Adair nodded. "As you say, there'll be some people who don't want Billy here. Or for Billy to receive amnesty. Word will spread fast. There may be some people who decide to harass him."

"Or lynch me," Billy said.

Adair nodded. "That's a possibility, too. There've been a lot of lynchings in this area in the past few years."

"I can assign a guard," Conlon said.

"I'd appreciate that."

"A good shot," Billy said. "That's what I need. Somebody who stays sober and is a good shot. So nobody'll bother me."

"You're really going to stay out of the saloons?" Conlon said.

"Believe it or not, Conlon," Billy said. "I want this amnesty. I want to settle down same as my friend Pat Garrett always talks about."

"You know Garrett?" Conlon said.

Billy nodded. "He's a good man."

Conlon had known Garrett slightly for the past few years, and he didn't much care for him. He was one of those tireless self-promoters the West was filled with. Crooks Conlon could deal with—hell, he'd been a crook himself—but self-promoters wearied him quickly.

Conlon stood up. "Well, I'll get things set up in the next couple of hours. Tell your friends to expect a deputy to be staying on their front porch for the next few days."

"You're a good man, Marshal," Lew Adair said expansively. Conlon noted how often Adair glanced longingly at his writing desk. He was like a man just aching to be with a special girl.

"I appreciate that," Conlon said. This wasn't going to work. There was no controlling Billy. Billy couldn't even control himself. This was a crazy arrangement. The amnesty was a stupid idea, and leaving Billy to his own devices was even more stupid.

"I'll walk out with you, Marshal," Adair said. "I'll be right back, Billy."

Billy gave Conlon a good-bye smirk. "You tell your deputy I'll be a good little boy, Marshal."

As they went down the waxed and gleaming hall to the front of the house, Adair said, "He's just a big, overgrown kid. He's more talk than anything else. The Mrs. says he just likes to talk tough but that inside he's actually a very decent lad."

"That's him, all right," Conlon said. "An altar boy at heart."

Adair laughed. "You really don't like him, do you?"

"No."

"Why?"

"Because he's a killer. He'll kill anybody who gets in his way."

"So you don't share my wife's benign view of Billy?"

"Afraid I don't."

When they got to the front porch, Adair extended his hand again and then said, "I really do appreciate this, Marshal. I know you don't agree with me, but I appreciate your professionalism."

But Conlon wasn't paying much attention to the governor's words. He'd just seen sunlight glint off a metal shaft. The shaft of a rifle barrel poking out of a window in the house across the street.

He said, "You know who lives across the street?"

"Family named the Conways. Good religious people."

"You know anything about them?"

"Not much. But I do know they're not home. They had to go to a funeral in Clovis."

"Makes sense, then."

The governor was baffled. "What does?"

"You tell Billy to stay inside and not leave till I tell him to."

"I sure wish you'd tell me what's going on, Marshal."

"I'll be back in a few minutes. You go back inside now."

Conlon left the porch and started down the walk, careful to walk slowly and casually. To the disinterested observer, he was simply a man heading back toward the center of town in no particular hurry. He reached an alley and then walked across the street where alkali dust powdered his boots. When he was in this section of alley, his pace changed. He moved quickly now. He crossed the backyards of several houses. Luckily, no one was outdoors to ask him questions. When he reached the rear of the large stone house he was looking for, he trotted up the lawn to a large screened-in back porch. He walked on tiptoe now, crossing the porch to the back door. It was unlocked. He went inside. He found the servant, a Mexican woman, bound and gagged on the kitchen floor. Her eyes glowed with relief and gratitude when she saw him. He put a silencing finger to her lips and then untied and ungagged her. She whispered, "Upstairs." The drapes were pulled tight against the heat of the day. A sweet incense had been burned here recently. The furnishings were outsize and comfortable looking. He moved quickly, once again on tiptoes, taking the stairs one careful step at a time. He moved down the hall until he reached the third door on the

right. He heard a man cough. This was the room. He
would have to be quick. The man had a rifle, and he
wouldn't take time to note Conlon's badge. Conlon
readied himself. Deep breath. Steady grip on his six-
shooter. He raised his right boot and stomped it
against the door. The slab of painted pine flew inward. The gunnie was crouched at the window, his
rifle trained on the front of the house where Adair
was staying. He didn't have time to move effectively.
Conlon was on him, slamming the barrel of his
weapon across the back of the gunnie's head, knocking both man and rifle to the floor. Conlon crouched
next to him, his six-shooter pressing one of the man's
eyeballs.

"Who are you?" Conlon said.

"You're the law, huh?"

"Answer my question."

The man's breath came in gasps. He had a doughy,
morose face, brown eyes both aggrieved and angry,
and some kind of skin rash across his throat. "I'm
legal."

"What the hell's that mean?"

"I'm a bounty hunter."

"Shit," Conlon said, disgusted that he hadn't figured this out before the man told him. Of all the problems with bringing Billy into town this way, Conlon
hadn't even thought of a bounty man stalking him.

Conlon stood up. "Get up."

"Like I said, I'm legal."

"You were going to kill him, huh?"

"Dead or alive," the man said, getting to his feet.
"That's what the law says."

"And then you'd get your name in all the dime
novels."

"Don't give a damn about that. Just want the

money. Got wiped out farmin' last year in the drought. Got three kids to feed. I'm doin' anythin' I can to make money."

"Including killing people in cold blood?"

"That's what *he* does, isn't it?"

They were in a girl's bedroom. There was a canopy bed. Everything was yellow and bright.

"Sure wish my little girls had a room like this," the man said.

Conlon sighed. He wanted to hate the sonofabitch. But he couldn't. Not quite.

"You're a U.S. Marshal, right?"

"Yes. Why?"

"That means you don't have no jurisdiction in this town."

"I'm also acting sheriff. Appointed by the town council."

"Shit."

Conlon said, "I'm ordering you out of town."

"Who the hell's gonna miss him? There's ten thousand dollars on his head, and I got all them mouths to feed."

"What's your name?"

"Greaves. R. C. Greaves."

"Well, R. C. Greaves, you get your ass out of this town and you keep it out, you understand?"

"I'm legal."

"Not in this town you're not."

Greaves glared at him. "You got any kids?"

"We're not talking about me. Now take that rifle and get the hell out of here."

Conlon followed Greaves downstairs. "I could run you in for tying up the maid."

"She's a Mex."

"What's that got to do with anything?"

"Where I come from," Greaves said, "you tie up a Mex and nobody gives a shit."

He made sure to scowl at the Mexican woman as he walked through the kitchen.

"He's a bad one," the woman said.

"Yeah, he is."

"He called me names. Filthy names."

"I'm sorry."

"I am so appreciate. You come and help me. I will say special prayers for you to the Virgin."

He smiled. "I could sure use them."

23

BACK AT THE governor's, Conlon said, "We forgot to take bounty hunters into account."

"That's what he was?"

"That's what he was," Conlon said.

"Those bastards," Billy said. "Those stinking bastards. I killed one of them once. You hear about that one, Marshal?"

"Nope," Conlon said, "and I don't particularly want to."

"You're sure a hard fella to like, you know that?" Billy said.

Conlon said, "I'll go to my office now and get everything set up. The guard should be out there by mid-afternoon."

"Thanks again."

"How'd you like it?" Billy said to Conlon. "Some sonofabitch followin' you around tryin' to kill you?"

Oh, he was a real pleasure, Billy was. A real pleasure.

24

"THE BACK DOOR stays locked," Conlon said. "You got that?"

"The back door stays locked. Right," said the nephew, Larry Glencoe.

"And the only people who are allowed through the front door are the couple who live there. You understand?"

"I sure do, Marshal."

"And you keep watching the street for any people who act strange. Remember?"

"Oh, I remember good."

"And what if Billy wants to leave?"

"Oh. Right. Billy don't *get* to leave."

"That's right. Billy doesn't leave. And if he tries—"

"I hold him at gunpoint and send the kid across the street running to fetch you."

"Good. Now how about when you need to go to the outhouse?"

"I go ask the mister to watch the front for me."

"Right."

"But what if I have to grunt?"

That's what a lot of the people out here called sitting down. Grunting.

"You just tell Mr. Ryerson you'll be a little longer."

"A little longer," Glencoe repeated dutifully. "Got it."

On his walk back to town, Conlon had stopped by the Ryersons and talked through everything. He wished the Ryersons were watching Billy instead of the nephew.

"So, you all ready to go?"

"All ready, Marshal. The wife's bringing me by a piece of pie and a cee-gar for supper. That all right?"

"That's fine."

"It's blueberry."

"The pie?"

"Uh-huh. Raspberry's my favorite, but she don't have no good raspberries, so she made blueberry."

"Makes sense."

"The cee-gar's a Corona Special. Got it at the Murphy-Dolan store. It's a good one."

The poor Ryersons, Conlon thought. He sure hoped that neither of them decided to step out on the porch and have themselves a little chat with the nephew here.

"Well, I'd better be going, Larry."

"She could bring you by some pie if you wanted some," Larry said.

Conlon sure hoped the Ryersons didn't step out on the porch for a little conversation.

25

Lying bastard.

Billy had in mind the fancy-pants bastard Governor Lew Adair.

Billy had been led to believe that the Ryerson house was a nice, big one where Billy would have his privacy. But it was a small house with small rooms and the only privacy that Billy could see was hiding in the basement. Then there were the "prayer hours," as the plump, gray-haired and ever-busy Mrs. Ryerson told him, four different times per day, right at the top of a given hour, when they got down on their knees and praised the Lord. In the evening, she said, they sang hymns. A fine-looking boy like yourself, Mr. Billy, I'll bet you have a real nice voice.

Lying bastard.

What was Billy going to do in a place like this?

He went up and lay down on his bed, making sure not to take his boots off so they'd smudge up the white bedspread.

You had to pay one hell of a price to get yourself an amnesty, there was no doubt about that.

He thought of women, he thought of money, he thought of his gang days back in New York. He could actually *smell* New York, good and bad smells alike, cabbage and sweet perfume and the grass on the baseball field, garbage and dog shit and hot dogs with mustard, and see all the pretty immigrant girls, Irish and Jewish and German and Italian, and hear that symphony of dialects and tongues. Someday, when he was nice and settled on his farm, he'd have a little money and he'd spend it on going back to New York and the old neighborhood. See his old friends. A lot of them would be dead now, of course. Or in prison. But there'd be a few left, anyway, and they'd find a tavern conducive to recollecting the old days, and they'd sit there till they tipped over feeding each other memories and lies of the past.

By then, he'd be long shut of this place.

Cheery Mrs. Ryerson knocked on his door. "Would you like some hot water for a bath?"

"Not right now."

"Would you like some coffee?"

"Not right now."

"Would you like some soda pop?"

"Will you get the hell away from my door, you nosy old bitch?"

There was a long silence.

"I was just trying to be pleasant." Tears strained her voice.

"Just leave me alone."

"Oh, my Lord. Your language."

And then she was gone, paddling down the hallway. No doubt she'd go downstairs and find her gawky, bald husband and tell him all about the bad language their guest had used.

They'd probably sink to their knees right on the spot and pray their stupid asses off.

He was back in jail again. Only in this particular jail, the person in charge was a sweet-faced old lady who had prayer hour four times a day.

MAE COULD SEE she had hurt his feelings. When Conlon looked over at her, he tried to look cool, disinterested. But the pain was there to see, and she knew she was the one who'd put it there.

But what choice did she have? She liked him, too, and if she liked him enough, her life would get complicated. Right now, all she had to worry about was Billy, and how she was finally going to kill him.

She said, "I'm going down and getting a piece of candy. You want some, Marshal?"

She'd been busily working at her desk during the past hour. This was only the second time she'd spoken to him since she'd come to work at eight this morning. He looked surprised at the relatively cordial tone of her voice.

"No, thanks."

She wanted to say more, something that took that hurt from his eyes. But she knew she'd just make a fool of herself trying.

She stood up and went to the door.

She was halfway across the threshold when he said, "I guess I'd take a twist of licorice."

She turned to him, smiling. "Black or red?"

He smiled back. "You decide."

IN THE NEXT forty-eight hours, nothing remarkable happened in town. There was a Mexican girl in the poor section who was now three weeks late with her baby, a drunkard told a priest in confession that the devil himself had visited him in his room the previous night, and a whore in one of the saloons got a five-dollar tip from a thirty-one-year-old who had until this night been a virgin.

Billy bitched. He bitched to the Ryersons and he bitched to the guards who stood on the front porch. Larry Glencoe, one of those guards, tried to mollify Billy with pie but had no luck. Mrs. Ryerson tried to mollify him with cake. She had no better luck.

Conlon spent most of his working hours trying to figure out Mae. Sometimes she was nice; sometimes she was cold. Her mood didn't seem to depend on anything he said or did. She shifted moods inexplicably. Three times she brought him licorice. Seven or eight times she refused to speak to him no matter what he said to her. When he confronted her, she calmly said that she hadn't heard him. He felt sick, miserable.

In the evenings, Conlon sat in one of the saloons telling tall tales of his days as a New York policeman. He even managed to work in stolen jewelry, loose women, and a yacht. It was a way of keeping him and his drinking friends amused.

Mae chose to walk by the Ryerson house. She knew that R. C. Greaves, a bounty hunter, had already tried to gun Billy down. She planned to have better luck. She would do it in the dead of night. As a former tomboy, she easily climbed out on the sturdy limb of a maple in the backyard of the Ryerson house. She spent both nights watching Billy move around in the flickering lamplight of his room. This was where she'd shoot him from. Getting away would be easy. Nobody would ever know who'd done it. Certainly nobody would suspect sweet, quiet Mae who worked in the sheriff's office.

Bill Stockton, the county attorney, had still not come up with a plan to get rid of Billy. He'd be thunderstruck with an idea and then gloat over how easy it would be to pull it off. But then, as reason set in, he began to see the flaws in it. All his plans were just too damned easy to trace back to him. And thus to Barcroft. If he implicated John Barcroft in anything, he'd be dead within hours.

Out at the Tunstall ranch, Jimmy Dobbs arranged a nice service for his friend Sam. He invited the girl who'd caused Sam to get killed, but she sent a note saying it'd just be too sad to be there. He hired a man who claimed to be a preacher to come and say some prayers while they were putting Sam in the ground. The ranch hands all stood around the fresh grave. By this time, they'd come to hate Billy just as much as Jimmy did. But, unlike Jimmy, they knew better than to entertain ideas of avenging Sam's death. Billy would just shoot you dead and then laugh his ass off about it. Billy was an asshole. Jimmy lay in the bunkhouse at night thinking of ways to get back at Billy. He wanted to make it good. He could backshoot him, but Billy wouldn't suffer. And suffering was what Jimmy hoped to visit upon Billy. A lot of it.

The old men who played checkers in the shade and the fourth grade boys who were members of the Billy Pecos club both talked about the same thing—how

much fun it'd be to go out and see Billy in the flesh.
They all joined other townspeople in finding an excuse to drift by the Ryerson house and gander in the
windows for a sign of Billy. Several claimed to have
seen him, but these were well-known liars who had
also told stories such as seeing Geronimo and personally seeing Jesse James gun down people. The fact
that none of these liars was over the age of eight made
their stories seem even more unlikely.

And so it was the night the real trouble started . . .

28

BILLY COULDN'T TAKE it anymore, and who could
blame him?

If the Ryersons weren't having prayer hour, then
they were at the upright piano in the parlor singing
hymns. And if they weren't singing hymns, they were
wandering around their tiny, tidy home cooing love
names to each other, "Lambykins" and "Dearface"
being their two favorites. You would've thought that
a couple of old farts like this would've given up the
love names a long time ago.

What Billy wanted to do was run downstairs and
empty thirty or forty guns into them. Or douse them
with kerosene and set them on fire. Or drop them into
a pit filled with rattlers. Listening to them scream
would be a lot of fun.

The missus kept trying to get him to pray. The
mister kept trying to get him to talk about any famous

gunnies he may have known. If you asked him, the mister would of course tell you what bad and un-Christian men gunnies were. But this didn't dissuade him from sounding like an awestruck little boy when he asked about them.

Billy sat in his room. About all he'd accomplished the last two days was getting a sore back from lying on the bed so much. And masturbating. He must've set some kind of indoor championship. He felt like a little kid back in New York City, worried his mom would come in and catch him.

Dusk came, and his mood grew even worse. He smelled the dying day and watched his window darken. Moms called the little ones in from playing their final sweaty games of tag and hide-and-go-seek and pom-pom-pull-away. Neighborhood dogs started their lonely barking, and he felt disconsolate. Maybe this amnesty thing was crazy. Maybe he wouldn't even get it. Maybe Stockton and Barcroft would queer the whole thing. Barcroft had the local power to do it, that was for sure.

Billy lay on his bed aching for the taste of whiskey, the touch of womanflesh (and the scent and taste of womanflesh, as well), and that half-giddy feeling of pushing through the batwings and having a whole sa-loonful of people recognize you and step back in sur-prise and fear. There were cards to be played and punks to scare and songs to sing (when he was drunk enough) with the player piano or the darkie banjo player.

And here he was trapped in the deathgrip of Lam-bykins and Dearface.

They were now starting their religious tent show for the evening, leading off with some hymns in the parlor.

He grabbed his pillow and slapped it tight over his face, taking special care to press it tight over his ears.

But it didn't matter. He could still hear them.

Mercifully, he dozed off.

When he woke, they were still downstairs singing. Full night painted the windows now, the autumnal stars bright against the dark sky.

He sat up and rubbed his face and then went over to use the chamber pot. Then he stood at the window wishing he was a bird who could just fly away.

Then he saw the tree limb.

How he had *missed* seeing the tree limb before startled him. All this time he'd been thinking about how he was going to escape from this place when all he needed to do was look out the window.

No need to sneak down the stairs. Or tie a blanket to the bedpost and let himself down the side of the house.

The larger branches of the maple brushed the back of the house. He'd have no trouble opening the window and simply leaping, monkey-style, out to the branches and then down the tree. Simple and fast.

Lambykins and Dearface were going to be very upset.

He went down the hall and cleaned up.

Lambykins knocked. "Are you hungry, Billy?"

"No, thanks, Mrs. Ryerson." He figured he could afford to be polite now that he was getting out of here.

"Do you need a fresh towel?"

"No, thanks, Mrs. Ryerson."

"Would you like to see the newspaper?"

"No, thanks, Mrs. Ryerson."

"Did you read that religious pamphlet I left in your room?"

"Yes, I did, Mrs. Ryerson."

"Did you enjoy it?"

"Yes, I did, Mrs. Ryerson. Very much."

"Well, there's roast beef and rhubarb pie downstairs if you change your mind about eating."

"Thanks, Mrs. Ryerson."

"Oh, don't thank me, Billy. I'm just doing what any good Christian would do. Isn't that what it says in that pamphlet?"

"Yes, Mrs. Ryerson, that's *exactly* what it says."

"Well, don't forget about the roast beef and the rhubarb pie if you change your mind."

"I won't, Mrs. Ryerson."

"The mister and I are going to sing a few more hymns and then retire for the evening. You can always join us if you'd like."

"Thank you, Mrs. Ryerson."

Then, praise the Lord, she was gone.

And Billy was back in his room putting on a clean shirt. And contemplating all the fun he was about to have.

He edged up the window. The soft night suffused him with breezes and aromas almost sexual in their power. He looked down at the ground and realized that it was farther down than he'd thought. Leg-breaking distance for sure. So he'd have to use all his monkey skills. Back in New York he'd been the most agile member of his street gang. But that had been a few years ago.

He put a foot on the window frame and started to pull himself up, and then the knock came.

"Billy?" the mister said. "Wondered if you'd like to sit in the parlor with me and tell me a few more stories about the gunnies you've known. Guess you can tell I've got kind of a weakness for them stories of yours."

Billy sighed. "I'm not feeling too good."

"You want me to have the missus come up and give you something?"

"No, just a headache is all. Just need some sleep."

"You ever know Black Bart?"

"Nope, but I knew a bunch of gunnies who knew him pretty well."

"That's who I'd like to talk about next time," the mister said. "Black Bart. They tell you any good stories?"

"Oh, yes. They told me some real good ones. Now I'd kinda like to get back to sleep."

"Don't blame you. Those dratted headaches can make a fella plain miserable."

He paddled away down the hall.

Black Bart. Billy smiled. Old fart sounded like a little kid. Please c'mon 'n tell me about Black Bart, Unca Billy. Please!

He raised his right leg up again and fitted his foot to the window frame. Then he raised his left leg and was soon squatting whole in the window frame. He looked up at the half moon and the spray of stars. He felt good. He had some excitement in his life again. Then he made the mistake of looking down. Every time he looked, the ground looked farther away. Broken leg would sure hobble him. Here he gets an amnesty and what happens? He's gimped up and can't enjoy it.

But he couldn't stay here. Oh, he'd sneak back in later. But he needed at least four, five hours away. Find a saloon with some shadowy corner and keep his own company. Just sort of sit back and take it all in. Little bit of whiskey so he didn't get in no trouble, and a blond prairie girl with big melons for company, and he'd be just fine. He wouldn't bother nobody, and nobody would bother him. All he had to do was jump out the window to the farthest-reaching branch, the big, sturdy-looking one . . .

C'mon now, Billy, you chickenshit. Jump.

But he was frozen. Stomach knotted. Fine sheen of cold sweat on his forehead. This wasn't as easy as it'd looked.

Jump, Billy. Jump.

Deep breath. Hard swallow. Clenching sphincter.
Jump, Billy.
He jumped.

He was mid-air with the terrible feeling that he was
falling fast. His hands reached out and clawed some
purchase of the extended branch, leaves and bits of
gnarled maple shearing off in his grasp. The branch
wasn't as strong as it had appeared. It started dipping
toward the ground, Billy cursing, grasping, grappling,
groaning. What he did was climb the damn thing.
That was the only way he could avoid being hurled
to the ground by the dipping end of it, the branch all
the time creaking and crying, as if it would snap at
any moment and dash him to the earth. Had to keep
moving. Just like climbing a rope, scaling up the
branch until he found its stronger sections, sections
that wouldn't spill him below. He smelled tree bark
and leaves and sap. His palms were being ripped
bloody. But he kept working his way upward until he
clung to the tree itself, hidden amidst the leaves and
other branches. He needed to know if somebody had
heard him. He stayed still as he could, swallowing his
hot gasping breath, arms wrapped around the tree.

Sounds: barn owl, baby crying, horse hooves clop-
ping down the sandy street, the missus at her piano
warming up for the night, angry man shouting now
at crying baby.

But no sound of the deputy out front running
around to the back to see what was going on.

Billy was pretty messed up, and it pissed him off.
He'd gotten clean and combed and now he was all
sweaty and mussed. He kicked the tree. You sonofabitch, look what you done to me.

But he remembered seeing a clear clean creek not
too far from here. He'd stop there on his way to the
saloon. Get himself back in order. He sure did want

whiskey, but he equally wanted a woman. He surely did.

He waited ten more minutes and then eased himself down out of the tree.

Then he was free again and hurrying down the alley to the fast-running creek.

29

THE FUNNY THING was, Conlon hadn't realized he was lonely until he met Mae. It was kind of like being innocent. Here he'd been wandering the West since his days as a dishonest New York cop, taking fleshly pleasure where he could find it but never really understanding that he was lonely. Oh, once in a while he'd see a sweet young mother and her baby and get nostalgic about the early days of his marriage, before he'd become a complete shit. Or he'd see a bunch of couples walking arm-in-arm down by a river or in a park somewhere and he'd feel a bit isolated. But never really *lonely*.

Then Mae, damn her, went and took his innocence away.

The truth was—and this was a truth he knew too well—he was quickly developing something not unlike and something that might easily be confused with and something right on the very cusp of being . . . love.

As evidence, look at him tonight.

When he got done with his paperwork, he'd gone

for his usual supper and then for his usual after-dinner walk with his big stogie. The few people who stopped to talk to him wanted to know about Billy, to make sure he was no threat to the town, and to express their opinion on Billy being granted amnesty, him being a killer and all.

And then he went over to the boarding house where Mae lived.

He felt like a lovesick seventh grader.

He walked past Mae's place four times in an hour, not quite sure which window to look at, not knowing which room she was in.

He wondered if she saw him out there on the lamp-lit street. And if she saw him, what did she think? Surely, by now, she must have sensed his feelings for her.

A couple of old men, who were more shadow than substance, sat on Mae's porch in rocking chairs. You could hear their rocking chairs squeak and see the burning fire of their own stogies. Conlon could feel their eyes on him, assessing. They'd know who he was, of course. By now, everybody knew the acting sheriff. He just hoped they didn't know why he'd been past here four times in the past hour.

But his fourth time past, a giggly old-man voice said, "You're wastin' your time, son. She ain't home."

He hadn't been called "son" in twenty years. But that wasn't what bothered him. It was that they knew his secret. That he was looking for Mae. They'd tell her, of course, two old men like these would take abiding and pure delight in kidding her about the law-man who had the sweets on her.

And so he hurried on through the darkness, em-barrassed. He was some lawman, all right, carrying on like a silly kid, keeping a street vigil in front of his loved one's house, the way he had so long ago in

front of a New York tenement where one Suzie
O'Shay had once lived. He'd been so lovesick that
his mom put him to bed thinking he'd come down
with influenza. They'd even brought the doc in. But
Conlon had been too ashamed of himself to explain
that he was carrying on this way because he'd learned
that Suzie was in love with Teddy Parnell, who lived
down the street from her. He'd stayed in bed three
days and three nights and only when his oldest sister
Nell came in and told him that this was how love was
some times—Nell fell in love several times a year,
like the seasons—did he have the faint hope that
someday he'd feel better again, the irony being that
six years later Teddy Parnell and he were cops together in the same ward, and good friends, and Conlon became the godfather of the third child Suzie
O'Shay bore Teddy.

He wished he had Nell to talk to tonight. Maybe
she could make him feel better about Mae, the way
so long ago, on a soft summer night when the kids
played stickball in the moonlight, she'd made him
feel better about Suzie.

He did the only sensible thing a man could do.

He went to a saloon.

The place was so crowded that nobody paid him
any special deference. He got himself a bottle and he
got himself a glass and he got himself a table way
the hell in the back of the place. A girl came over,
but she wasn't Mae, so what was the point? Then a
couple of gamblers came over and wondered if he
wanted to be fifth for poker, but he knew he'd never
be able to concentrate. He sat and sipped. He wasn't
a heavy drinker. He'd taken a whole bottle more as
a dramatic gesture than anything else, the way men
did in dime novels when their souls were troubled.
Even lawmen were susceptible to the histrionics of
the yellowbacks.

An hour later, when he had just poured his second drink, he saw one of the nephews wriggle his way through the crowd. He'd spotted the marshal and meant to talk to him. This particular nephew was not a deputy. He just sort of hung out around the jail with the other nephews hoping to get *hired* as a deputy.

"God, I been lookin' for ya everwhere," the nephew said sweatily. "You're a hard man t' find."

Conlon got nervous. Nephew or not, the kid looked as if something was really wrong.

He said, "You know my cousin out to guardin' Billy?"

"Yes. What about him?"

"Well, his wife, Esse Lou, she made a cake this afternoon and asked me to truck a piece on out to him. You know, like a suprise kinda like."

"Will you please get to the point?" The men were shouting at each other. The crowd was so loud that the men had to escape.

"He ain't there, Marshal."

"Who isn't there?"

"Billy! He snuck out!"

A few moments later, Conlon and the nephew were quick-stepping their way out the door.

30

THERE WERE TWO types of places to look for Billy: the whorehouses and the saloons. The nephew took the former and Conlon took the latter.

Conlon knew he didn't dare ask if anybody had seen Billy. That would start a panic. A lot of townspeople would see it as their nightmare come true, a gunnie of Billy's murderous nature and inclination walking free among them.

Conlon solemnly and silently passed among gamblers, whores, drunkards, toughs, gunnies, would-be gunnies, retired gunnies, miners, cowboys, and decent townspeople who sure as hell shouldn't be hanging out in such places—not if they planned on *staying* decent, anyway.

A drunken gunnie offered to fight him. Conlon kicked him in the balls and passed on.

A drunken whore offered to take him up to her room. She just made him lonely for Mae.

A sobbing drunken man beyond consolation wept because he'd gambled away his pay. Conlon gave him a dollar, all he could afford, and a pious lecture, and then escorted him the short distance home.

He went back to the middle of town and checked out the remaining three saloons.

No sign whatsoever of Billy.

So just where the hell was he, and how the hell had he gotten out of the Ryerson house?

Conlon decided to take all his anger out on the nephew who'd been standing guard and set off for the Ryerson place.

31

Oh, it was all so fine, so fine.

He couldn't, in fact, tell which was better, the sex or the whiskey, though he leaned slightly in favor of the sex because the Widow Gaines was something indeed.

Widow Gaines's husband had once worked for Tunstall. But he'd been killed breaking a horse. This was two years before Billy even came to these parts. Widow Gaines sometimes came to the ranch to visit the other hands and to talk about the days when her husband was still alive. During a couple of her more recent visits, Billy had been there. He could see that she found him appealing.

On his way to the saloons tonight, Billy, for once, actually thought through something he was about to do. If he went to the saloons, the word would soon get around. And that would bring the marshal. And that would mean that Conlon would, over even the objections of Governor Adair, throw Billy's ass in jail. And Billy would get to spend the next couple of weeks in the company of God's forsaken and forgotten people. You did not meet a high caliber of folks in the county jail.

That was when he remembered the Widow Gaines. And her eye-stunning bosom. And that sweet, shy smile. And those pretty eyes.

An old-timer on a porch told him where the Widow lived, and Billy went there posthaste.

She seemed more than surprised—she seemed

downright startled—when she saw him in her doorway. Behind her, in the lampglow of the tiny but orderly house, two little girls in pigtails and nightshirts played a game of checkers. Billy put their ages somewhere around eight or nine.

She invited Billy in, offered him the remnants of her supper, which he declined, and then offered him the remnants of her whiskey bottle, which he accepted.

The girls went to bed in a back room just after eight o'clock. Billy sat in a rocking chair sipping whiskey and listening to the Widow say prayers with the girls and then kiss them goodnight and then tell them again, for about the sixtieth time it seemed, how much she loved them. Then she left the room, closing the door.

Billy just sat there sipping whiskey and wondering if she could see the enormous erection he had snaking around in his corduroys. He hoped so.

Took him an hour but he finally got her on the floor. Took him another half hour to get all her clothes off. But before she actually let him inside she jumped up and went to the wall and turned pictures of her husband and Jesus around so they couldn't see what she was about to do. She said she couldn't do anything if they were watching her. Billy didn't care. It gave him his first good look at her naked ass, her standing on tiptoes to turn the pictures around, and boy she had a beauty.

By now, the effects of the whiskey were settling in. He was at just the right point where the hooch enhanced his performance and gave him an even greater appreciation for the woman beneath him. She smelled so pretty, and her flesh was so damned silky.

He went three rounds, drinking a lot of whiskey between his spates of lovemaking. She wanted to

talk—hell, even whores wanted to talk—but as usual
Billy was able to *look* as if he was listening while not
actually hearing much of what she said. That she
shouldn't have done this. That he was the first man
she'd done it with since her husband died. That she
sure hoped Billy didn't have any kind of whore disease or anything like that, that that was maybe how
God would pay her back for being so sinful, her girls
sleeping sweetly in a nearby room, and her carrying
on this way and all, her naked and everything with
Billy inside her. Maybe God would give her a disease,
and everybody in town would know she had the disease, and the teachers would send the girls home from
school and tell them to never come back because of
her mother's disease, and even the parson would tell
her that she was no longer welcome among decent
people. And it would serve her right, when you came
right down to it, serve her right for doing what she'd
just done with Billy. She just sure hoped he didn't
have a whore disease. And Billy, sort of half-assed
listening to this, real bored, just wanted her to shut
up so he could gaze in rapt rhapsody upon her wonderful breasts.

Finally, with the Widow still talking and not seem-
ing to wear down at all, Billy stood up and said he
was going to step out and take a piss, and her saying
we have a chamber pot, and him saying right back,
no, I need a little air too. Her looking hurt a bit and
him laughing and saying, I'll be right back, I promise.

32

"YOU DIDN'T HEAR him?"

"Nope."

"And didn't see him?"

"Nope."

"Then how did you know he was gone?"

"Some of the kids down the block, they seen him runnin' and came'n told me."

"Just great."

"You kind've pissed at me, Marshal?"

Conlon sighed and walked down off the front porch and looked far down the sandy, lamplit street. It was such a sweet night. He should be in his room with the breeze coming through the window reading his Sir Walter Scott book. He loved those books. He wasn't an educated man, but he was a reader.

Conlon walked around back. The nephew and the cousin started to follow him but he snapped, "Stay there!"

They glanced at each other with smirks on their faces.

The backyard was beautiful in the moonlight. A tomcat sat in the grass, watching him.

Conlon wanted to satisfy himself the way any professional lawman would want to—by figuring out just how Billy had managed to escape. It didn't take a genius to figure it out, either. From the window to the tree branch. Lot of leaves on the ground, meaning he'd probably had some trouble, shredding the leaves in the process.

But the satisfaction he felt was momentary at best. Now that he knew how he'd escaped, he was right back where he'd started. Just where the hell was Billy, anyway?

He had just reached the front yard again when he heard a voice shouting, "Marshal! Marshal?" Somebody on the street, running this way, sounding excited, scared.

"Sounds like somebody's looking for you, Marshal," cousin said.

"No shit," Conlon said.

The runner was a skinny young man in britches worn too high and suspenders worn too tight. He was buck-toothed, sweaty, and gasping for breath.

"Terrible thing happened, Marshal, and they need you real bad!" His voice came in hot bursts.

"What happened?"

"The Widow Gaines!" the young man said.

"What about her?"

"Oh, it's terrible, just terrible!" the young man said.

"Just calm yourself," Conlon said.

"Sorry," he gasped.

"It's fine," Conlon said.

The young man shook his head in apology and touched his fingers to his riled chest. He kept sucking air deep down inside himself and finally said, "Her little girls, Marshal, they was runnin' down the street in their nightshirts, Marshal! Some sumbitch cut the Widow's throat and then run off!"

33

CONLON HEARD THE mob before he saw them, men and women alike, *angry* men and women, shouting affirmations at a deep male voice that was urging them to "Do the right thing—and I don't have to tell you what that is, do I?"

The nephew said, "Looks like we won't have to worry about it, Marshal, whatever it is. A good ole-fashioned lynchin' settles things right fast."

Yes, Conlon thought, there was nothing like the company of professional peace officers to inspire confidence in the law.

Against the night, torches flamed in a semicircle as a crowd of fist-shaking people moved on a woman with a shotgun and a man cowering next to her.

The woman was Mae. The man was Billy.

Before them on the grass lay the bloody form of a dead woman, the red smear across her face and throat glistening in the dancing torch light. Off to the side, huddled against a plump woman in a long dark nightgown, were two little girls.

Conlon drew his six-shooter and fired twice into the air. It was the fastest way to get the mob's attention.

The shots didn't have the immediate impact he'd hoped for. A flank of the mob continued to approach Mae and Billy.

Conlon shoved his way through a tangle of people and took his place next to Mae.

"You gotta help me, Marshal," Billy said. "These people wanta kill me."

Conlon took brief enjoyment in seeing Billy scared. Always nice to see bullies frightened. But this wasn't a time for moral judgments, much as Conlon, like most people, loved to make them.

Now it was time to haul Billy's ass out of here.

Crowds had always scared Conlon. Even when his mother used to take him to the open-air market, the sheer number of people terrified him. He was a cop when the so-called draft riots took place, thousands of young whites resentful because they were being conscripted into the Civil War, resentful because they didn't want to fight for darkies whom they hated in the first place, expressing their resentment by hanging Negroes from virtually every lamppost they could find. Conlon had tried to stop the mob, but they soon smashed his head in with stones and trampled his body. He was in the hospital for three weeks. He remembered the faces of the punks—youths who would be too afraid to beard a copper on their own were made bold and fierce by the mob.

He looked at these people and saw the same thing, average folks who might be decent enough individually but who'd become momentarily insane because of mob pressure. Easy enough to understand why the dead woman would affect them this way, but this was no way to deal with it.

He lowered his six-shooter until it was pointing at the wildest looking of the crowd, a beefy, black-haired man in an eyepatch and a pair of Indian breeches. His name was Seretti, but he worked hard to look like an Indian.

"You take one more step, Seretti, and I'm going to drop you right on the spot," Conlon said.

To make his point, Conlon took two steps toward

Seretti. He raised his weapon and pointed it directly in Seretti's face.

"He killed her," Seretti said. He was drunk but coherent.

"If he killed her, the law'll take care of that."

"The law!" somebody shouted. "You mean like Adair givin' him a pardon?"

"You people need to go home," Conlon said. "This is just making things worse."

"You can bet Sheriff Glencoe would've let us have him," somebody else shouted.

Yes, Conlon thought, and gotten himself a nice bonus from John Barcroft for doing so.

"I want you people to break up, now," Conlon said, "and go on back home."

The apple caught him squarely in the middle of the forehead. It was a hard, red apple the size of a baseball, perfect for throwing. It didn't even break, just smacked into Conlon and fell to his feet. The impact was considerable and knocked him back half a foot or so.

Seretti mistook this as a good time to move on Conlon. He lunged at the lawman, grabbing for Conlon's gun arm as he did so. But even with the pain of the apple still numbing his forehead and nose, Conlon was able to defend himself. He brought his knee straight up between Seretti's legs. Seretti cried out and made a grotesque face. Conlon put his hand over the face and pushed Seretti to the ground.

A couple of other toughs started toward them, but Mae was there with her shotgun, putting it in their faces and forcing them back.

Billy gawked nervously at each torch-lit face in the crowd. A man of his reputation should be able to trade on that reputation in a circumstance like this. But not even the women looked afraid of him now. They just wanted to get their hands on him, get a rope around his neck, and watch him shit himself and dangle till the crows came and ripped out his eyes and the young ones came at first light and stood staring up at the dead man who took his gunnie rep with him to the grave.

But they didn't get their chance, not with both Conlon and Mae advancing nice and slow on them, pushing them back and back and back until they reached the sandy street, their torches now lighting the houses on the other side of the block. Their anger was sputtering now. A few of them still flung curses at Conlon and Mae, and later in the saloons they would talk beerily and bravely of what they would have done if they just got another chance. But for now, not wanting to argue with a U.S. Marshal, they began to sputter much like their torches. Conlon said to leave the two girls here—he'd take care of them.

It took ten minutes to disperse them, but finally they were gone, nothing more than torchlight now in the long narrow street leading back to town.

Mae had hog-tied Billy so he couldn't escape. He lay on his side next to the dead woman.

"She got them ropes so tight, she's cuttin' off my circulation," Billy said.

But Conlon barely heard him. He was staring at the dead woman. Somebody had thrown a blanket over her. She was naked beneath. She had good facial bones, the same bones in the faces of the little girls. The crowd had taken the light and the noise with them, like a parade vanished into the night. Now there was just the moonlight and the natural songs of night, sweet birds in the trees, and solemn frogs by the creek in back.

Mae had the girls over by a tree. She was talking to them very quietly. One of them suddenly started sobbing. She rushed to Mae, and Mae picked her up and walked her around the way she would an infant.

The little girl clung to Mae's neck with little girl stick arms.

Conlon went inside and looked around. The front room was a mess. There was a lot of blood soaking the couch, where the woman must have died. He went to the back of the house. Neither the kitchen nor the bedrooms had been damaged. Apparently, the violence had all taken place in the front room.

Conlon was walking down the narrow hall when he saw the knife on the floor. It had been kicked into a deep shadow.

He got down on his haunches and struck a match.

The pearl-handled dagger was filthy with blood. So was the floor around it.

Conlon dug out his handkerchief. He carefully lifted the knife by the handle and just as carefully carried it outside.

"When the hell you gonna cut me loose?" Billy said.

Conlon walked over to him and showed him the knife. "Look familiar?"

"You know it looks familiar," Billy said. "It's mine."

"This is probably the knife that killed her."

"So?"

"Well, that makes it really likely that you killed this woman."

"I didn't kill her, Marshal. I really didn't."

"Then who did?"

"That's the hell of it," Billy said sincerely, "I can't remember."

Part Two

34

"THIS IS ALL bullshit."

"Yeah, you've said that before, Billy. About six hundred times."

"I didn't kill her."

"You've said that, too."

"But I get the feeling you don't believe me, Conlon."

"You were there with her. She was killed with your knife. You had blood all over your shirt and your trousers and your hands."

"I told you. I just bent over her. To see if she was alive."

Conlon sighed. It was one in the morning, and he was tired. He and Billy had been in a small room in the sheriff's office for the past three hours. Billy kept rolling cigarettes and saying he had to go to the toilet. Which meant that Conlon had to walk him down the hall, walk him out the back door, walk him out into the alley, and let him go.

Conlon said, "You were outside emptying your bladder."

"That's right."

"And you turned and—"

"He was there."

"He?"

"Yeah, 'he.' There something wrong with that?"

"You told me you didn't see the face or didn't get much of a look at the body, but you're sure it was a 'he.' "

"There was a bandana over the face."

"Yes?"

"And a slouch hat on."

"Yes?"

"And a bulky coat."

"Yes?" Conlon sighed. "I'll take your word for it that it was a 'he.' If he was even there."

"What the hell's that supposed to mean?"

Conlon took his pipe from his mouth. "It means, Billy, that I don't necessarily believe you."

"Why the hell not?"

"Why the hell not? You want to start with the fact that you're wanted in eleven states? Or that you've held up at least seven banks? Or that you've killed as many as twenty people?"

"A lot of that stuff's exaggerated."

"Right. You've probably only killed *nineteen* people."

"Well, I'm telling you one thing, Marshal, I didn't kill this woman."

Conlon leaned his head back. He wanted to be in bed. He wanted to be tumbling down the long dark winding staircase of sleep. He leaned forward and said, "Nobody believes you, Billy."

"I'm not known for killing women."

"True. But that doesn't mean you're incapable of it."

"I was having a good time. Why would I kill her?"

"You didn't have to force her to have sex?"

"Force her? She practically tore my clothes off." This was the only time he smiled tonight. "I've got that effect on women."

Conlon stood up and walked over to the small oblong window. Empty alley. Hungry dog wandering left-right, right-left in some kind of weaving pattern only he understood. He looked lonesome and sweet in the silver glow. Even the garbage waiting for the pickup man was blessed by the moonlight.

"How the hell did I ever get into this?"

Conlon turned around and looked at Pecos. He had his elbows on his knees and his head in his hands.

Conlon said, "We need sleep."

"I won't be *able* to sleep."

"Sure you will."

Billy looked up. "I been in jails before, Marshal. They talk all night."

"There's only two people up there, an old colored man on a vag charge and a guy who's so drunk he won't be awake till noon. C'mon, Billy, let's pack it in for the night."

35

MAE WAS AT her desk when Conlon got there in the morning. She'd put the coffee on and was sipping from her battered tin cup. She glanced up and nodded "morning" and went right back to her work.

Conlon got himself some coffee and went to his desk and sat down and said, "I was here until almost two."

She kept on working through her papers. "Good."

"We had a real long session, Billy and me."

Working.

"And I've come to a conclusion."

Working.

"I don't think he killed Mrs. Gaines."

Stopped working. Instantly. Looked up at him sharply. "What?"

"I don't think he killed her."

"Of course he killed her."

"Why 'of course'?"

"Oh, let's see now," she said. She had one of those rubber thumb things that made it easier to flip through papers. She took it off and set it on her stack of papers. "Maybe because he was the only other person there, besides her kids. Or maybe because it was his knife that killed her. Or maybe because he was found in the house with blood all over him. Or maybe because everybody knows he's a killer."

"You really hate him, don't you?"

"That doesn't matter here."

"You've never told me why you hate him so much."

"Like I said, Marshal, it doesn't matter. All that matters is that you don't think he killed her."

Conlon took his pipe out and put it, unlit, into his mouth. He drew on it, savored the sweet taste that had accrued in the bowl over the years. He said, "The thing he wants most is that amnesty."

"So?"

"So why would he jeopardize the amnesty by doing something like this?"

"Because he's insane."

"I don't think so."

"All right. Because he was drunk, and she did something that made him mad."

"According to him, she practically tore his clothes off."

"According to him."

He leaned forward and said, "You think you'll ever tell me?"

"Tell you what, Marshal?"

"Why you hate him so much."

"Like I said, it doesn't matter."

"It matters to me."

"Why?"

"Because we're supposed to be professional."

"I see."

"And we're supposed to keep our personal feelings out of professional business."

"Human beings aren't built that way."

"Law officers are. Or should be."

"I'm not a law officer."

"No, but you work in the jail. And that means you have certain responsibilities."

She glared at him and said, "That was a nice little speech, Marshal. Now I need to get back to work."

He went back where one of the nephews was sweeping out the cells. Billy was still asleep, curled up like a baby. The other two prisoners had been shunted to the courtroom an hour earlier.

Not that he paid much attention to what he saw, for he was still seething from his confrontation with Mae. She could make him crazy faster than anybody he'd ever known.

He went to the front office and stood at her desk.

After a long minute, she looked up. "Yes?"

"It's because I asked you to dinner, isn't it?"

"What's because you asked me to dinner?"

"The way you changed."

"I wasn't aware I'd changed."

"Oh, you're aware, all right. You and me got along just fine until I asked you to dinner. Then you started all this."

"All this what?"

"You know all this what."

Then she shocked him by grinning this great grin that had the effect of a punch. "Anybody ever tell you you're cute when you're mad, Marshal?"

"I want to take back my dinner invitation."

"Good. That's a good, constructive idea."

"And I never plan to ask you to dinner again."

"Fine. I'm all for that."

"Now can we go back to the way we were?"

"I'll be happy to."

A few minutes later, feeling just awful about everything, knowing now that any hope of romance was out of the question, Conlon put on his Stetson and went to visit County Attorney Stockton.

36

THERE WAS NOTHING like a good beating to make you feel better about yourself.

Ever since Ronnie Pritchett had snuck away last night and seen things he oughtn't to, he'd been feeling pretty bad. Them demons was in him again. It was them demons that had rizz him from his bed and snucked him out of the house and pranced him out and about the town. And it was them demons that made him see what he oughtn't to have. Oh, Lord, God, he wished he hadn't seen it.

His father didn't find out that Ronnie had snuck off. Any time Ronnie Pritchett found himself possessed by them demons, and did something he shouldn't have, the good Reverend Pritchett found out about it and responded accordingly.

But not this time.

His father had taken extra whiskey to sleep last

night because his rheumatiz was so bad. (Ronnie knew that his father wouldn't drink all the time unless it was something God wanted him to do, the good Reverend being in direct and constant communication with the Man in the Sky.)

Thanks to the extra whiskey, the good rev had slept through clean till the rooster crowed. And by then, Ronnie was back home. In bed.

Just the other afternoon, knowing that them demons that drove him were still inside him, he went into the kitchen where his scarecrowlike father sat with one skeletonlike hand on the bottle and the other on a glass sloshing with whiskey. Every time the good Reverend gulped, Ronnie was fascinated because his father had an Adam's apple half the size of a baseball, and it was fun to watch it go up and down, like some sort of county fair amusement.

"Pa, I got demons in me," Ronnie began, and then told his father about how those demons wouldn't leave him after he snuck back home this time. He told Pa about leaving the house, about the demons screamin' inside his head and tellin' him all sorts of dirty stuff about women's breasts and the soft hot thing between their legs. (He didn't tell him about how sometimes he snuck over to watch the widda woman Gaines take off her clothes and slip into bed on hot nights.)

In that place they'd put him, they didn't know how to administer good beatings, them guards and them nurses. They'd slap you or kick you or push you down stairs (he once broke three fingers on his left hand) but they didn't know how to drive the demons out, not even when they caused you to bleed a lot, like when they cracked his head open pounding it against that floor that time.

But his father the good Reverend, God's hand

guided him when he give you a beating. God's hand guided him real good.

He used the barber strap until the welts started to bleed and until Ronnie started puking and feeling like he was going to faint. And then he started crying "Lord! Lord! Forgive me!" And that's when he could feel the demons start to leave, the hand of the Lord guiding the Reverend's hand and pushin' those demons back to the fires of Hades where they belonged.

Now, it was morning, and his father was sitting in the kitchen with one ape-knuckled hand on the bottle, the other on the glass, and his Adam's apple going up and down, down and up, above the line of his collar. Ronnie knew he should tell Pa about last night—what he saw and all—but he didn't think he could handle another beating.

His father said, "I chase them demons off?"

"You sure did, Reverend. And I sure thank you for it."

His father liked to be called Reverend. By everybody. Even Ronnie's mother, before God had told him to cane her to death, even Ronnie's mother had called him Reverend. There had been some talk of maybe charging the Reverend with something, but the religious folk in town stuck up for him and said the sheriff didn't have no right dallyin' with God's plan. He'd summoned Irna, and all the good Reverend had done was make sure that she got herself dispatched up to the pearly gates.

"Kin I go down to the creek by the bridge, Reverend?"

The Reverend tossed down another drink, his Adam's apple so big and fierce it looked like it'd just tear through his skin. "You say your prayers?"

"Yes, sir."

"You go to the bathroom?"

"Yes, sir."

"And you didn't touch yourself down there in no sinful way?"

"No, sir."

"And you ain't got no *Police Gazettes* stuffed under your mattress?"

"No, sir."

He looked up at him. "I don't want to have to do no demon-banishin' today. You think them demons are comin' back, you run over to the church and go to the altar and pour the sanctifyin' water all over yourself. You hear me?"

"Yes, sir."

"Because beatin' them demons out of you is a lot of work. It tires me out."

"I really appreciate you doin' it, though, Reverend. I surely do. Otherwise them demons'd be with me all the time."

A few minutes later, he was on his merry way toward town.

37

SOFT. THAT WAS the first word that came to mind when Conlon met Bill Stockton. The plump cheeks, the plump belly, the soft damp hand. Soft. The wounded eyes didn't help. He looked as if he expected to be beaten at any moment. He was the perfect employee for a man like John Barcroft.

The county attorney's office was small, orderly, and quiet. The women in the outer office took note of Conlon but went immediately back to their work. Stockton led Conlon back to his office, another small space filled with a collection of wooden office furnishings that didn't quite match. An outsize, framed painting of President Rutherford B. Hayes imposed itself on the room. Hayes looked as though he had indigestion.

Once they were seated, Stockton said, "I want to thank you for breaking up that mob last night. That could've been a very dangerous situation."

"It may be a serious situation again," Conlon said. "That's one of the reasons I'm here."

"Oh?"

"I want you to give John Barcroft a message for me."

"Is there some reason you can't do that yourself?"

Conlon said, "You see him more often than I do."

The implication had the desired effect on Stockton. A flush came to his chipmunk cheeks. "I know him socially. Not professionally."

"If you say so."

"I'm not sure I like that tone of voice, Marshal. The county attorney isn't allowed to have friends?"

Conlon sighed. He felt a little sorry for Stockton. There was no other place in the West where a weak man like Stockton could add county attorney to his résumé. You needed somebody like Barcroft who wanted his own man. He'd give you the title if you'd give him your soul.

"I apologize," Conlon said. "I haven't had much sleep, and I'm looking for somebody to blame it on."

Stockton smiled. "I've had a lot of nights like that, myself."

Conlon said, "I imagine Barcroft's happy that Billy won't be getting his amnesty."

"I haven't talked to Mr. Barcroft, but I'm sure he's very upset about Mrs. Gaines's death. She was a good woman. Billy will finally get what he's been deserving for a long time."

"I don't think he killed her."

"My Lord," said Stockton. "You're serious?"

Conlon nodded. "Yes."

"But of course he killed her. He may have been drunk and not aware of what he was doing. But of course he killed her."

"I think somebody else killed her and made it look as if Billy did it."

"Marshal, that is nonsensical."

"Billy has a lot of enemies in these parts."

"Who, for instance?"

Conlon calculated the effect of his words. "Barcroft, for one."

"That's absurd."

"Not everybody out at the Tunstall ranch liked him, either. Maybe it was somebody from out there."

"He killed her, Marshal. There is no doubt of that at all. No doubt."

"I don't mean to pull rank on you, Stockton. But I was a New York homicide detective for several years. I worked on more than seventy murder cases in my time. Sometimes, things look too neat, and that always makes a good detective curious. This one looks too neat."

"He was drunk, and she wouldn't have sex with him, and he tore her clothes off and killed her."

"That isn't the way Billy tells it."

"Well, what do you expect him to say, Marshal? As I said, he may have been so drunk that he doesn't remember it. But he killed her. His knife. All the blood."

"He's got a big knot on the back of his head."

"So? That just means she hit him with something while she was defending herself."

Stockton might be a weak man, but he was a middling-fair lawyer. He was arguing his case well.

"Or the real killer knocked him out," Conlon said, "and then took Billy's knife and killed Mrs. Gaines with it."

"Or he struck his head on something when he fell over backwards after killing her. Mrs. Gaines's daughters said they found him unconscious on the lawn next to their mother—those poor little girls. Apparently, he'd chased Mrs. Gaines outside. She was already half-dead, most likely, and then he finished her off on the front lawn."

Stockton was gaining in poise and self-confidence. This little court trial in the abstract was doing great things for his self-esteem. "I just can't believe you'd take Billy's word for things. You're a savvy lawman, Marshal."

"It's just too neat, that's all. That's why I believe him."

"Aren't things ever neat?"

"There's a difference between neat and too neat."

A knock. "Excuse me, Mr. Stockton. Somebody from the courthouse ran over and said Judge Michaels would like to talk to you. I guess Bolan isn't doing a very good job this morning." Bolan was a tyro in the county attorney's office. Conlon had met him a few times. He was young, confrontational, and genuinely annoying.

"I'll be there in a few minutes," Stockton said.

Conlon stood up. "I appreciate the time, Mr. Stockton. I just wanted to let you know that I'm going to spend a little time on this. I have to admit that there's a good chance Billy did it—that my instincts are wrong. But at least I want to satisfy myself before I close the case."

"You're being a professional, Marshal. Nothing wrong with that."

Stockton walked him back to the courthouse. They talked about an upcoming baseball game in a nearby town.

38

MAE WAS FEELING pretty good, actually.

She was sitting under a tree down the street from the courthouse and the jail, a copy of *Peterson's La-dies' National Magazine* in one hand and an apple in the other.

She was feeling relieved.

For a while, she was afraid she was going to get involved with Conlon. She *wanted* to get involved with Conlon. At least a part of her did. And she'd wake up in the middle of the night and find herself suffocating. Literally smothering. And she knew why. Because her own desires were betraying her. She was losing control of her life and letting Conlon take over. And she was betraying her one true calling in life: to take Billy's life from him. This was the best chance she would ever have, and she could not let her feelings for Conlon get in the way.

"My pa says magazines are sinful," Ronnie said.

She looked up and smiled. Big innocent overgrown boy-man like Ronnie. She liked him in a pure, simple, completely trusting way, the way she liked cats and dogs.

"Your pa says a lot of things."

Ronnie grinned. "Yeah, I guess he does. I had me the demons again, but my pa, he beat them out of me."

"Oh, Ronnie." She put her magazine down and patted the grass next to her.

He sat down. She knew he had a crush on her. It was sweet.

They didn't say anything for a time. The air was busy. Butterflies and horseflies and birds. The dusty alkali street was busy, too. Wagons and horses and children bright as flowers.

She said, "Your back hurt?"

"Not so bad."

"I don't know why you let him do it to you."

"I *want* him to. I got me the demons. And anyway, he don't want to."

"Oh?"

"He says it tires him out."

She couldn't help it. She laughed. "Yes, I guess I could see where beating somebody could tucker you out."

"I don't know what I'm gonna do when he passes."

"Why?"

"Why?" Ronnie said. "Well, who am I gonna get to beat me when he dies?"

"I guess I never thought of it that way."

"I think of it that way all the time." He put his head back against the tree. "I snuck out last night."

"Demons?"

"Yeah. They just kept tellin' me to sneak off, so I did."

"Where'd you go?"

"Oh, you know. Just around town."

She angled her head to look at him. He sounded evasive. She knew she was his best and most trusted friend. "You have a secret, Ronnie?"

He swallowed hard. "Yeah, sort of, I guess."

"I don't think you've ever had a secret from me before, have you?"

"I guess not."

"It must be some secret."

"My pa said I shouldn't never stick my nose into other people's business."

"He actually said that?"

"Yeah, why?"

"Well, he sticks his nose into other people's business all the time."

"He does?"

"Sure he does. He's always telling people they're sinners and always telling them to change their ways."

"He only does that because God tells him to."

She shrugged. He loved his father so much. It was heartbreaking. "Oh, Ronnie, I wish I was as sweet as you are."

"I'm sweet?"

"You sure are."

"Sweet as honey?" He was grinning.

"Sweeter than honey. I just wish you wouldn't let your pa beat you."

"He only does it 'cause I ask him. Because of the—"

"I know, I know. Because of the demons."

"Well, it's true. I've got me the demons. Just like some people have got them the head lice or the shingles."

She slipped her railroad watch out of her Levi's. Time to head back to the office. It wasn't suffocating any more, now that she and Conlon had struck their bargain. Now that she was back to concentrating on killing Billy.

"Need to head back, Ronnie."

"I sure do like sittin' with you."

She leaned over and gave him a sisterly kiss on the cheek. "I sure do like sittin' with you, too, Ronnie."

On the way back to the sheriff's office, she wondered idly about the secret Ronnie was keeping from her. It probably wasn't important. She put it quickly out of her mind.

39

JUST BEFORE NOON, Conlon rode out to the Tunstall ranch. He had to pass by two armed guards to get inside. They took a lot of pleasure in making him identify himself and his intentions. What could be more fun than pushing a U.S. Marshal around?

The first thing he heard about was some bogged cattle down by the river, several hands having been down there since just after dawn. A chip wagon passed as he dismounted, the cattle chips triumphantly odorous on the clear air. But the chips were worth the smell. They made great, cheap fuel. A rough string—unbroken horses—was being led into a rope corral by a heavyset Mexican whose eyes radiated hatred on sight of Conlon's badge. Probably assumed every law official in the area was in John Barcroft's pocket.

He found Jimmy Burke in the barn, shoeing a horse. Billy had told him that maybe Jimmy knew something. He identified Jimmy as an enemy.

"Mr. Burke?"

The sad-faced man in need of a shave said, "That'd be me."

"Name's Conlon."

"I know who you are." He went back to his work.

The barn smelled sweetly of fresh hay and horse shit. Here in the shadows it was five degrees cooler than outside. Cowboys came in and out, getting tools and horses.

"You hear about Billy?" Conlon said.

"I heard."

"He told me that you hate him."

Burke's face turned up to Conlon again. "Sam was a good man. He had honorable intentions toward that girl. He was real stuck on her. Sam was the kid you killed the other night."

"I didn't have a hell of a lot of choice."

"You should've killed Billy instead. He was the one who pushed Sam in that direction."

The horse started switching its tail with metronomic violence as Burke finished up the job. When he was done, he put the hoof back to the earthen floor and stood up straight. "She was over here last night. To see Sam's grave. She was a mess."

"What's her name?"

"Trudy. Why?"

"Trudy what?"

"Trudy Demmel."

"You know where she lives?"

"She lives in the next county. But she's got an aunt in town, and she's staying there for a few days."

"You know the aunt's name?"

"McCarty, I think." Then, "Why all these questions?"

"Just following up on a few things."

"Because Billy told you to?"

"Where were you last night?"

"Me? Why?"

"You ask a lot of questions," Conlon said.

"So do you."

"So where were you?"

"In the bunkhouse reading. Until around eight-thirty or so."

"What happened at eight-thirty?"

"There was a commotion among the cattle out in the field."

"And that's where you went?"

"I checked it out. By then, the boys had it pretty much in hand."

"Then what?"

"Then what?"

"Then where did you go?"

A hand came in and grabbed a pitchfork. He was gone again in moments.

"Then I went for a ride."

"Why?"

"I was still thinkin' about seeing Trudy. How mad she was and all. I figured a ride would calm me down.

"You went alone?"

"Sure."

"You see anybody while you were riding?"

"Nope."

"What time did you get back to the ranch?"

Burke shrugged. "Eleven, eleven-thirty."

"Long ride."

"Like I said, Marshal, I needed to relax."

"Billy have a lot of enemies out here?"

Burke leaned back against the edge of the stall. "About the only one who ever liked him was Tunstall hisself. They really got along."

"What about the other gunnies? They didn't like him?"

"Not so you'd notice. Billy made real sure they knew he was the boss."

A cowboy stuck his head in the barn and said, "Jimmy, they said they need you down by the river. They're havin' some trouble with them horses."

"Be right there." Then, "He's finally gonna pay the freight."

"Billy?"

"Yeah," he said. "Billy."

40

MAE SPENT THE rest of the afternoon trying to figure out how she was going to kill Billy.

The way she planned it, she'd shoot him with a horse standing by. She could be out of town long before Conlon suspected who the real killer was. A lot of people wanted to kill Billy.

The trouble she was having was figuring out the best way to do it.

One of the nephews would doubtlessly be in the office all night, so just sort of drifting back there and killing him would be impossible.

Another way she'd thought of and rejected was poisoning his food. The trouble was that you couldn't always rely on poison with a doctor around right here in town. She'd seen two or three people survive poison when they should have died.

A third way was to pretend to befriend him. Help him escape. Then, when he escaped, shoot him in the back. The trouble with that was that any number of things could go wrong. He might really escape, for one thing. And then she'd have to start looking for him all over again.

She was hauling some garbage out the back door

when she heard a couple of the prisoners talking, and that was when the idea came to her. Their voices drifted through the barred window in the stucco-sided wall.

Of course. All she needed to do was stand on a stool, sight down a rifle, and kill him right through the barred window. His cell was directly beneath. If she waited until late enough, town and prisoners alike would be asleep, and she could pull it off simply and with no chance of getting caught.

Around four o'clock, she was feeling pretty good, sitting at her desk and zipping through her paperwork.

"I never heard you do that before," Conlon said.

"Do what before?"

"Hum."

"I was humming?"

"You sure were."

"I'll be danged. I didn't even know I was doing it."

"Oh, you were doing it, all right, and doing it nice, too. You've got a nice voice."

"Well, if I do, I got it from my ma."

"Oh?"

"She had a purely wonderful voice."

"Well, now you've got the voice."

"She always sang at church. And at the county fair, one of the traveling actors—he was doing all these Shakespearean readings—he told her she sounded just as good as anybody he'd heard in Chicago or Kansas City."

He smiled at her. "It's good to see you happy again."

"It bother you?"

"Does what bother me?"

"My humming?"

"Heck, no. I like it."

"Good," she said, " 'cause I'll do some more of it."

She knew how unseemly it was to feel this good about killing a man. But she couldn't help it. She just couldn't help it at all.

She started humming again, this time "Little Brown Jug."

41

AN OLD NEW York literary agent—a man who had been both a publisher and an editor—had once given Lew Adair a piece of sage advice. "It's like not being able to get a hard-on, Lew. The more you worry about it, the worse it gets. So when you get stuck on a page, don't just sit there and stew about it. Get up and do something else. Just relax."

Governor Lew Adair was pacing. He couldn't find anything else to do, so he walked back and forth in the big sunny room he'd converted into his office.

Ordinarily, late afternoon was the time when he got most of his writing done. He had dealt with all the day's problems, and he was ready to work.

But not today.

Billy Pecos kept intruding upon his thoughts. He'd sit at his desk, pen poised, ready to work on the great chariot race that was the centerpiece of the book—and what would happen? Billy would happen. Billy's smug, ironic face. Billy's air of violence. Billy's slightly crazed blue gaze.

Billy Pecos had turned Lew Adair into a laughing-stock.

Here, Adair had gone around the territory talking up his great amnesty idea. *All we do is give the men on both sides the right to wipe the slate clean and start again, and the violence is over.*

You're crazy, a lot of sensible people had told him. *You don't go around giving gunnies amnesty like this. First chance they get, they'll kill somebody else, amnesty or not.*

Not these fellows, Lew Adair had said confidently. *I've got a sense these fellows'll make the best of it.*

So what does Billy do?

He has sex with a woman and then cuts her throat.

He could hear the laughter all over the territory. They already distrusted him: what kind've fella writes books, anyway? Women write books; not men. Not *real* men.

And real men also don't have ideas like giving amnesty to gunnies. Especially to Billy Pecos, for God's sake.

Well, Governor. You just couldn't wait to get him to town and start the process moving along. And look what he does. And that mob last night was just the beginning. You walked the streets at all today? You heard the way people are talking? The Widow Gaines was a respected woman. So what if she was having a little sex on the side? You want to cast the first stone? You want to call her a whore? A woman like that needs some fleshly pleasure every once in a while. She made the same mistake you made, Governor. She thought he'd be different with her. She thought she could use her considerable charms to turn him into a decent human being. At least for the night. But we know better than that, don't we, Governor? The Widow Gaines was a good woman, with two of the sweetest kids you could ask for. And what does the sonofabitch do? You should've seen her throat, the way he cut it. That's the way the Apaches cut a white man's throat.

He paced. He looked out the window. He picked his nose. He scratched his head. He scratched his butt. He thought longingly of the chariot race. Best scene he'd ever written. Well, *half*-written. He hadn't finished it yet. He should be finishing it now. But how could he after what Billy did? How could he when he knew people would be snickering at him when he walked down the street? Got any other brainstorm, Governor? Maybe you could turn all those warriors loose from the reservation and invite them to come over and pillage our little town.

He sat down at the desk again, took his pen in hand, and looked at the blank piece of white paper. Bent, ready to begin setting words to page. And saw an attractive woman with her throat cut.

The first thing he had to do tomorrow was visit her kids and make some kind of provision for their future. Find a family who'd take them in. Set up a little trust fund for them. In a very real way, he had taken their mother from them.

The chariot race. The sound of the vast crowds in the coliseum. The cheering. The fearful and angry face of Caesar.

Good Lord, what a scene!

And not a word came.

He prayed to the Christian God, *his* God. He prayed to the non-Christian muses. To the bitch goddess herself.

And not a word came.

He thought of the advice of his New York friend. Don't worry about it. Just relax.

Just relax. Easy for him to say, the pompous old twit. He was a publisher and editor. He didn't have to experience the cold sweat of the empty page. The despair of not being able to write.

Just relax.

Billy. It was Billy's fault. He'd like to march right
down to that jail, drag him out of his cell, and lynch
him right on the spot.

Then he'd be able to write. To finish the chariot
race.

Billy would be dangling from a tree, and the chariot
race would be finished with the main character triumphant. And people would forever forget Adair's
idea to grant hardened gunnies amnesty.

He took a series of deep breaths. Just relax.

He closed his eyes and put his head back against
his desk chair. Just relax.

Then he opened his eyes and sat forward, almost
sexually ecstatic with the prospect of putting words
to paper.

But when he picked up his pen and sat forward,
nothing came.

Nothing, nothing, nothing.

42

THE TINY HOUSE smelled of lard-oil lamps and a pet
pig badly in need of a rain storm. The pig had not
yet reached full size. It sat in a corner of the front
room, watching the humans talking to each other. The
pig liked it when people got up and did physical
things. But watching conversation was boring.

The man with the silver thing on his leather vest
said, "I don't plan to upset them."

"But you *will* upset them, Marshal Conlon. How could you not? Making them go through it all over again?"

Conlon looked over at the pig. For some reason, the thing unnerved him. It was as if the pig was *watching* him. Spooky little beast; it smelled bad, too.

Mrs. O'Riley had been a good friend of Mrs. Gaines. She took the Gaines girls when she heard what had happened to the mother. She was understandably protective of them now that they were staying here in her house. But Conlon felt it was necessary to talk to them.

"I won't keep them long," he said, "and if they start to get upset, I'll stop asking them questions. How's that?"

Mrs. O'Riley was a plump but pretty woman in a faded gingham dress. There was a large crucifix with a long, drooping piece of palm hanging behind it. Palm Sunday. Conlon thought back to his old New York parish, the triumphant sound of the organ, the heavy heady scent of incense, and all the pretty little Catholic girls coming back from the communion rail, heads bent, hands folded. He'd had a million crushes when he was a little boy.

"No more than five minutes."

"All right."

"And if they start to cry—"

"Then I stop questioning them."

Mrs. O'Riley stood up, nodding severely to him. "Wait right here."

"You know, ma'am," Conlon said, "you would've made a good prison warden." He smiled.

"I don't appreciate that remark," she said. "I'm trying to protect two little girls."

"I was just trying to be funny, Mrs. O'Riley."

"I know what you were trying to be, Marshal."

She glowered at him and went to get the little girls.

43

ANY TIME AFTER two in the afternoon you could hear the player piano music from the saloons and the casinos.

Billy lay on his jail bed, listening to it.

The girls wouldn't be in the saloons quite yet. They'd come a few hours later, on toward dusk. But there would be liquor and cards and the pleasure he took in strutting around just so people would know for sure who he was.

Hard to strut around in a jail cell.

Hard to feel good when you remembered the mob that had been seriously thinking of lynching you.

Hard to even sleep when your prospects were so bleak.

The thing that really got to him was that nobody had come here from the Tunstall place. His so-called friends. Where the hell were they?

The colored man in the next cell said, "You hear that music?"

"I hear it, old man."

"I bets they be havin' a good time."

"Shut up."

"Why, listen, boss, all I said was—"

"And all *I* said was shut up."

The colored man sat down on the bunk, looking almost forlorn. Billy was the only other prisoner in the jail this afternoon. Got awful lonesome when you didn't have nobody to talk to. The colored man lay down on his bunk and rested his forearm over his eyes. Sometimes he almost wished he was back in Alabama. There had been some damned good times on that plantation he'd grown up on—the dances, the parties given by the slaves on another plantation, and the girls. Oh me, oh my, all them purty purty girls. But then the colored man would remember the other things, the fear just *seeing* the plantation boss inspired, his baby brother being sold off to a plantation six hundred miles away, and, worst of all, being branded just the way cattle were branded. The colored man had a big welted B just above his right buttock. The August Burton plantation, that's what the B stood for. Then all his sentimental memories vanished. The plantation had been a shit hole, and no matter what happened to him out west here—he'd been arrested on a vag charge, after jumpin' off a freight train about fifteen feet away from a deputy—anything was better than goin' back to Alabama.

"Sorry I told you to shut up."

"Aw, that's all right," the colored man said. "You got a world of trouble, boss."

"I didn't kill that woman. All the people I killed, and now they're gonna get me for somebody I *didn't* kill."

"Them law peckers, boss. They don't care who done it or who didn't do it. They just want somebody to hang is all they want."

"All the people I killed, and now they're gonna get me for somebody I *didn't* kill."

"I knows how you feel," the colored man said sadly. "I sure do knows how you feel, boss."

44

THE GIRLS ARE afraid of him.

How can you blame them? Somebody sneaks into their house and kills their mother. They hear her scream, hear her die. They run to her, but it's too late. They are helpless children in the vast, dark, terrifying world of adults. The last time they see her, she is on the grass outside, dead.

At the moment, they seem beyond tears. There is a chalky deadness to their prim, sweet little faces, all pigtails and gingham and shoes two sizes too big, the way pioneer mothers always buy shoes, so the kids will have growing room and the shoes will last many years.

He is an adult and is therefore part of the conspiracy that took their mother from them. The small Sears circular sofa is big enough to hold them both. They sit there holding hands, Susan, nine, and Carolyn, ten, watching him with a grave suspicion that will never leave their eyes, no matter how old they get. They know the worst secret of the universe now, and it is a secret the darkness will never purge from their minds.

He says, "I'm sorry I have to ask you questions."

They stare and say nothing.

"Which of you woke up first the other night, when your mother was screaming?"

"I did," Carolyn says.

"Did you hear anything except her screaming?"

"I don't know what you mean."

"Was the man saying anything to her?"

"No."

"I know who the man was, though," Susan says. The main difference between the two girls is the opulence of Susan's freckles. Otherwise, they are virtually twins.

"You do?"

"I saw him."

"When?"

"I woke up earlier."

"I see."

"And I walked up to the front room."

"Were they there?"

"Yes."

"What were they doing?"

The two girls look anxiously at each other. Susan says, "My mom was being bad."

"Bad?"

"She was committing a sin," says Carolyn.

"A sin?"

"She was on the floor with the man," Susan says. "They were kissing."

"That's why God punished her," Carolyn says. "Because she was bad."

"That's true," Susan said. "We heard Reverend Pritchett talking to Mrs. O'Riley last night."

"And that's what he said?" Conlon asks.

Carolyn nodded. "He said she was a bad woman and God was paying her back."

Reverend Pritchett, Conlon thinks, the man who drives the demons out of his son by beating him.

"He said she was going to hell and not to heaven," Susan says. "Do you think that's true, Marshal?"

"I'm sure it isn't. From everything I hear, your mother was a very good woman."

"If she was a good woman, then how come the Reverend says she was bad?" Carolyn asks.

Conlon does the adult thing and changes the subject. "I'm sure she's in heaven, girls." Then, "Tell me about the man you saw."

"Billy Pecos?"

"You're sure that was the man in the front room with your mother?"

"Yes. I saw him."

"How about later, when you heard her screaming? Do you think it was Billy, then?"

"Yes."

"Did you actually see him?"

"No."

"Then how can you be sure it was him?"

"I just know is all."

"How about you, Carolyn? Did you see him?"

"No."

"Did you see any man?"

"Huh-uh. I was real sleepy. Then when we seen my mom—" Tears fill her eyes. "I just remember the smell."

"The smell?"

"He smelled like my dad used to."

"I guess I don't understand," Conlon says.

"My dad was going bald," Susan says. "He used this hair stuff on his head."

" 'Hair-Gro'," Carolyn says. "He always bought it at the barber shop."

"And that's what you smelled, Susan?"

She nods and looks up.

Mrs. O'Riley has appeared in the doorway. "I need the girls to help me now, Marshal. I'm afraid your time is up."

There isn't much he can say to that now, is there? You should never argue with a woman holding a pig.

He shakes the hands of the girls and adds, "Thanks, Mrs. O'Riley."

"Say good-bye to Petey," Carolyn says, her tears gone now.

"Petey?"

"Petey the Pig," Mrs. O'Riley says, as if Conlon is just about the dumbest guy in the territory.

"Oh, the pig."

"Yes, Marshal. The pig."

"Good-bye, Petey."

The girls giggle. Their laughter is silver. He leaves them.

45

THERE WAS A time in his life a couple thousand years ago—or so it seemed—when he still lived in New York, that Conlon used to think the murder victims he dealt with were playing jokes on him.

True, he'd grown up in a very rough neighborhood, but he hadn't seen much death. Violence, yes, ohmygod violence. But not actual death.

So sometimes as a young cop, when he'd been kneeling next to an unmoving body that didn't show any outward signs of violence, he'd think: *This is a prank. Any moment now he'll get up and go* boo! *And make an ass out of me.*

But they never did. Not even the ones whose wounds were so tiny even the docs had a hard time finding them.

But as the years went by, and his cop's eyes became more practiced, Conlon learned about the *air* at a murder scene.

The air was different. The molecules had been altered in some inexplicable but very real way. His first surmise was that the temperature was cooler than it was everywhere else. But no, that wasn't it. His second surmise was that the *texture* of the air was different. But no, that wasn't it, either. And when he finally *did* hit on it, finally *did* figure it out, his first impulse was to reject it.

Having been raised a Catholic, Conlon didn't have any trouble accepting such concepts as the Virgin Birth and Three Persons in One God and Christ rolling back the huge stone after rising from his death.

But he did have trouble accepting ghosts.

And that was the conclusion he'd come to about murder scenes. That the ghost of the deceased hung around for several days after, kind've checking things out, *observing* if you will, just how the cops were handling the investigation. And maybe eavesdropping on what their former friends had to say about them now that they had passed; maybe hearing things they wished they hadn't.

Ghosts.

Conlon never shared this insight with anybody, of course: *Say, Captain, did you ever notice any ghosts hanging around your murder scenes?*

Such things were not expressed, not if one hoped to continue as a proud member of the New York Police Department.

But the ghosts were true—at least, for Conlon— and now as he stood in the small house where the Widow Gaines had lived, he felt her unearthly presence.

She didn't speak to him; they never did. Nor did she put on a white sheet and flit about the house trying to scare him. They never did that, either. But, dammit, she was *there*, and he knew it.

The house hadn't been cleaned up yet. Blood-splattered walls, furniture-scraped floor, lamp-smashed corner. The violence had started in here and quickly gone outside. By now, all the neighborhood dogs, cats, possums, and raccoons would have had a taste of the blood staining the ground out front. By now, all the neighbors would have paid their head-shaking and tongue-clucking respects: the poor woman, and those poor, poor girls.

He went through the house slowly, the way he'd been trained back in New York, and he didn't find a damned thing. Or thought he didn't, anyway. As he was leaving the house, just to the side of the front stoop, he saw it. At first he wasn't even sure what it was. Wasn't sure it was important at all. But what the hell, he hadn't found anything inside, so maybe it was worth the trouble of actually bending over, actually walking his fingers over to it, actually picking it up. Just because he was forty-six didn't mean he should start getting lazy and careless the way so many law men did.

What it turned out to be was the heel piece from a western boot, that eighth-inch piece of leather that capped most good heels. It was fairly new and didn't show much wear at all. Sometimes a heel piece like this would have a brand stamped on it, but there was no brand on this one.

It didn't necessarily have to be the killer's, of course. The first boot he'd check would be Billy's. It might belong to him.

He spent a few minutes in the yard, standing next to the blood. He *felt* her. Oh, she was there, all right. The ghost of her was, anyway.

Couldn't you just give me a hint, Mrs. Gaines? He thought. *Just a small hint and make this easier on both of us?*

But that was something else ghosts didn't do. They

didn't cooperate. In fact, they were about the most
uncooperative types of beings he'd ever dealt with at
a murder scene. Absolutely no help at all.

He stood there in the sunlight for a while longer,
a little Mexican kid and his scruffy dog standing in
the fusty street watching him, and then he headed
back to the office.

Nope, Mrs. Gaines wasn't going to be any more
cooperative than any other ghost he had ever dealt
with.

46

AT FOUR O'CLOCK that afternoon, just as Conlon was
making his way back to the office, Jimmy from the
Tunstall ranch was explaining how good a friend
young Sam had been, and how Billy Pecos had caused
his death. The man listening to Jimmy was R. C.
Greaves, the bounty hunter Conlon had earlier told to
leave town.

Jimmy wasn't much of a drinker. Back in Ohio,
he'd been a good Lutheran of the Missouri Synod,
and the Missouri Synod did not hold with liquor.
When his wife and kids had been alive, Jimmy never
touched a drop. But these days he needed something
to fill the hollowness. So he drank. And on those
nights when he drank enough, he also ended up at
one of the town's whorehouses. Some nights, too
drunk, he needed a little help to get fully erect. But
most nights, he didn't have no trouble at all. The sex

lasted five, six minutes at most, but the guilt hung on
for long and dreary days afterward. How could his
life have come to this?

R. C. Greaves was a different breed altogether
when it came to drink and sex. No guilt for him. Hell,
all he wanted to know was where he could get more
of both of them. And right away.

These two, then, are the men who get things rolling
on this particular day. It is barely five in the afternoon.

"You couldn't've asked for a nicer kid than young
Sam," Jimmy says wistfully. "He always put me in
mind of my own son."

"And Billy screwed his girl."

"Practically screwed his girl right in front of him."

"That damned Conlon shoulda shot Billy insteada
Sam."

"That's what I told him," Jimmy says, "that arrogant mick bastard."

All around them is the noise of saloon and casino,
laughter of saloon girls, barking curses of losers, high
yipping exclamations of winners, slap of poker hands
being thrown down, gurgle of whiskey being poured;
and over all is the player piano, playing endless
happy, prancing tunes, loud enough to put a hairline
fracture in an eardrum if you stood too close.

Not that either hear any of this. By this time, even
without the words being spoken, they are conspira-
tors, intense, insular, isolated in their growing self-
righteousness and rage.

"You know what?" Bob Wylie says, finally getting
around to the real point of all this. Wylie is an aux-
illary sheriff and a self-styled authority on Western
life, particularly anything pertaining to gunfighters.

"What?"

"I'd kill the sonofabitch for free."

"Conlon, you mean?"

"No, not Conlon. Billy."

"Lynching's against the law."

"Think of the distinction."

"Distinction?"

"Yeah, this little town bein' the one that finally hanged him."

Jimmy, even this drunk, is cautious. He doesn't want to be the first one to actually *say* it out loud. "You're talking about . . ."

Wylie shakes his head. "You *are* tryin' to shit a shitter." He leans very close to Jimmy and stage-whispers, "Lynch the sonofabitch. *That's* what I'm talkin' about."

"Gosh, I never thought of that," Jimmy lies.

"And I'll bet there's twenty, thirty other men in this town who feel the same way we do."

"You know somethin'? I'll bet you're right."

"The way he treated your friend Sam and all."

"Hell, the way he treats *everybody*."

"We wouldn't have no trouble findin' the men."

"Nope," Jimmy says. "I surely don't think we would."

"They did four of them at one time last year in Montana. Four of them. And I seen the pitchers, too. Four of them, two buck niggers and two Mexes, dragged 'em right out of the jail and strung 'em up. The way I get it, the sheriff even unlocked the cells for them, long as nobody said he played any part of it, him bein' a lawman."

"Four of them."

"Isn't that somethin'?" Wylie says.

"It sure is," Jimmy says, imagining Billy swinging from a tree. "It sure is somethin', all right."

47

THIS WAS THE third time the killer walked past the good Reverend Pritchett's house. Each time, the good Reverend was screaming and shouting. Strange, crazed man. The argument going on inside his own head. The demons he beats out of his son trouble him, too.

When the killer was not thinking about what poor odd Ronnie Prichett saw, the matter of guilt came to mind.

It was a known fact, at least in Sunday school lectures and the sort of melodrama favored by the masses, that nothing affected you or ate at you or tormented you worse than guilt. Killers shouted their guilt from the gallows; dying men whispered their guilt from deathbeds. All wanted the same thing—relief from the ferocious battering pressure of having sinned.

The thing was, the killer did not feel any guilt at all, ferocious or otherwise.

Got up this morning, tended to the usual routine, pondered again and again what had happened last night, and felt . . . nothing.

Well, not exactly *nothing*. Felt fear of being identified as the killer. Felt fear of the townspeople if they ever figured out what happened. And who was behind it. Felt fear of what the loved ones would forever think if they knew the truth.

But felt, miraculously, no guilt. No pride. No glee. But no guilt, either.

Maybe it was what they called a delayed reaction. You're walking down the street and you happen upon one of the Gaines children. Or you hear a church bell tolling and you know it's for her. Or you see the hearse working its way up the hill to the graveyard, and you realize in there is the vibrant woman you turned into an already-deteriorating corpse. Then the guilt would come. And it would suffuse you. Become inescapable. Even asleep you would be forced to relive last night over and over again.

But for now . . .

The killer almost feels guilty for not feeling guilty. Now that's a good one. Feeling guilty for not feeling guilty.

Ronnie Pritchett is on the porch, the front door opening and him stepping out to call for his cat, "Here Carl! Here Carl!"—that being about the strangest cat name you could ever imagine, Carl. Ronnie really belongs back in that home where they put him for a while. People like Ronnie shouldn't be running free around town. People like Ronnie are a real threat to the community.

And then the killer thinks: I killed a woman last night, and I'm saying *Ronnie* is a threat to the community? Now there's another good one for you.

The cat comes up on the porch, a shaggy old calico tom. Ronnie picks it up. Holds it the way he would an infant. Rocks it. Talks to it. Carl. What a crazy name for a cat.

And then some instinct—some hunch—makes Ronnie look up across the narrow dusty street and see . . .

The killer.

Ronnie doesn't react right away. Doesn't run inside, as if frightened. Or make a face. As if challenging the killer in some way. He just holds Carl, always gently rocking him, and stares across the street.

The good Reverend starts shouting for Ronnie to come back inside. "Are you forgetting what the Bible says about those who would disobey their father?" screeches the old man. "Do you know the hottest flames of hell are reserved for those who disobey their parents?"

This makes Ronnie move. Clutching Carl even tighter, he turns around, opens the front door, and disappears inside the house.

The killer is not happy.

Ronnie is a very fearful person. Even little kids can scare him off.

Why, then, didn't Ronnie cower when he saw the killer? Hadn't the killer put the fear of God in Ronnie last night?

48

A DOG HAD bitten a seven-year-old boy, and the boy's mother wanted the dog run out of town. Two men had been unloading wagons of dry goods when a masked bandit appeared and demanded all the money they had. A dowager reported a window peeper. And a lonely old man, well known to local law, said that he had seen a monster at his window last night.

These were some of the matters waiting for Conlon when he got back to the office. No wonder he'd never wanted to be a town sheriff. It was like being a rookie cop again.

The one good thing about all these problems was

that they were on paper, written up as reports. Mae had handled them all in her usual quick and competent way. The dog bite was barely a scratch; the infamous "masked bandit" was Randy Sullivan once again needing beer money (so said Randy Sullivan, who was now sitting in a cell); the window peeper turned out to be the dowager's next-door neighbor who'd been looking for his daughter's cat last night; and as for the monster, Mae had given the lonely old man a cup of coffee and sat him down and let him talk about his rheumatiz, his daughter in Omaha who never wrote him any more, and how much he missed his deceased wife. Finally, she kissed him on his bald, liver-spotted head and sent him on his way.

"You should be a judge," Conlon said.

"I'm just nice to people is all. That's the trouble with too many lawmen. They aren't nice."

"Being around criminals tends to make you *not* nice."

"Then you should do something else. But don't take your bitterness out on the public."

He laughed. "I take that back about you being a judge. I think you should be mayor."

He noticed how much easier it was between them now. And it made him feel good and bad at the same time. His fingers wanted to hold those slim shoulders of hers, and his eyes wanted to look deep and tenderly into hers, and he wanted to say some of those ridiculous things you said when you were young and giddy and in love.

She said, "Billy had a bad spell this afternoon."

"Bad spell?"

"Started shouting that he didn't kill that woman. Saying we should let him go. Then he sat down on his bunk and cried."

"He really cried?"

"Like a little child."

"You don't sound real sorry for him."

"I'm not."

"God, Mae, you really do hate him."

"Yes, I do."

"Maybe he didn't kill the Gaines woman. You ever think of that?"

"Even if he didn't, he's killed lots of other people."

"That isn't how the law is supposed to work."

She smiled. "I thought you said I'd make a good judge."

He nodded. "I think you would. But for some reason, you have a hard time being fair-minded about Billy."

She walked over to his desk and sat down. "I let the old colored man go."

"Good. Long as he left town."

"He left. I had one of the nephews take him over to the station."

"Who else is back there?"

"Randy Sullivan."

"Who's he?"

"He sticks up people when he runs out of drinking money. People tell me he's harmless. Sort of a town joke."

"He use a real gun?"

"Yes."

"Then he isn't harmless, and he isn't a joke. Anybody ever prosecute him?"

"I guess not."

"Well, then, we're going to be the exception."

"He seems like a decent guy, actually."

He bristled and tried to stop his voice from sounding harsh, but he couldn't. "You're ready to lynch Billy without being sure that he even killed that woman, but you're willing to let a man go free who robs people at gunpoint. That's a little inconsistent, Mae." He was right, of course. She was being inconsistent. But he'd spoken too angrily. "I'm sorry."

She looked stunned by the ferocity of his earlier words. "No, that's all right. And you're right; I am being inconsistent."

She started to turn back to her work. He touched her frail shoulder. It damned near broke his heart; oh, boy, was he a mess over this girl.

"I'm sorry."

"It's all right. You think I can't handle criticism?"

"I just shouldn't have snapped the way I did."

She reached over and patted the hand resting on her shoulder. "It's all right, Marshal. I'll probably survive." She gave him a sweet girl smile. "I really will."

Then she turned in such a way that his hand slid away from her. He gathered himself again. "There a cobbler in town?"

"Tiny shop out in back of the livery."

"Think they're still open?"

"Should be."

He went to the door, snatched his hat from the peg. "I'm sorry about snapping at you."

"It's fine, Marshal. Really."

But it wasn't fine. He felt all roiled up inside. No, it wasn't fine at all.

49

YOU HAD YOUR ankle jacks, which were half-boots with ten holes for lacing; you had your bluchers, which were also half-boots preferred by men who spent a lot of hours in the saddle; you had your brogans, which were ankle-high and the shoe wear of choice for Southern plantation owners who bought them for their slaves; and, of course, you had your cowboy boots, every kind of bootskin, bootstyle, and bootheel imaginable. These were for the men.

For the women, you had your adelaide boots, which had fur around the tops; you had your balmorals, which were front-laced, and were worn by women and men alike; and you had your boots so long and narrow they required what was called boot hooks to pull them on.

There were many more shoe fashions than this, of course. But Furner wasn't exactly Denver. Furner, in fact, wasn't even Wells Springs.

Conlon liked the smells of polish and dye and new rubber. He liked the big, thick, industrious hands of the cobbler, and the way the woman had silver shoe nails sticking out of her teeth and the polish-smudged apron she wore. This woman was like a painting, and she reminded Conlon of why he'd come to prefer West to East. There was a purpose one sensed out here—of survival, of goal, of *meaning*—that one rarely saw back east. She was gray-haired and stout, and when she smiled hello at Conlon she did so without troubling the angle of the nails in her teeth. No small accomplishment. INEZ SIMMONS, PROP. said the sign on the counter.

She put down the woman's shoe she'd been repairing, blew the nails into the palm of her hand, and said, "Help you?"

The small shed-like structure tilted slightly under Conlon's weight.

"You're a big one," she said. "Ronnie always says you're like one of those gunfighters in the dime novels."

"You know Ronnie?"

She nodded. "Very well. He's a nice boy. I hate it when people pick on him. Especially that crazy father of his."

He put out his hand. "Name's Conlon."

"Right. The U.S. Marshal. Just so's you know, John Barcroft is a friend of mine. My husband and me used to work this place together. Then he had a stroke last year, and I thought we'd have to shut down. John Barcroft stepped in and wrote out a check so I could buy this little place. Supposed to be a loan. When my birthday come around, I got a note from him tellin' me the debt was absolved. Far as I'm concerned, he's a damned decent man, and I don't want to hear otherwise, not from you or anybody else."

"All right."

"I think they should hang that Billy first chance they get. Lew Adair never should have let Billy come to town. And then puttin' him under house arrest instead of puttin' him in jail. That was just crazy."

"Maybe Billy didn't do it."

She laughed. She had a booming, warm laugh, and he liked her despite his better judgment. "Yes, Mr. U.S. Marshal, and maybe I can flap my arms and fly."

"You're that sure, huh?"

"If he didn't do it, who did?"

"That's what I'm trying to figure out."

She studied him a moment. "Sounds like you've thrown in with the Tunstall bunch."

"I haven't thrown in with anybody, believe it or not. I'm just doing my job."

"Good. Then how can I help you?"

Now that she'd identified herself as a Barcroft partisan, Conlon knew better than to tell her where the heel cap came from. He said, "This came off my boot this afternoon. Just wondered if I could get a replacement?"

She took the cap in her big, purposeful hands, turning it over, examining it carefully. "Funny it'd come off."

"Why's that?"

"Looks almost new."

"You got another one?"

"You don't need another one. I can just nail this back on. But it's funny."

"What is?"

"This doesn't look like it came off the boots you're wearing."

He had to be careful here. "What kind of boot you think it came off?"

"A handmade riding boot. Not necessarily all that expensive. But handmade."

He smiled. "You're good. How'd you guess?"

"The design pattern on the bottom. If factory turned out those little Vs there, they'd be perfect. Couple of these are a little bit bigger than the others. Somebody made a mistake. Machines don't make mistakes like that."

"Well, I'll bring the boots in with me tomorrow. Left them back in my room. Just wanted to make sure you could put the cap back on."

She studied him again and said, "You're a sneaky one."

"Sneaky?"

"You no more own the boots this cap came off than I do."

"I don't, huh?"

"No, you don't."

"Then who does?"

"I wouldn't have the slightest idea. All I know is that you don't."

He put the cap back in the pocket of his vest. "I appreciate your time."

"He's a good man."

"Barcroft?"

"Yep. And don't believe anybody who says otherwise."

He still liked her but had no idea why. "I'll try to remember that."

50

MAE COULD HEAR them trooping down to dinner. The people in the rooming house where she stayed were almost a family. They couldn't wait to get together at day's end and discuss all the things that had happened to them and then decide what they'd do that night. They always talked—over coffee and pie at the end of the meal—as if they had some great choices to make for the night's entertainment. But their choices were actually few. They could sit around a checkerboard smoking their pipes and cigars, or they could play a few hands of penny poker, or they could sit on the front porch in rocking chairs (the lucky ones got to sit on the creaking porch swing, but you had to get there very early to get such a hallowed seat) and talk politics or baseball or town gossip—or, in the last week or so, of Governor Adair and his damn foolish amnesty. It was nice on the porch: a breeze all the way down from the mountains, seeing the fireflies, and the night in all its velvet darkness, sweet and cool and aromatic, and there was a human laziness in everybody's voice, a sleepy day's-end laziness that was nice to hear.

She lay encased in her isolation on her bed. It was a coffin, her isolation, a coffin as real as any as you'd find in an undertaker's back room.

Tonight was the night. Finally.

She wondered what would become of her afterward, after it was done and she was long gone from here.

A knock. "Mae?"

Mrs. Johansen, the widow who owned this house. "Yes?"

"There's cake down on the porch."

"No, thanks, Mrs. Johansen. I'm still full from supper."

"Still full? Why, child, you barely ate."

"I guess I'm not feeling too well." She needed a quick lie. "My visitor just started to arrive."

"You have visitors in there?"

Visitors were strictly prohibited. Strictly.

Mae smiled. "My 'monthly' visitor, Mrs. Johansen."

"Your monthly—" A pause. "Oh, you mean—"

"That's what I mean, Mrs. Johansen."

"Then no wonder you looked so pale at supper tonight. Are you having cramps?"

"Not so far."

"Well, if you need anything, just let me know."

"I will, Mrs. Johansen, and thank you."

"Rusty nail water works for cramps sometimes."

Cramps and unwanted pregnancies. The word was that rusty nail water worked wonders on both of these troubles. But Mae had never known a single case where drinking rusty water actually helped.

"I'll keep that in mind."

"I'd better get back downstairs."

"Thank you again, Mrs. Johansen."

"Mr. Carter—you know, the new boarder—he's going to tell us about his days as a street car conductor in Baltimore."

"I'm sorry I'm going to miss that."

"I'm sorry, too, Mae. Now don't forget about that rusty nail water."

"Oh, I could never forget that, Mrs. Johansen."

The landlady went back downstairs.

Mae smiled to herself. Mr. Carter's experiences as a street car conductor in Baltimore. Sounded like something you might hear at a tent show, some stout man in a three-piece suit being stentorian and stuffy as all hell.

Then she was back to her isolation. She tried very hard not to think about Conlon. She'd never see him again after tonight, and that made her feel sad. She could see his face when he would finally figure out it was she who killed Billy. He wouldn't know what to do. He was obviously in love with her. But he was also a lawman. Would he come after her? Would he shoot her if he had to? Could he? She wasn't sure. He wasn't a man of large and dramatic contradictions, but you could never quite predict how he was going to respond to something.

Then it was time to start getting ready. She still had hours left, but she wanted to be ready. All ready.

She took the Colt from her drawer and sat on her narrow cot in the soft flickering lamplight. She used the gun oil first, and then the Winchester gun grease,

which worked just fine on any kind of weapon. Her
father used to order it from the Sears catalog, three
tubes at a time, $1 per tube plus postage. She had an
image of her father sitting in his rocker, cleaning and
oiling his weapons. She used to stand in the doorway
to the side of him late at night and just watch him,
and love him and feel more secure and loved than
any child ever had before, and he wasn't even aware
of her being there. That was the funny thing, him
radiating this sense of love and protection and not
even aware that she was there in the doorway watching him.

She wondered if Conlon had any kids. He'd never
told her anything about his past. But somehow she
suspected he was a father.

She had the sense that he'd make a good one.

51

CONLON SAID, "WHO told you that?"

"Fella."

"What fella?"

"Don't know. Just a fella I was drinkin' with."

"He say who was behind it?"

"Nope. Just said two other fellas."

Conlon had stopped back in the office after supper.
He was doing some paperwork when the door opened
and a beefy black-bearded man came in. He wore
dark, dusty clothes and smoked a cigar.

"Only reason I mention it, Marshal, was I seen one once."

"Lynching?"

"Yep. Guy shit his pants so bad it was running out of his trousers. Splattered shit all over'n folks who was standin' close by. Took him a while to die, too. His neck didn't get broke right or somethin'."

"You think you could find this fella again?"

"Aw, hell, Marshal, I got to get home. The old lady'll kick my ass as it is."

This was the kind of talk he had to put a stop to immediately. Lynch talk took on a life of its own. Conlon had never seen a lynching and didn't plan to start now.

"What'd he look like?"

"The fella?"

"Yeah."

"Big blond guy. Most likely a Swede. You know, they all come here together couple years back. Had a scar across the bridge of his nose. Looked like barb wire done it."

"Now tell me again what he said."

"Said they was gonna lynch Billy around ten o'clock tonight."

"Was he drunk?"

"Not so's I could tell."

"So you took him seriously?"

"Didn't see no reason not to."

Conlon stood up and put forth his hand. "I want to thank you for coming here, Mr. Montgomery."

"You gonna go find him?" Montgomery said, shaking Conlon's hand.

"I'm going to try."

"I sure wouldn't want to see another one. A lynchin', I mean."

"There isn't going to be any lynching."

"He's a big sonofabitch, Marshal. I got to tell you that."

"Big or not, there won't be a lynching."

Conlon walked him to the door. "You just go on home to your wife now, Mr. Montgomery. And thanks again."

Before he left, Montgomery pointed to a rifle case on the east wall. "That your sawed-off?"

"Yes, as a matter of fact."

"You gut-shoot a man with that, you'd put a mighty big hole in him."

"You sure would."

"You ever use it?"

"Not on a human being. Target practice, I did."

"That's a mean-lookin' sonofabitch." He smiled sadly. "But then so's the Swede."

"I'll worry about the Swede, Mr. Montgomery. You worry about your family. G'night, now."

"G'night, Marshal. And good luck."

"Good luck to you, too, Mr. Montgomery."

And with that, he closed the door behind the man.

52

IT WAS HARD to say just where Jimmy and Wylie met Swede. Jimmy and Wylie were switching saloons every hour or so, recruiting men as they went, and then all of a sudden, somewhere in their beer fog, there was Swede, talking as if all this was *his* idea and he was in charge of things. Neither Jimmy nor

Wylie was about to argue. Swede looked as if he could not only take your gun from you, but bend it up every which way, and then swallow it whole.

Swede stood at the plank bar, facing the batwing doors, talking to a group of drunks who now numbered in the thirties. Swede was six-five, with blond curly hair, a badly broken nose with a scar like a white snake across the bridge, a red-and-black checkered shirt, and dusty Levi's held up by the widest suspenders most of the men had ever seen.

He didn't do all the talking. In fact, he was more like a master of ceremonies. He grabbed Jimmy, for example, and said, "You tell dese here boys about your friend Dave."

"His name was Sam," Jimmy said, gently, not wanting to rile Swede.

"Jus' tell 'em," Swede said irritably.

It was kind of like a piano recital a kid put on. But instead of music there were syrupy words about what a paragon Sam had been. Seems like the Pope would be bestowing sainthood on Sam any day now. And instead of the applause a kid would get, there was this rumble of cursing and threats and the flash of guns in the air. Swede knew about these things, knew just how to build them. This was his history, or part of it. He hired out as a troublemaker in the territory. Sometimes this meant breaking legs, and sometimes this meant stirring up trouble against Indians, sheep men, cow men, Eye-talians, Mexes. Swede didn't care, just as long as the money was good.

Swede next pulled Bob Wylie to the fore. Men didn't take to him the way they had Jimmy. You sensed Jimmy's sadness—the death of his family would always be in those sad-dog eyes of his—and you sensed that he'd really cared about the youngster Sam.

But Wylie was the kind of man their mothers and

wives had always warned them to stay away from. He just had that look. Shifty was the common word for it. He told some highly unlikely—and heroic— stories about himself and how his brand of law was making this world safer for every virtuous woman and every tot west of the Mississippi. To hear him tell it, in fact, the West could not have been settled but for upstanding, visionary men such as himself. "You do it for money!" somebody shouted from the back. And the crowd started to turn on him. But Wylie was quick. "Not this one, I don't. A lawman don't get paid for helpin' with a lynchin'. This here punk, this Billy, he's a threat to everybody who ever drew a breath, and that includes his so-called friends!"

The men still didn't like him. Swede saw this quickly and stepped in front of Wylie and said, "He's a good man to have with us tonight. Just keep that in mind."

"That Conlon," one of the men said, "he looks like a mean one."

"You leave Conlon to me," Swede said.

"What time we goin' to the jail?" somebody else said.

"About ten-thirty," Swede said. "And in the mean-time, I suggest you do yourselves some more drinkin'."

He had a big, open smile and let it loose on the crowd. He'd made them forget Bob Wylie and start thinking again of Billy and drinking.

The men settled into their drinking. Swede, Jimmy, and Wylie found themselves a table.

53

BILLY COULD HEAR the saloons from his cell. The music and the laughter, mostly.

Moonlight lay barred lines of shadow across his bunk. He was the jail's only prisoner. He'd been lying down for the last hour. He had the despair of a hangover and badly wanted a drink.

He kept trying to remember walking out the widow's door. Trying to remember anything about his attacker. Trying to remember what, if anything, he'd seen or heard as he'd been clubbed into unconsciousness.

He was lying there in the shadows with his grief and sorrow when he saw something flutter down to his left. Something white. Like a little bird.

He half-leapt from the bunk, just in time to see a somewhat ridiculous face at the high, barred window behind him. Young man. Looked crazy or slow—or maybe both. Back in Brooklyn, Billy'd had a cousin who was slow. That kid had always scared Billy.

The face was gone.

What had fluttered to the floor was a small white piece of paper, brilliant white in the gloom.

Billy snatched it up, read it.

MR. BILLY PECOS, I KNOW YOU DIDN'T KILL THE WIDDA WOMAN. YOUR FREND.

That was it.

Who the hell had that eerie face at the window belonged to, and why was he writing Billy notes like this?

54

VOMIT, URINE, AND blood.

New York or Waco, it didn't matter. Saloons were the same. And if you hung out in them long enough, that's what you smelled. Vomit, urine, and blood.

Except for prisons, the dirtiest fighting anywhere took place in saloons. Fights that made you look away. Fights that made you sick to your stomach.

You saw wives come to saloons and pull their husbands away from whores. You saw ministers and priests come to saloons and beg the workers not to spend all their family's money. You saw sad little kids come to saloons and try to pull their fathers away from the demon rum.

Conlon had been one such sad little kid. The old man'd had a fondness for the bottle. No doubt about that. The old lady'd be in bed two, three times a week crying her eyes out as she muttered her rosary, and every time she'd say, "I don't care if he dies in one of those dives," Conlon would get scared and start crying himself. He never could understand his feelings about the old man, hating him and loving him as he did. The old lady had gotten cancer when she was thirty-eight years old. Conlon was fourteen at the time, and the old man just went totally to hell, staying drunk all the time, sobbing and sobbing and sobbing about what a miserable sonofabitch of a husband he'd been, and finally one night taking his cop pistol and blowing out the back of his head, killing himself before the old lady died, which was seven months later in the hospital, and all this being funny as hell, the old man's guilt, since he'd never paid any attention to her and was always running around in his uniform and cribbing the free favors of prostitutes. It was then that Conlon learned one of the most confounding and perplexing lessons of life—you never knew what was really inside anybody's head. Watching somebody's behavior could be misleading as hell.

About the time he entered the fourth saloon, the ghosts of his father and mother were dancing all around Conlon. He felt like a little kid, just as vulnerable to his dead parents as he was to the living Mae.

The din, the dour faces of the gamblers, the daunting smoke of the place was something he wanted out of as soon as possible. He went over to one of the big mick bartenders—white shirt sleeves rolled up beefy black-haired arms, fists all ready for fun—and said, "You know anybody they call Swede?"

"I just come on, Marshal," the mick said. "Better talk to Shanahan."

"Who's he?"

"Redhead down the bar."

He walked down the bar. All the drinkers took note of his face and badge. A lot of smirks. Men didn't like to show how much they feared authority. Made them lesser men. Smirks were easy.

"Shanahan?"

The redhead was pouring whiskey. He looked up and saw the badge and grinned. "All right. I admit it.

I stuck up that stagecoach this afternoon. And tonight I'm gonna rob the bank.' "

The drinkers along the bar found all this stuff just plain hilarious. This was better than smirking at a lawman.

"You know a man named Swede?"

The redhead surprised him. He ended his routine. "Know who he is."

"Seen him tonight?"

"Earlier."

"How much earlier?"

"What's he done?"

"Nothing I know of."

"Then why would you be lookin' for him?"

The redhead winked at one of the customers, and Conlon realized that the mick was still putting on a show, just a different kind now. Now he was playing tough-guy while he poured whiskies out of a bottle.

Conlon moved quickly. Ripped the bottle from the mick's hand and poured it all over the bar, so that the liquid was running over the sides.

"You sonofabitch," the mick said.

The other bartender was drifting this way.

"When was he in?" Conlon said.

"You shoulda answered his question, Shanahan," the other bartender said. "The boss always cooperates with the law. You know that. He's gonna make you pay for that whiskey."

"He's the one poured it out," Shanahan said sullenly.

"You want to try and collect it from him, do you?" the other bartender said. Then, "The Swede was in about an hour ago."

"I thought you didn't know him."

"I just remembered who he was."

The two men stared at each other.

"You see him," Conlon said, "ask him to stop over at my office."

"That I will, Marshal. That I will."

Conlon turned and walked out of the saloon, the drinkers making space for him.

Behind him, Shanahan said, "I ain't payin' for that bottle, McGinty. You just try'n make me 'n' see what happens."

55

MAE COULD SMELL the pipe smoke and tobacco smoke and hear the soft shadow voices of the people on the porch. Creak of swing, thrum of rocker back and forth, forth and back, Mr. Bridgerly telling his railroad stories again, cut off by a blizzard on a mountain pass he was tonight, and a baby being born in one of the back cars, and a poker game between Wild Bill and three of the Belizzi Brothers going on in another, and one engineer's hand so frozen he was thinking of cutting off two of his fingers, they was so frozen. "Now how was that for a predicament?" Mr. Bridgerly always liked to say, being he savvy storyteller he was. And like children, they'd always ask, "So then what happened, Mr. Bridgerly?" And he'd tell them, of course, with smooth practiced ease, having told the story many times before. But that was all right because he never had the same ending for any story; he changed it every time. But nobody minded. They weren't looking for truth; they were looking for entertainment, something to complete their sleepy after-dinner satisfaction.

Mae stood just inside the front door, listening to them. How content they sounded. How peaceful. Their heads would touch their pillows tonight, and they'd sleep like children. Wouldn't lie there dreaming of killing Billy, getting so agitated that sleep became impossible. She wanted to be one of them—my, oh my, did she—lulled on swing or rocker, just listening to old Mr. Bridgerly's gorgeous lies, a truly happy person.

Mae was here a lot of nights, listening this way, wanting to go out on the porch and join them. But somehow she could never quite make herself go out there. She wasn't one of them and never would be, much as she wished she was.

She turned away, then, and made her way through the house and to the back door.

Devil sat on the kitchen table, one of 1,736 places that he was not supposed to be in this house. Devil was an old tomcat, pure black, and he did what he damned well pleased. Mae thought he was funny. He had impish green eyes and a strange little expression that she swore was a wry smile. She was usually partial to dogs, but Devil had taken her heart and refused to give it back.

She went over and petted him. "Looks like tonight's the night, Devil. I don't think I should be petting you. You're supposed to be bad luck. I guess I won't be seeing you any more, Devil."

From behind her, a voice said, "Now, why won't you be seeing him any more, Mae?"

Mae turned her head. "Oh, I didn't know you were there, Mrs. Johansen."

"Just came to get more tea." She came into the kitchen, formidable as always. "Now why would you say a thing like that to Devil?"

"I was just making a joke," Mae said, thinking quickly.

"A joke?"

"I meant that if you saw him on the table, he wouldn't be around here much longer."

Mrs. Johansen smiled. "Did you hear that, Devil?"

Devil didn't look impressed.

"Now you get down, you bad cat."

Devil still didn't look impressed—it didn't help that Mrs. Johansen was talking to him in baby talk— and in fact looked directly up at her and yawned.

"Oh, you," Mrs. Johansen said, and picked him up and plopped him down on the floor. He landed on springy paws and then walked calmly away.

"Say, you look like you're ready to go out, Mae."

"I thought I'd go for a walk." She was glad she'd stuck the gun inside the magazine she was carrying.

"But you were feeling so bad a while ago."

"Still am, Mrs. Johansen. But I think some air will do me good."

"Mr. Bridgerly is going to tell us about the time he was captured by the Indians."

"I'll bet it's a good one."

"Personally, I prefer the story when he was captured by the Comanches. The one where he's captured by the Sioux isn't as good. The one with the Comanches, there's this beautiful Indian girl he falls in love with. She helps him escape, but then she's caught and put to death by the medicine man who secretly wants her for himself. But he's really angry and forgets how much he loves her and stabs her right in the heart."

"That's some story."

"I still like the sea monster one best of all."

"Mr. Bridgerly saw a sea monster?"

"Oh, my dear, not only *saw* a sea monster. But killed one."

"How do you kill a sea monster?"

"It wasn't easy, let me tell you. All he had was his pocket knife."

Mae smiled. The power of storytelling always amazed her. It was almost a religious experience, to be caught up in a make-believe story but to accept it completely out of sheer will and faith. Storytelling could wonderfully distract the mind and, in so doing, heal one's soul. To some, Mr. Bridgerly was a foolish old man. But to people like Mae and Mrs. Johansen and the other men on the porch, he was a shaman.

"Well, I'd better get going, Mrs. Johansen."

"You sure you feel all right to walk?"

"I'll be fine. Honest."

"And you're taking a magazine with you?"

Another deft lie: "Just returning it to Mrs. McCain is all. I'll walk right past there tonight."

"Just don't be gone too long."

Mae smiled. "No, Mom, I won't be."

Mrs. Johansen laughed. "I do sound like your mom sometimes, don't I?"

"Well, everybody needs a mom," Mae said, "and you make a good one."

She nodded good-bye to her landlady and set off.

56

DEPUTY LARRY GLENCOE had picked a bad night to strut around in the fancy new western shirt that had arrived in yesterday's mail from Denver.

Usually, Larry liked to swagger around town and

see how many comments a new shirt got before he made up his mind about it. The white shirt with the blue piping had gotten more than thirty compliments the first couple nights Larry had worn it. The saloon gals loved it. He'd gone upstairs with one of them and been careful to take off the shirt before he jumped into bed with her. His wife had a nose like a hound dog. She could smell poontang on him from three blocks away.

But there was a bad feeling tonight.

And in every saloon he stopped in for a free schooner of beer, his usual rounds for the evening, all he heard was angry talk about how Governor Adair should never have started this amnesty business.

And in every saloon he went, he could hear the anger the Swede had left in his wake. The Swede was good. He was like a Saturday night preacher. He could get all frenzied up, all bug-eyed and sweating, and so pissed off they couldn't quite control themselves any more. That damn Swede. Someday somebody was gonna bust that sonofabitch's head wide open with an ax and good riddance. Larry hated tension like this. People started shooting when they were in this kind of frenzy, and Larry sure hadn't signed on to get shot. The range war had skewed everything. Guy couldn't even strut around in a new shirt no more and get hisself some nice compliments. Larry, I swear, you get handsomer ever time I see you, one of the saloon gals had said to him the night he'd first worn the blue shirt with the white piping. The blue even cut down on his gut some, or at least it seemed to when he stood before the mirror and inspected himself.

But tonight—

They were out on the lamplit street in little knots of twos and threes. Usually, they'd be inside with the gals and the gambling and the alcohol. But tonight they were on the street glaring at Larry as he passed

by them. And there weren't any deferential words for
the chubby deputy, either. No, sir, not tonight. Tonight they looked at him not as the dopey but harmless nephew of the sheriff but as an extension of Lew
Adair himself.

Out on the streets in little knots of twos and threes.
This was how a mob often formed, slowly at first,
then faster as the drinks were thrown down faster and
the rage grew.

Larry wondered if Conlon knew about this.

He tugged up his pants, pressed a hand against his
gut, as if that might flatten it some, and continued to
walk down the middle of the street, well aware of the
men watching him with great scorn and malice.

Damned range war. A man could get hisself killed.
And who the hell wanted to do somethin' stupid like
that?

57

CONLON WAS READING the letter. That's how it was
in his mind: The Letter. He'd gotten maybe a hundred
letters in his lifetime, but this was like no other. This
was the first and only time his eldest daughter had
ever written him.

The letter was now three years old. He'd read it so
many times that the paper was wearing thin. Real nice
penmanship, a sweet girly penmanship, blue ink on
off-white paper.

Dear Dad,

I keep having dreams about you. Mom finally said it would be all right to write you. I'm twelve now. I'm not sure this letter will even reach you. I'm sending it to the U.S. Marshal's office in Washington, D.C. Mom said they'd know how to get it to you. Mom said she thinks you're out west. We read a lot about Indians. I have nightmares about Indians. So do a lot of kids in my school. Just so you know, my step-father treats me real, real well. He never hits me or anything. And when he yells at me some-times, he always apologizes. He's nice to mom, too. I have a picture of you. I sleep with it under my pillow. Mom says I was too young to re-member you but I think I can remember your voice. Sometimes in my dreams I hear your voice and I start crying. I don't know why. Mom is helping me write this letter and she says it's enough now. I guess I'd better go. I love you, Dad.

Love, Susan

He always cried.

It was a funny thing.

You'd think that after you'd read something so many times, it couldn't touch you any more.

But Susan's letter always touched him. Always.

He was just putting the letter away, just snuffling tears up into his nose, when the front door opened and Larry Glencoe came in.

Larry was wearing a new cowboy shirt. He mail-ordered them from Denver and looked stupid and fat and show-offy in them. One thing a good lawman did was stay quiet: quiet in voice, quiet in action, quiet in attire.

Larry looked like one of those gleaming trick-pistol artists that you see in a circus. He said, "They're gonna try and take him out of here."

"That's what I hear."

"I'd better go get my kin."

"What for?"

"What for? Hell, Marshal, there's gonna be a pack of wolves descendin' on this place tonight."

Conlon folded up Susan's letter and put it in his shirt pocket. "I'm giving them another half hour."

"For what?"

"To show up here."

"And then what?"

"Then I take my sawed-off shotgun and go talk to them."

"The Swede's behind this."

"I know he is."

"And the Swede works for Barcroft."

"I know that, too."

Larry shook his head. "My uncle, he had him a real good relationship with Barcroft."

"He had more than a 'good relationship,' Larry. He took his orders from him."

"I don't know why Barcroft'd turn on the sheriff's office now."

Conlon went over to the gun case, grabbed himself a box of ammunition, came back, and sat down. "Barcroft wants Billy dead because Billy killed some of Barcroft's men. A lot of townspeople want Billy dead because they hate gunnies and want to use him as an example. The man they call Jimmy from the Tunstall ranch wants him dead because Billy killed Jimmy's best friend. And a whole bunch of other people want Billy dead to piss off Governor Adair and show him what they think of his amnesty policy. So it isn't just Barcroft. It's the whole town."

"That's why we need my kin."

Conlon said, "No offense, Larry, but your kin'd be more trouble than they'd be worth."

"Meaning what, exactly?" Larry was getting mad.

"Meaning they're not professional lawmen."

"You mean they're stupid?"

"Nope. I just mean, they haven't been trained to handle situations like this."

"Trained? What the hell's 'trained' got to do with anything? What we need tonight is men who can shoot good."

Conlon opened the box of bullets and started filling his Colt. "I have to handle this my own way, Larry."

"Well, I'm sure as hell not gonna stay here and get my balls shot off with you."

"That's up to you, Larry."

"My cousin Mo, he's one of the best shots I've ever known."

"Does Mo happen to be sober tonight?"

"Well, he's sober by his lights."

"That isn't real reassuring."

"Well, there's Deke. He don't have no problem with the bottle."

"Deke's crazy, Larry. Didn't I hear that he used to strip naked and then run through town firing his guns?"

"He was just havin' a good time was all, Marshal. He just gets a little high-spirited once in a while."

Conlon said, "No, thanks, Larry."

"Well, there's Bob and Rick and—"

"No, thanks, Larry." He nodded to the door. "If you're going to leave, you'd better make it now. No telling when that mob's going to show up."

Larry looked disgusted. "Mr. High and Mighty. Mr. U.S. Marshal. Nobody in these parts is good enough for you." He smashed his hat to his head. "Well, I just want to see your face when they all show up tonight with torches and a hangin' rope, Marshal. I just want to see what you look like then."

And with that, Larry left.

Conlon stared at the door a minute, and then went back to getting his Colt good and ready.

58

IT WASN'T GOING to work. Not if she hoped to escape, anyway.

This afternoon, it had all looked neat and easy to Mae. The town would be pretty dark. Nobody would be idling around the jail. She could kill him quick and clean.

But she hadn't realized how bright it was around the jail. And how many people stumbled past on their way home. And just how loud a gunshot would be.

It wasn't going to work.

The night air was soft. It'd be a good night to go to bed early and yawn and stretch like a cat and sleep with a light blanket on.

She went over and sat on the front steps of the jail and watched up and down the street. There'd been rumors all day about a mob forming. The small groups of people she saw out in front of the saloons confirmed the rumor. She wondered what Conlon was doing. She knew he was inside. She felt sorry for him. A mob usually killed the peace officer first and then raided the jail. She should be here to help him.

But Billy had to come first. She had waited so long, so long.

The mob might deprive her of Billy, though. That was her main concern now. She didn't want the mob to have the honor. She didn't want to defend her father through the deeds of a lynch mob.

She was still thinking about how she could get to Billy when Larry Glencoe came up.

"He in there?"

"Conlon?" she said.

He nodded.

"Sonofabitch."

"What happened?"

"What happened? What the hell you think happened? I offered to gather up some of my kin so we could hold off the mob, and he all but told me he thought my kin was a bunch of monkeys."

"Larry," she said, "your kin *are* a bunch of monkeys. I mean, no offense."

He shook his head miserably. "I ain't sayin' they're the brightest folks in the world. Or the most responsible. Or even the cleanest, the way some of them smell. But they're better'n nothin' when a lynch mob's comin' at you."

"I guess I never thought of it that way. Better than nothin', I mean."

"He thinks his shit don't stink is his problem."

"He's a professional lawman, Larry. He knows how to handle things. He was a detective back in New York."

"Yeah, and he don't let you forget it, either."

She looked at him. Larry was a dope, but he was good hearted and could be reasonably competent at certain moments. "He'll need all the hands he can get tonight."

"You gonna help him?"

She lied. "Sure."

He sighed. "Guess I'd better help him, too, then."

"I'm sure he'll appreciate it."

"They can't help if they're stupid."

"Oh, Larry," she said. "I'm sorry."

"Or they smell bad sometimes."

"Now, that they can probably help."

"Huh?" Larry said.

"Not being bright isn't their fault. But being dirty is. They can always take baths."

"They say it gives 'em rashes."

"Rashes?"

"Yeah. That's what they say, anyway. They think it's the water that gives it to 'em."

She stood up and slid her arm through his and gave him a hug. Larry was stupid, but he was sweet-stupid, and that wasn't a bad thing to be at all.

"Let's go talk to Conlon," she said.

59

AS THE GROUPS of twos and threes collected into a larger group, it was obvious that Bob Wylie was going to be its leader. The Swede had already headed back to the Barcroft ranch. His work was finished here.

While Wylie was not the smooth and subtle rabble-rouser the Swede was, he had two things working in his favor. One being that Billy was genuinely hated in this town for murdering the sheriff, irrespective of the fact that the sheriff had killed some of Billy's friends in cold blood. Two being that at this time of

night, the mob was sufficiently liquored up to pretty
much act on its own.

Wylie thought he was going to get both the reward
and the reputation that accrued to Billy's killer. He
had no intention of seeing Billy hang. He was going
to manufacture a moment when it looked necessary
to cut Billy down with a gun. Wylie had contrived
such moments many times in the past. He just had to
keep an eye out.

The mob numbered thirty or so. A couple of men
had lighted torches. The torches looked dramatic as
hell, but they didn't add any more light than the lamps
were already spreading through the night.

The mob was already incoherent: voice piled on
voice in an ugly cacophony of curses, threats, and
enraged babble. Rifles, pistols, knives were waved in
the air. The mood was orgasmic, rushing to a climax.
Tears of ecstatic frenzy could be seen in the eyes of
some men; others laughed with glee; one man even
wet his pants. Could there be anything more plain fun
than lynching a man? There were decent men among
this number, of course, law-abiding, fair-minded,
even generous and compassionate men who truly believed that this was the only way they could handle
the situation with Billy. If they didn't make an example of Pecos for killing their sheriff, the town
would become overrun with gunnies, the irony being
that the crowd consisted of both Tunstall *and* Barcroft
supporters. This was lynching's dark little secret—
that it was sometimes done by honorable men for jus-
tifiable reasons. But far more often, as was the case
tonight, the mob was made up of drifters, gunnies,
drunks, and scared little men who wanted to feel
manly.

By this time, the mob was pulling people out of
their houses and sleeping rooms and saloons the way
a parade would have. Onlookers started lining the

streets, fascinated. There were even a few little kids. And lots of dogs and cats and pet pigs. And whores and all three of the town's preachers and the two little nuns who worked with the local Indians.

Hell, it *was* a parade of sorts, the way the men had started marching up the middle of the street, headed for the jail. So what there warn't no tubas? So what there warn't flags flapping in the breeze? So what there warn't no fancy marching uniforms like that day the past governor visited here? So what? If anything, it was *more* exciting than a parade. Do you get to see a showdown between a lawman and a mob in a parade? No. Do you get to see a prisoner being dragged out of the jail? No. Do you get to see a man get hanged from a tree and have his eyes all bulgy like a frog's and maybe even see him shit himself? Hell, no, you don't. Why, in fact, come to think about it, this was *much* better than a parade.

Much better.

60

"You hear 'em, Marshal?"

"I hear 'em, Larry."

"Sounds like a lot of them."

"Sure does."

"Comin' up the street now."

"Yep. Right up the street."

"To the jail."

"You don't have to stay, Larry. I appreciate you

comin' back. But you've got a family to think about."

"I just want you to think better of my kin is all, Marshal."

"I'll tell you what, Larry. After tonight, seeing that you came back and all, I'll think a whole lot better of your kin."

"You really will?"

"I really will. You didn't have to come back here tonight. But you did. That tells me something about the kind of people who raised you. The kind of kin you have."

"I appreciate that, Marshal. I truly do."

Conlon sat behind his desk, the sawed-off shotgun in his lap. "Where's Mae?"

"Fixin' up the back door. She said one of the locks needed to be screwed down tighter."

Conlon nodded. Mae was a fair handyman. She was a hell of a lot handier than Conlon, anyway. Every time he used a hammer and a nail, he walked around for days with a swollen purple thumb.

"God, listen to 'em, Marshal."

There was a hellish din in the streets now. The sound of hate and rage. Conlon's bowels turned cold and he swallowed hard. Even in New York, you had lynchings from time to time. They were scary as hell, especially if you were one of the few lawmen up against the mob.

61

BILLY HEARS THE mob, of course.

Kinda difficult to mistake it for anything else with all the shouting, cursing, and the slapping of feet on dusty streets.

By his estimation, they're one block away. Or so.

He's heard a lot of stories about lynchings. Never actually saw one, though.

A colored man in the next cell says, "I'm gettin' scared, Mr. Billy. You gettin' scared?"

"What the hell you think? 'Course I'm gettin' scared. Conlon! Conlon!"

He's been yelling off and on for the past five minutes. But no Conlon.

Billy has this terrifying thought: maybe Conlon's thrown in with the mob. He's heard of that. Lawman throwing in with the mob. Conlon doesn't like him, that's for sure. The cold way he looks at Billy. The cold way he speaks.

"They lynched my brother down in Georgia."

"Oh, great," Billy says. "That's just what I need to hear."

"They was gonna hang me, too, but then the sheriff, he stopped 'em. Tole them all I was a good boy. That it was my brother that was the bad nigger."

Billy lunges at the bars, trying to get to the colored man. They just brought him in this afternoon. Another vag colored man. "I don't want to hear no more! You understand that!"

The colored man, who looks old and whipped and

worn and sad as all hell, he says, "I'm confessin' to ya, Mr. Billy. In case they mean to hang me tonight, too. I ain't never confessed this to nobody and I gots to now. I gots to."

"What the hell you talkin' about?"

" 'Bout my brother, Mr. Billy. He wasn't the bad nigger. *I* was. I was the one broke into that house and killed that white woman."

But the mob is out front of the sheriff's office now, and the last thing on Billy's mind is some colored man's confession.

"Conlon! Conlon!" Billy screams, gripping the bars, literally trying to tear them apart. "Conlon! Conlon!"

62

CONLON SAID, "GUESS it's time."

"Yeah," Larry Glencoe said. "Guess it is."

He looked at Conlon and said, "I just want to see my wife and kids again is all."

"I really appreciate you doing this, Larry."

The first rock slammed into the front door. It sounded more stark and violent than a bullet would have.

Conlon hefted his sawed-off. "I'll go out and face them. You hang back by the door."

Larry nodded. "I actually learned some things workin' with you, Marshal. And I appreciate it."

Another rock against the door. The crowd, already

restless, working itself in the early stages of froth.

"Bastards," Larry said.

"Let's go."

It was like a couple of unknown actors walking out in front of the nastiest audience in the West. The torches could have been footlights.

Conlon stood on the boardwalk in front of the sheriff's office, looking out at the mob, mentally taking their count. Thirty-eight or so, from what he could see. Plenty of men to overrun himself and Larry.

Bob Wylie and Jimmy were right up front. Faces were painted gold from the torches; the air stank of the kerosene-soaked rags that kept the torches burning.

Conlon walked to the edge and said, "Clear them out, Wylie, or I'm going to run you in. He's my prisoner. I don't have any choice except to protect him."

"Meanin' what exactly?" Wylie said.

"Meaning that I don't necessarily like him any better than you do."

"Then let us have him," Jimmy said, in a gentler tone than that of Wylie. He sounded like a reasonable man, until you stopped to think what he was talking about.

Another crowd was forming now, the one behind the mob. The onlookers. It made Conlon sick to see that children were in that crowd. What the hell kind of parents would turn their kids out for something like this?

Conlon said, "I know what he did to your friend, Jimmy. And I appreciate the fact that you don't blame me for what happened. But this isn't the way to handle it."

"I told you he threw in with the Tunstall crowd," somebody in the mob said.

"Just turn him over, Marshal," Wylie said.

Conlon lowered his sawed-off right at Wylie's chest. "You'll die before anybody else does, Bob. You better keep that in mind."

"Yeah," Wylie said. "But you'll get it right after I do. Right, fellas?"

They voiced hearty assent. By this time, they were as eager to get their hands on Billy as Wylie was.

Larry Glencoe stepped forward, standing next to the marshal.

"Aw, Larry," somebody in the crowd said, "you're a goddamned joke and you know it. Why don't you go home and screw yer old lady'r somethin'?"

The crowd found this mighty humorous.

Larry lowered his Winchester. He covered Jimmy with it.

"Let's just see how serious you are, Marshal," Wylie said. "I'm gonna take a step forward, and let's see if you shoot me."

"I'll do more than shoot you," Conlon said, "I'll kill you."

"In cold blood?"

"In cold blood."

"Right in front of all these witnesses?"

"Right in front of all these witnesses. I've already warned you to break up and head back to your saloons. Now I'm warning you not to come any closer."

"But I'm *going* to come closer."

"Then you're going to die."

"Look how scared Larry is," somebody else said.

"You shit yer pants, did you, Larry?" somebody else said.

"Everybody move forward a step when I do," Wylie said.

A more ameliorative voice in the crowd said, "Just turn him over to us, Marshal. He's just gonna hang, anyway. Why should you and Larry here have to die for him?"

"Get ready," Wylie said. "We're all gonna take a step forward and see if the Marshal's got any real balls."

His bowels still felt cold; and if the light were better, they'd be able to see his hand trembling on the sawed-off.

"You men're going to be sober in the morning," Conlon said, "and then you'll have to face what you did."

The two things happened almost at once, the rock that hit Conlon on the right side of the face and the bullet that hit Larry in the forehead.

Just before the rock landed, Conlon had time to see a man two-down from Jimmy suddenly raise his pistol. Whether he meant to actually fire, it was hard to tell. The man next to him, apparently fearing that his friend really was going to fire, grabbed at his friend's gun hand. And the Colt went off.

It was then that Conlon was struck on the side of the head with the rock, a piece of native stone about the size of a softball. The impact blacked him out for a moment. He felt his eyes go blind, a terrible pain arc across the top of his skull, and a rush of cold air fill his nostrils. It had been a perfect throw, and he was paying the price.

But even more than his personal pain, he kept hearing that lone gunshot, the one that had taken Larry down, echoing and echoing in his ears. There were other sounds, of course, many other sounds—curses, more shouting, women screaming, a din of confusion and panic, two lawmen were down and this was suddenly a very terrifying evening—but somehow the only one with any gravity and substance was that lone gunshot.

And then he was crumpling to the walk. And there were shouts. And the flat slap of shoes running around the side of the jail. And all the time he was fighting the darkness that rushed at him. And all the time the mob was jumping over him, slamming back the front door and surging inside.

And then the darkness, complete now—the darkness . . .

He was sitting in his chair behind his desk. A woman he didn't recognize was gently daubing a wet cloth to the cut he'd suffered above his right ear. There was blood on the right shoulder of his shirt. It had also leaked into his ear. He pushed in the tip of his little finger and brought it back and looked at it. His head hurt, and the taste of blood was in his mouth and throat. Apparently, he'd bit in the inside of his mouth when he'd fallen over.

The woman said, "You got hit pretty hard."

He was up and out of the chair.

"Hey," she said. "Hey. You should stay sittin' down for a while."

He stalked to the front door and flung it wide open. The first thing he saw was the hearse. It was a fancy one, with glass sides. Two men were loading a blanket-draped form into the back of it.

Conlon started to step off the boardwalk but then had to grab on to a hitching post to stay upright. A wave of dizziness almost knocked him off his feet.

Jimmy came over and said, "You want me to help you back inside, Marshal?"

Conlon surprised everybody, especially himself, by finding the strength to raise his fist and plant it into the middle of Jimmy's hard-scrabble face. He wasn't finished, either. He drove a second punch deep into Jimmy's stomach. Jimmy gasped, turned to his right, and almost instantly started puking up all the beer he'd had in the last seven hours. As he doubled over to make vomiting easier, Conlon kicked him in the ass, sending him sprawling into the dirt, an arc of puke preceding his contact with the earth.

Conlon turned around, ready to start in on the other two. But he didn't recognize either of them. They were just two drifters who'd parked it here the past few weeks. Following the bank failures of the last two years, there were a lot of drifters in the West. They weren't necessarily bad people; just aimless, unemployed ones. "Where's the rest of the mob?"

"Some guys went after them."

"Who's 'them?' "

They looked at him as if he was joking. Then one of them said, "Say, that's right. You were out when it happened."

"When what happened?"

"When Wylie and Greaves ran around back and found out he was gone."

"Who was gone?"

"Billy, Marshal," the first man said. "Billy."

"How'd he get out?" Conlon said.

"Colored man told us the girl took him out of the cell at gunpoint," the second man said.

"The colored man still in there?" Conlon said.

"Far as I know."

Conlon went back inside. He had a dizzy spell just before he reached the interior door leading to the cells.

"You better rest, Marshal," the woman said.

"No time."

"That's a pretty deep gash."

He looked over at her. "I've had worse. But I appreciate your concern."

The colored man was there, all right. Larry had brought him in earlier for trying to sneak into the back of a café and steal food. He sat calmly on his cot and stared up at Conlon.

Conlon said, "Mae took him?"

"Yessir, if that's her name."

"She say anything about where they might be going?"

"Nope."

"She say anything at all?"

"Just that she'd kill him if he tried anything."

"How'd they'd get away?"

"Guess she had two horses out back waiting."

"Sonofabitch." All Conlon could think of was how she'd reacted to Billy any time Conlon made mention of him. Her anger. Conlon wondered what the hell was going on here. "Billy say anything?"

"He just looked grateful."

"Grateful? Why would he be grateful when somebody's got a gun on him?"

The colored man smiled. "Well, sir, I reckon I'd rather face a pretty girl with a gun than a lynch mob with a rope any day."

Conlon smiled. It hurt. He'd taken a serious chunk out of his inner cheek. "I guess I'd have to agree with you there, my friend."

Conlon held up the keys. Jangled them. "You go over to the livery."

"You lettin' me go, you mean?"

"Yep. You go over there and sleep the night and be out of this town by dawn. You understand?"

"Oh, I understand. I understand real good, Marshal."

The colored man grabbed his jacket and was out of the cell the moment Conlon opened the door.

Conlon dropped some coins into the man's hand. "Take this around to the back of that café you were sneaking into. There's enough here for a good meal."

"Yessir, and thank you."

Conlon nodded. The man beat his way out the back door.

Part Three

63

BY DAWN, SOMEBODY had turned up a Navajo man who'd done a lot of tracking in these parts for the Army. He agreed to try to find the tracks Mae and Billy had left.

Somebody else turned up a man who'd just come into town and said he'd seen two riders near his ranch just before sunup. Conlon took down the directions the man gave him.

All this time, a posse was being put together. A couple of the men in the mob had nerve enough to show up, still drunk and surly; at gunpoint, Conlon put them both in a cell.

Just as he was coming back out of the sheriff's office, a spare prairie woman, all angular jutting bones and crazed blue eyes, stepped out of nowhere and delivered unto Conlon a slap so hard it rocked him on his heels. The woman then stalked off.

"Larry Glencoe's mother," one of the posse men said. Twelve men and their horses lined the street outside the sheriff's office.

Conlon had guessed it was Larry's mother. A time like this, the loss still so raw, so utterly unbelievable, a lot of people needed somebody handy to blame. Conlon was the logical choice. He didn't blame the woman at all. And maybe it was his fault. Maybe if he'd brought in Larry's kin, maybe Larry wouldn't be dead now. He thought of all the mean things he'd said about Larry and felt like hell.

He said, "Everybody got his orders straight?"

The men nodded. These were older, gentler men than the saloon-types that had made up last night's mob. There were merchants here, and a minister, and a couple of farmers, and an Indian agent. They were good, sensible citizens intending to do a good, sensible job. They weren't out for glory or money. And they weren't out to kill anybody. Conlon had divided them into four groups, each of which would fan out from town in a different direction. He had also told them that he wanted both Mae and Billy returned alive if at all possible. He still didn't know what the hell Mae was doing, springing Billy at gunpoint that way.

Without any deputies for backup, Conlon had no choice but to stay in town. He believed that the men were responsible enough to be trusted. He made note of the time they left: 6:37 A.M.

64

FROM UNDER THE shadowy overhang of the livery down the street, Ronnie watched the posse leave. It was exciting to see all the men sliding their rifles into their rifle scabbards and all the animals fresh and ready to go. He wished he could be one of them. Being in a posse would be fun.

But not fun, he realized, if you had to pursue Mae. He loved Mae. She was his best friend.

Then Ronnie remembered why he was here. He was going to talk to the marshal, tell him what he'd

seen the other night at the Widow's house, tell him
that it wasn't Billy who'd killed the Widow at all.
He'd tried to write him a letter, figuring it'd be easier
than telling him in person—the marshal being a man
who scared the hell out of Ronnie, as did all people
who had authority over him—but he wasn't much of
a writer and gave up after several tries.

He was just about to start across the street to the
sheriff's office when he saw someone he recognized—
recognized all too well—suddenly appear and walk
into Conlon's office.

65

THERE WAS NO *good* time to see County Attorney Bill
Stockton. But an especially *bad* time was this early
in the morning, and on an empty stomach.

Stockton, not even completely inside the office yet,
said, "You let him escape!"

"That's just what I did, Stockton," Conlon said,
calmly seated behind his desk. "We rolled the dice to
see who got the jail keys, and I lost. So Billy just
rode on out of here."

"Why the hell would your deputy take him away?"

Conlon frowned. "I'd like to tell you that I think
she was afraid he'd be lynched. But to be honest, I'm
not sure why."

"Oh, great," Stockton said. You could see where
he'd cut himself shaving. And his usually neat attire
had been thrown on too hastily at this point, the cel-

luloid collar not quite flat on the left side of his neck, the cravat slightly askew, the vest not completely buttoned. "Just great!" He leaned across Conlon's desk so that their faces were only inches apart. "Do you know what John Barcroft's gonna do to me when he finds out Billy's gone?"

Conlon almost felt sorry for him. There'd been a few times in his life when Conlon had known boss-fear. When he'd had to creep around, trying not to be noticed; and having to live in ass-kissing dread every time he'd been in sight of the boss. It was a miserable, awful, degrading way to live.

"It isn't your fault," Conlon said.

"No. But he'll *make* it my fault."

Conlon sighed. "Yeah, I suppose he will."

Stockton paced. Then he went over and grabbed the coffee pot off the potbelly stove, only to find it was way too hot to touch without a cloth to protect his fingers. "Oh, shit!" he said, sucking on his hand, the heat-pain filling his eyes. He looked like a kid.

"I'm going to get him back," Conlon said.

"You didn't even go with the posse. How the hell you gonna get him back?"

"That's my business," Conlon said. "You worry about Barcroft." Then, "I hear you knew her."

"Knew who?"

But Conlon could see that Stockton knew damned well whom he was talking about. "The Widow."

"Of course, I knew her. Everybody in town knew her."

"That's not what I'm talking about, and you know it."

Stockton started to make fists of his small hands. "I don't know what you're suggesting here, Marshal, but I don't like it. Not at all."

Conlon got up from the desk and started around it. A man like Stockton could be intimidated easily once he lost authority. And the way he was fidgeting and backing toward the front door, Stockton was obviously nervous.

"She was a beautiful woman, Stockton."

"I'm a married man."

"She was still beautiful, Stockton. And married men get tempted all the time."

"I know there were rumors about us—"

Conlon matched Stockton step for step. He would back Stockton right up against the front door.

"Maybe you got jealous—"

"—no!"

"—or maybe you wanted it over with—"

"—no, dammit!"

"—or maybe she was going to tell people about you two . . ."

And that was when Conlon heard the gunshot. This early in the morning, there wasn't much competing noise, so the shot was not only loud, it was also startling, the way only a gunshot can be.

"What the hell was that?" Stockton said unnecessarily.

But Conlon was already pushing him out of the way and heading for the street.

There were more horses than people awake at this time of the morning. You could hear them in their livery stalls and in the rope corrals down behind the livery.

Then somebody was shouting, "Over here, Marshal! Over here! Somebody shot Ronnie Pritchett!"

66

RONNIE WAS PROPPED against a stucco wall in an alley filled with garbage. The early morning flies were already hard at work.

Ronnie's eyes were shut. He wasn't moving. The shot had entered his body just to the left of his heart. Blood seeped out of a dark hole in his shirt. You could still smell the gunpowder in the air.

Two men knelt next to him. One checked his pulse. The other talked to him. Uselessly.

Conlon had just reached them when he heard a voice behind him. "Better let me in there first, Marshal."

Young Doctor Talbot looked spry and awake. The only sign of sleepiness was some green nocturnal goop he had in the corners of his eyes. At least his nose wasn't running. He carried his Gladstone bag in his right hand and a Colt in his left. When he saw that the situation was in hand, he opened his Gladstone and dropped the gun inside. "Never know what you're going to run into."

Conlon and the other two men stood aside as Talbot went to work on Ronnie.

Talbot went over the various pulse points, opened Ronnie's left eye, and moved his face close to the wound for a better look. "He needs to be taken over to my office."

"He going to make it?" Conlon said.

"I don't know."

"Wonder what he was doing up so early?" Conlon

said. "I don't usually see him around until later in the day."

"He said your name, Marshal," one of the men said.

Conlon recognized the pair as workers at the wagon works. Good, dependable laborers. Plaid shirts, sleeves rolled up; corduroy pants.

"Yeah," said the second man, "he said he needed to talk to you."

"He didn't say anything else?"

The first man shook his head. "The blood was pretty bad by then. He drifted off."

"What were you two doing around here?"

"Shortcut. On our way to work."

Conlon figured out the path they'd take from their homes to the wagon works. This probably was a pretty convenient shortcut. "I don't s'pose you got a glimpse of the man who shot him?"

They both shook their heads.

"You hear anything?"

"Not really," said the first man.

"Except the gunshot," said the second.

"Oh, we heard the gunshot, all right, Marshal. We weren't very far away. That's how we got here so fast."

"We really do need to get him to my office," Doctor Talbot said, standing up again, brushing dust from his knees. "I need to get that bullet out of there as soon as possible."

"We can carry him over if we get goin'," said the first man.

"Otherwise, we'll be late, and Nevins, our boss, he's a grumpy sonofabitch."

"He always likes to dock ya," explained the first man. "And dock ya good. I guess he figures it'll impress the guy who owns the place."

"The prick," said the second man.

Conlon wasn't sure which was the prick, Nevins or

the man who owned the place. Right now, it didn't matter.

"I'm going to look around here," Conlon said.

The two men picked up Ronnie.

"Easy with him," Talbot said. "You don't want to make him worse."

"We should have a stretcher," the first man said.

"I would've brought one," Talbot said, "but I couldn't get it in my bag. Now, c'mon you two. Go easy with him."

Young Doctor Talbot clearly enjoyed giving orders. The problem was he had a sort of whiny voice, and the orders came out with a certain petulance.

After they were gone, Conlon spent twenty minutes looking around for anything the killer might have dropped. By now, there was a small, sleepy, yawning crowd in the street. Whenever somebody would come into the alley, Conlon would shoo them away, as if he were dealing with annoying little mutts.

He found nothing, not even a spent cartridge, not even a clear set of footprints. The problem was that there were too many footprints. This seemed to be a well-traveled alley for some reason.

When he left the alley, he saw that the crowd had just started to disperse. The menfolk all had jobs to get to soon enough; the womenfolk had homes to tend to. "Ronnie Pritchett was shot here this morning. Do any of you know anything about this?"

Quick, anxious glances at each other, and then the remaining crowd members also started to drift away.

Nobody knew anything. As usual.

67

JESUS WAS IRRITATED. That was in some of the small framed paintings. In others, he looked not just irritated but downright pissed off.

The way these cheap reproductions depicted Jesus told you a whole lot about the good Reverend Pritchett's view of Christianity. This wasn't Christ the gentle, tolerant, compassionate, *forgiving* man—be he simply man or son of God, it didn't matter—this was some mutant variation on the real Jesus, some dark, ominous, savage zealot who took pleasure in the pain and misery of mankind.

Conlon sat in Reverend Pritchett's small parlor. He'd come over to tell the Reverend that his son had been shot. The Reverend's only response had been, "Demons! I knew I should have beaten him last night! God has punished me now! He may take the life of my only son!"

And then he vanished into some other part of the house.

Conlon had been left on the doorstep. He'd invited himself inside, which is where he saw the parlor gallery of glowering Jesus paintings.

The Reverend suddenly appeared, smelling heavily of freshly imbibed whiskey.

"I'd best go see him." When he'd come to the door, the man had worn a plain shirt and trousers. Now he wore the black suit and collar of his calling.

"I wonder if I could see his room."

"He sleeps on the back porch most of the time."

"Then I'd like to see that."

"Why?"

The good Reverend did not intend to make this easy.

"Maybe I can learn something about who shot him."

"God's messenger."

"I see."

"Punishing me for being remiss."

"For not beating him?"

The good Reverend scowled. "I hear your skepticism and sarcasm, Marshal. Your law is secular and profane. The law I follow is divine. I wouldn't expect a man like you to understand it."

"I understand that whipping your son isn't anything to be proud of."

"Perhaps not according to your law, Marshal. But under my law—the one and only law that matters in the entire universe—it is something to take great pride in."

How do you argue with that? Conlon thought. Guy believes he's in direct contact with God. Anything you say, he says God told him you're full of shit. Makes for a short argument.

Conlon said, "I'd like to see his room."

"I would like to get to the doctor's office to see my son."

"You don't need to be here, Reverend. I won't steal anything. I promise."

"Maybe my son isn't the only one who needs a whipping, Marshal. You seem to have demons of your own."

"A lot of them, in fact, Reverend. But if you don't mind, I'll take care of them myself."

Pritchett said, "I'm not much enamored of that young doctor, either. I'm told he's not a church-goer."

"Reverend," Conlon said with astonishing patience, "you go see your son."

He took the man by the elbow, guided him to his own front door, and said, "I'll talk to you later."

The back porch contained a cot, a few yellowbacks, small toys running to Civil War soldiers and marbles, and a small photograph of a pleasant but somewhat sad prairie woman. She looked not only sad, Conlon thought, but weary, too. This had to be Ronnie's mother. The good Reverend could make anybody weary.

He found the three crumpled papers over in a corner where a black-and-white kitten was batting one of them around. She looked up at him with sweet curiosity and then pawed at him playfully when he started picking them up.

He lifted her up and touched her pink nose to his. He remembered his daughter doing this all the time with *her* kitten.

When he set her down, she sat next to his right boot and looked up at him with her fetching little face.

"Let's see what we have here," he said. The Reverend would probably think he was possessed, talking to a kitten like this. At least the kitten wasn't talking back. Then Conlon would *really* be in trouble.

He uncrumpled the first paper.

Deer marshul
I seen who kiled

That was all. He uncrumpled the second paper.

Deer marshule
I no people dont think Im smart

That was all. He uncrumpled the third paper.

**Deer marshule
I seen who killed the wido the other night**

Conlon took the papers, flattened them out as well as he could, and stuck them in his back pocket.

Over the next few minutes, he picked things up and looked under them: sheets, a pillow, a blanket, a book, an empty box, a shirt, and a stack of magazines. Nothing hidden beneath any of these things. He'd likely found all there was to find, and that was plenty.

He hurried out of the house and over to the doc's office where Ronnie was being kept.

68

MAE HAD BEEN here a few times before with Ronnie. He called it his favorite hiding place.

The small ranch house had been burned down in a battle with some Apaches long ago. The woman who'd survived had decided to live in town. Her husband and son dead, life out here would be too hard and too frightening.

Even the outbuildings had been burned down. The grounds looked like a graveyard of blackened wood and ash. In the silence of midmorning, a sharp whistling wind played like souls of ghostly children among the carnage.

On the way out here, Mae had hit Billy three times with the butt of her rifle. The last time, she'd hit him especially hard. He was at last docile.

She ground-tied her horse and grabbed the rope from her saddle. She let her Colt lead her to Billy.

"Don't hit me no more," Billy said.

"Just get down."

"I sure don't know what you got against me, lady."

"I said just get down." It was obvious from the way she bit her words off that being around him was a trial. She wanted to kill him on the spot. But no, killing him quick and easy would ruin the moment she'd waited so long to bring to reality. Her hatred was a hungry monster, true. But better to rend Billy's flesh a bit at a time and feed the monster. Better for her, anyway.

Billy slowly dismounted.

"Try it and I'll kill you here," she said.

He'd been obvious about it, the thought that had just come to him. He'd be halfway dismounted, and he'd swing his right foot around and catch her in her gun hand.

"You're good, lady." He smiled down at her. "And pretty, too. I sure wish I knew why you hated me so much."

She stepped back so that he couldn't catch her with a foot.

He hit the ground.

"Hands up."

"Aw, shit, lady, you know I ain't got no gun."

"Hands up and turn around."

"Where the hell we goin', anyway?"

But he didn't want her to club him again, so he turned around and faced the charred remains of the house.

"Walk straight ahead."

"To the house?"

"To the house."

"Lady, it's burned down."

"I know it's burned down. Now move."

He moved.

When they reached the house, she said, "Now go left."

"Left? To the barn?"

"Just go left and shut up."

"I got to pee."

"We'll worry about that later."

"I'll bet if you needed to pee, we'd take care of it right away."

She hit him across the back of the head with the barrel of her Colt.

"Aw, shit!" he cried. "I told you not to do that again!"

And holding on to the back of his head with both hands, he did a kind of jig in hopes of allaying some of the pain.

She shoved him to the left, and then he was walking again.

They reached the barn and she said, "Inside."

Not that there *was* an actual inside to the barn. It was mostly foundation and burned walls. There was no roof, no doors. Shiny black crows sat on the charred remains of wall and watched them. Humans were a rarity out here these days. They were fun to watch.

"Now where?"

"Just stay where you are. And keep your hands up."

"Lady, you know how tired your arms get holdin' 'em up like this?"

She walked over to the right side of the barn. The earthen floor was covered with rotted ancient hay. She kicked some of the hay aside and got down on her haunches. All the time, she kept her gun aimed steady and true at Billy's heart. The barn floor smelled of damp earth from recent rains.

She used her free hand to find the small square door. She opened it quickly.

Folks out here sometimes combined root cellars and places to hide from Indians.

There was a gravelike coldness and dankness wafting up from the dark cellar below.

"Get over here."

"There'll be snakes down there."

"So? A big gunnie like you afraid of snakes?"

"Lady, I have *nightmares* about snakes."

She stood up and walked over to him. She put the gun right in his face. "Well, you get your choice, then. You either go down in the root cellar with me. Or I kill you right here on the spot."

"You sure are a hard-ass, lady. Anybody ever tell you that before?"

She put the barrel to his forehead. "Which one you want, Billy? The gun or the cellar?"

He sighed. "I'm not kiddin' you about those snakes." Then, obviously realizing that she just might kill him, he said, "All right, all right. I'll take the cellar."

She marched him over there, sent him down the ladder into dank darkness.

Then she slammed the small door, whipped the handcuffs off her belt, and handcuffed the two parts of the door's hinges together so Billy couldn't get out.

He started screaming, "Lady, it's dark down here! And I can hear snakes! I can *hear* 'em I tell you!"

She went to hide the horses.

69

As he approached the doc's office, Conlon could hear the good Reverend thundering inside. Other people looked up, too, startled and then amused by the incantations issuing from the bitter lips of the man. He felt sorry for the man, couldn't help it. Yes, he was a hateful, spiteful man, but inside the hate and spite was terror. The universe was a cruel and haphazard place. The only way the Reverend could deal with it was by clinging to all his biblical rules and beliefs, half of which he misinterpreted anyway. That was the part of the man Conlon felt sorry for. The fear part. The caveman-cowering-in-the-night part. The other part Conlon despised. The good Reverend would have fit right in at the Salem witch trials. He would have gladly burned his neighbors at the stake.

When Conlon went inside, the exasperated young doc met him in the front part of the office and said, "That sonofabitch is driving me crazy. And he sure isn't helping his son, either."

"What's he yelling about?"

"Casting out demons."

"At least he isn't whipping him."

"You should see that poor bastard's back. The son, I mean. Somebody should take the good Reverend outside some night and set him on fire."

Conlon smiled. "That part of the Hippocratic oath?"

"Take a look at Ronnie's back sometime."

"Let's see if I can do anything," Conlon said. "Oh,

did you get the bullet out? I forgot to ask."

"All that ranting and raving going on, no wonder you forgot." The young doc sighed. "I got it. But he's still in a lot of trouble. Fifty-fifty at best."

"Can he talk?"

"He couldn't a while ago."

Conlon nodded.

He went to the back of the small house the doc lived in. There were three small rooms. Conlon took the one next to the examination room.

Ronnie lay in a hospital-style bed. Covers pulled up to his neck. The room was tiny and white. A glass-fronted cabinet was packed with small bottles of medicine. Ronnie was unmoving, his eyes closed.

The Reverend swayed back and forth as he cried out to the demons who wanted the eternal life of his son. He was a spectral-like figure in his black garb, the pale skin, the cheeks still bearing the scars of youthful acne, the hatchet nose and beady steel-gray eyes almost luminous in their lunacy, and all the while that voice, that maddening, keening, crazed voice shouting out demons only he could sense. Pitiable and yet spooky at the same time.

Conlon gently took his arm. "Reverend."

But the Reverend ripped his arm from Conlon's grasp and continued, "Be gone thou evil spirit, thou art devil! Thou art unclean and cannot stand innocent before the Lord! Forsake my son and let him rest in the purity of the Lord!"

"Reverend," Conlon said quietly, and again tried to take the man's arm and lead him out of the room.

But the Reverend wouldn't go. Once again, he slipped Conlon's grasp and began importuning Satan.

"Reverend," Conlon said again.

And saw that it was hopeless.

Up came the walnut handle of his Colt. He brought it crashing against the back of the Reverend's head.

The man fell backward into Conlon's arms.

Conlon understood the hypocrisy of this, of course. He wanted the Reverend to quit pestering his son so *Conlon* could pester his son.

He dragged the Reverend out of the room where the doc waited. "What should I do with him?"

"In here," the doc said.

70

JIMMY AND R. C. Greaves were in a saloon. Jimmy felt it was vaguely sinful to be getting a snootful this time of day. Something in his prairie boy Lutheranism recoiled at the sight of all these weaving, wobbling drunks laughing it up when most folks were putting in a hard day's work.

R. C. Greaves was not similarly affected. In fact, he wished the girls were working because he could really do with having some quick sex (that being the only kind of sex R. C. knew about), it having been at least two weeks since he'd enjoyed himself. But, with no sex available, at least not till later in the day, Greaves said, "I'll make that sonofabitch talk all right."

"The way I get it, he's not conscious."

"Oh, he'll be conscious all right, time I get done with him."

Jimmy was no intellectual, but he was smart enough to know that R. C. Greaves was one of those people who talk to impress himself. Maybe that was the way he worked his courage up. Or maybe that was how he got his ideas. He just talked and talked and talked and eventually, amid six or seven thousand *bad* ideas, a good one popped up. And R. C. was just as shocked and surprised as his listeners were.

The trouble was that R. C. hadn't yet spewed forth a good one. He'd concentrated on bragging, mostly.

"Maybe he don't know where they are, anyway," Jimmy said.

"Oh, he knows."

"Just 'cause he knows her—"

R. C. shook his head. "He's sweet on her."

"Now how you know that?"

"Hell, I know when somebody's sweet on somebody."

Jimmy almost smiled. R. C. claimed to be an expert on everything else, why not on romance?

"So, even if he is sweet on her, what's that prove?"

"Proves that he'd tell her things."

"Like what?"

"Like hiding places, Jimmy. Damn, you're slow sometimes. Man's got to spell everything out for you, don't he?"

Consider the source, as Jimmy's momma always said to him. There was no sense getting riled about R. C. treating him so arrogantly. He treated *everybody* arrogantly. If the president of the United States walked in here right now (which, Jimmy had to admit, was a real unlikely event), R. C.'d walk right up to him and start tellin' him how to run the country.

"I'll do what you say to, R. C. All I care about is killin' Billy."

"I tole ya. I'm gonna give you 15 percent for helpin' me."

Jimmy shook his head. "Don't want no money, R. C."

R. C. did not look displeased. "You're a loyal friend. I got to say that for ya."

"It's time *somebody* killed Billy."

"Past time." He drained his schooner. "Guess we should head on over there."

Jimmy almost repeated himself, almost said 'The man's unconscious, R. C.' But what was the point? R. C.'d just smirk and say 'You let ole R. C. handle it.'

R. C. said, "You leavin' that?"

"Yeah."

"Perfectly good beer?"

"I just don't feel right, you know, this time of day and all."

"What the hell you talkin' about?"

"A man shouldn't drink till after sundown."

R. C. frowned. "Now who told you that?"

"My daddy."

"Well, your daddy didn't know what the hell he was talkin' about," R. C. laughed. He grabbed the schooner and poured it down into his seemingly bottomless stomach.

When he set the schooner down, he patted his considerable belly and said, "You don't catch old R. C. Greaves wastin' no beer, my friend. No, sir, you sure don't."

It was pure pleasure hanging out with R. C., Jimmy thought. Just pure pleasure.

71

MAE CAME DOWN the ladder backwards, pulling the trap door shut over her head. She kept her Colt trained on Billy.

"See you found the matches and the lantern," she said.

He didn't say anything. Just stood in a corner of the dirt cellar, which was roughly six by five, glaring at her. The room smelled of the grave. Neither of them wanted to think of the implications of that.

"You see any snakes yet?" She sounded merry, as if this were a lark.

"Nice and cozy down here, isn't it?" she said, indicating the room. Canned goods were stacked against one wall, some medical supplies against another. There were also a couple of rifles. No ammunition.

"Just what the hell you tryin' to do to me, lady?"

She smiled. "Make you mad."

"Well, you're doin' a damn good job."

She climbed carefully down from the ladder and walked over to him. "You don't know who I am, do you?"

He stared at her. "I didn't get you pregnant or anything like that, did I?"

"No," she said, and for the first time her bitterness came through. "I wouldn't let a pig like you put a hand on me."

And then she slammed her gun across his mouth, ripping a corner of his lower lip. He cried out and clamped a hand over his mouth.

But she wasn't done. She backed up a few steps so she could get a clean lift and then brought the toe of her boot into direct contact with his groin.

He was crying full out by now. Like a little kid. The sound of it sickened her.

"Who the hell are you?" he moaned over and over.

She sat down Indian-legged on the floor so she could watch him suffer. She'd done a very good job on him.

"You ever seen anybody gun-shot?"

"Just tell me who you are, lady."

"Long, long time before they die."

"Please. Just tell me what I done."

"Some men go insane before they die, the pain's so bad."

"I'm sorry for whatever I done. I really am, lady. I really am."

"I heard of a man who clawed his own eyes out, he was hurtin' so bad."

"Just gimme a hint, lady. Just a hint about what I done." He was still clutching his groin. Blood percolated in his mouth from where her gun barrel had cut him.

She said, "That's what I'm gonna do to you."

He started crying again.

"Now, how would that look in one of those yellowbacks, Billy? You crying after you let a girl beat you up? I'll bet people wouldn't believe it? Billy Pecos getting beat up by a girl? No, that's impossible. That's what they'd say, Billy. That it was impossible. But we know better, don't we, Billy? We know better."

He was still crying. "Just tell me what I done."

"I'll make you a deal, Billy. Before I gut-shoot you, I promise to tell you what you did. How's that?"

"Oh, Lord, Lord. This ain't happenin'. It can't be happenin'."

"Oh, I think it's happening, Billy."

"Maybe you got the wrong man, lady. You ever think of that?"

"Oh, I don't have the wrong man, Billy. That I'm sure of. That I'm *very* sure of."

"I'm beggin' you, lady, please. Please don't hurt me no more. Please don't."

She smiled. "Now that's something else that should never be in the book. About you begging a girl for mercy. That'd *really* disappoint your readers, Billy. Crying's bad enough, but begging? Oh, Billy, they'd never believe it." Her smile was even cooler now. "You sure wouldn't want to let your readers down now, would you, Billy?"

He lunged for her. And that was when she shot him in the shoulder.

72

THE TEMPTATION WAS to shake him. Shake him so hard that he woke up.

But of course, he wasn't just sleeping. He was struggling to live.

Conlon stood next to Ronnie and looked down at the unconscious form. Broken nose, probably thanks to some long-ago demon dispersing by the Reverend. Pimple-crusted throat. Chunk taken out of the left ear lobe. More pimples, like a band, across the forehead. His great sorrow was that he'd always be a boy-man, neither quite one or the other. The funny thing was

how peaceful his face looked now. No demons shrieking in his ears. No old man screaming at him for his
innocent sins. No townsfolk snickers or clucks of pity.
Peace on the boy-man's face.

Maybe it would be better for him if he'd just die,
Conlon thought. Maybe after a life—even a short
life—like Ronnie's, death would be a fetching escape.

That was the human side of Conlon.

The lawman side thought just the opposite. Ronnie's got to live long enough so that he can help me
find Mae. I don't give a shit about Billy. It's Mae I'm
worried about. Maybe she thinks she can handle Billy,
but she's wrong. Billy's at his worst when he's
trapped. That kind of man always is.

Conlon reaches out his hand. Touches Ronnie's
shoulder. Damp beneath the faded cotton shirt the doc
put on him. All of a sudden, as if somebody had just
dumped a bucket of water on him, Ronnie is sweating. The fever must have broken. Bullet fever.

"Ronnie."

Conlon almost smiles. He's trying so hard to be
gentle and caring, his voice is barely a whisper.

"Ronnie."

There. Louder. Stronger.

"Ronnie."

Up another couple of notches.

And now the hand gives Ronnie's shoulder a few
jabs. "Ronnie."

The eyelids move. To say they flutter is to exag-
gerate. They stir—the act just before the flutter.

"Ronnie."

Loud voice. Another jab.

Ronnie says, "You're the best dog I ever had, Chip.
I don't know why you had to go and play on them
railroad tracks."

And then he's crying. Not hard. Just a few crystal tears streak his cheeks.

"Ronnie."

Conlon feels heartened at first. Ronnie must be waking up.

Then Ronnie talks to his mom. "I got you this cup for your birthday, Mom. And I painted your name on the side of it. Dad said I misspelled 'Gretta,' but that's all right, isn't it?"

Another jab at Ronnie's shoulder. Maybe a little harder than Conlon intends.

He knows he should be patient, knows he should be considerate of the fact that this poor kid here may be dying.

But there's Mae. And he's scared for her, terrified for her. And the only person who can help him is Ronnie.

The doc looks in the doorway. "How we doing? Did I hear him talking?"

Conlon nods. "Yeah. To his dog and his mom."

"That happens a lot. When people have been wounded like this. They talk to people in their past a lot."

"I'm not sure he's going to wake up."

"I told you, Marshal. It's a long shot."

Ronnie moans, and they both turn their attention to him quickly. Ronnie licks dry lips, moans again.

Conlon glances at the doc.

"Just normal pain, Marshal. Doesn't mean anything one way or the other."

Conlon looks back at Ronnie. "I sure wish he could help me."

"How about the Reverend?"

Conlon shrugs. "I doubt he knows anything."

"Worth a try, I'd think."

"He still here?"

"Sitting in the outer office."

Conlon takes his final look at Ronnie. It's like looking at a book written in a language you don't know.

"Guess I'll go talk to the Reverend."

73

FIVE MINUTES BEFORE Conlon went into the room where Ronnie lay, Jimmy and R. C. Greaves walked up the alley behind the doctor's office.

"You go up to the back window," R. C. said, "and tell me what you see."

"Why don't *you* go up to the window? I don't take orders from you."

"No, but I'm a better lookout than you. I've had a lot more practice."

Jimmy knew there was no use arguing with Greaves. Greaves always had an answer that seemed logical.

It seemed logical, for example, that a man who'd been a bounty hunter for so long *would* just naturally be a better lookout than an inexperienced man like Jimmy.

But then when you thought harder about it, Greaves's retort made no sense. Standin' in an alley, lookin' up and down to make sure nobody came along and saw what you were doin'. Now how tough could *that* be? What kind of experience did you need to do somethin' like *that*?

But there was no point arguing.

R. C. Greaves always won the argument, no matter
how he had to bend and twist and otherwise totally
destroy courtesy, fairness, and logic. Maybe bounty
hunters had a code, and maybe twisting other peoples'
word was a part of it. Maybe they had a secret hand-
shake, too, the way them Catholic fellers did back in
Ohio, the Knights of Columbus.

"All right," Jimmy said, "but you keep a good eye
out. And leave that bottle alone."

R. C. carried a pint of shine on his person at all
times. He was like an infant who had yet to be
weaned off his momma's teats. "You leave my
drinkin' for me to worry about."

"I don't want nobody to see me."

"Like I say, Jimmy, you just go up to the window,
and I'll take care of everything else."

So Jimmy went up to the window. Actually, there
were two windows, but one was completely covered
with a heavy curtain. No point of even *trying* to peek
in there.

The other window, though . . .

Jimmy didn't have to get very close to see what
was going on in there. In fact, he had to duck behind
an outhouse so he wouldn't be seen.

Ronnie lay in bed. Marshal Conlon stood over him,
jabbing his shoulder, trying to wake him up.

Jimmy thought, *He's got the same dad-burned idea
we do. He figures Ronnie knows where Mae took
Billy.*

Jimmy looked back at R. C. Greaves.

R. C. was just stuffing his pint back in his rear
pocket. Broad daylight. And he's supposed to be
standing watch. And he's tipping the bottle.

Jimmy wished for the hundredth time that he could
find and kill Billy all by himself. He had no time for
men like R. C. But R. C. was wily and R. C. was cunning, neither of which Jimmy could claim among his

virtues. And he knew it. So he had to rely on him.

The young doc came into the room now and talked with Conlon. Then Conlon left and the doc attended to Ronnie again. The doc was talking to Ronnie, but Ronnie wasn't talking back.

Jimmy felt sure that Conlon hadn't learned anything from Ronnie. Conlon had looked frustrated as he left the room. But one thing was for sure—Conlon and the doc had a much better chance of getting Ronnie to talk than Jimmy ever did.

And now he saw how they could handle things.

He went back to R. C.

"I seen you take that drink, R. C."

"Well, good for you."

"That ain't no way to stand watch."

"You a preacher man or somethin' now, Jimmy?"

Jimmy sighed. R. C. always knew what to say. If he couldn't cut you any other way, he'd cut you with scorn, as he just had with Jimmy. He was not only wily and cunning, he was also fast. Jimmy just hoped Greaves was as fast with his gun—he'd never actually seen R. C. shoot anything—as he was with his mouth.

"Conlon was in there."

"What about Ronnie?"

"Out. That's the thing. Conlon was trying to wake him up."

"He's figurin' the same thing we're figurin'. That Ronnie knows where Mae's hidin'."

Jimmy felt good that R. C. had come to the same conclusion. It made Jimmy feel smart.

"So all we have to do—"

"—is follow Conlon," R. C. said, "wherever he goes."

"That's right," Jimmy said, "wherever he goes."

74

CONLON WENT OUT to the front office and sat on a wooden chair next to the one the Reverend occupied. The Reverend had his hands folded in his lap and his eyes closed and he was whispering what sounded to be prayers. He looked like a scarecrow with a terrible complexion.

After a time, he opened his eyes and glared at Conlon. "You're not a prayerful man, Marshal?"

"Sometimes."

"I'm praying that the demons leave my son's body."

"I've already said some prayers for Ronnie."

"I appreciate that."

"There's something I need to know, Reverend."

"And that would be what, Marshal?"

"Does he have any special hiding places?"

"He's a grown man, Marshal."

"But there's a child side to him, Reverend."

"The demons."

"All right. The demons."

"They want to keep him boyish so that he can't grow up and spread the true word about God Almighty."

"I see."

"That's how they punish me. By keeping him young that way. If I didn't beat him, God only knows what sorry kind of human being he would be."

"I can see where you're doing him a real favor."

"You think your sarcasm escapes me, Marshal. But it doesn't."

Conlon sighed. "I apologize, Reverend. What I need to know is about any hiding place he might have. Please think hard. Please."

"I can't think of any because there isn't any. Not that I know of, Marshal."

The young doc was in the doorway. "You want to come here, Marshal."

Conlon was across the room in moments. "Is he awake?"

"He's starting to get there, I think."

They went through the back room into the examination room.

75

MAE SAID, "IT hurt, does it?"

"You bitch."

"I could've shot you in the crotch."

"Just kill me and get it over with."

"You're starting to cry again, Billy. It's pretty disgusting, let me tell you."

"WHO THE HELL ARE YOU?"

She said nothing. Just sat there. Watching him. His arm was bleeding more slowly than she would've thought. It was almost disappointing. In the stuttering lamplight, his face looked glazed. He looked scared and young and sort of stupid, actually. She could imagine him all raw-faced and scrappy in a New York street gang.

Except he wouldn't be crying the way he was now. He would've been too proud to cry back then. But that was a funny thing, the older you got, the less pride you had about certain things.

Mae said, "If you really want me to, I'll kill you now."

"You know I don't want to die."

"Oh, really? Didn't you just ask me to kill you a minute ago?"

"You really are a bitch. A *real* one."

"You're confusing me, Billy. One minute you want me to kill you, the next minute you *don't* want me to kill you. It gets confusing."

Pain seized him, his whole body jerking. He lay his head down, eyes wide open, sweat sliding off him, beyond even tears now. "Oh, God," he said, "oh, God."

"I'm going to make you a promise, Billy."

"Just shut up."

"I'm not going to tell anybody about you crying and all. I think that's pretty decent of me, don't you?"

He just moaned and rolled his head miserably from side to side.

"You hear what I said, Billy? Don't you think that's pretty decent of me?"

He said nothing.

She walked over and picked up the canteen she'd brought along. Took a drink.

"I'll bet you want a drink, don't you?"

"I ain't gonna give you the satisfaction of saying yes."

"Well, then your answer's no?"

He licked his lips. A fever was setting in fast. The gunshot.

"I'd sure like to give you a drink, Billy, but you just told me you didn't want one."

"You bitch."

"You've got to come up with some new words, Billy. You're wearing that one out. You want me to teach you a few new ones?"

He was back to saying nothing.

"You want me to teach you some new ones?" she said again. And then she gave him her coldest smile. She'd waited a long time for this.

76

"HI, INEZ," ELLIE Stockton said.

Inez Simmons looked up from the boot she'd been slathering with polish and nodded hello. She liked Ellie. The Stocktons were nice people, even though Bill Stockton's job as county attorney could well have made him stuck-up to the ordinary people of the town.

"How're the kids?" Inez said.

Ellie's sweet face didn't brighten the way it usually did when Inez brought up the subject of the children. "Oh, you know how kids can get. Kind of wear you down sometimes."

No, this wasn't like Ellie Stockton at all. Usually she spoke with great pride and delight about her children. Also, she usually looked better, too. Today she wore a faded gingham dress. Her hair wasn't shiny and nice, either. And her pretty little face was pale and tired.

"Are you as busy as usual?" Ellie said, keeping the conversation going.

Inez nodded to a long row of shoes and boots on a table behind her. "Getting pretty far behind, actually."

"Maybe I'll just wait, then."

Inez laughed. "Some people I put to the head of the line, Ellie. You know that. People as nice as you and your husband, I take care of right away. So what can I do for you today?"

"Really, I can wait, Inez."

She was holding something below the line of the counter. Inez couldn't see what it was.

"Now, quit being ridiculous and put it up here and let me help you with it, Ellie."

"Well," Ellie said, "all right."

She put the black riding boot in the center of the counter.

"That's a handsome boot," Inez said.

"Special order, all the way from Denver," Ellie said. "Bought it for my husband right after we moved here. Problem is, he doesn't wear them that often because the heel cap keeps falling off."

Inez had a terrible feeling as soon as Ellie mentioned the heel cap. She thought of the lawman who'd been in here. Conlon. And what he'd wanted to know.

"Most of the time when it falls off, he feels it," Ellie said. "So we just glue it back on and it's all right for a while. But this time he couldn't find it. Guess you'll have to put a new one on."

Inez picked it up and pretended to give it her professional scrutiny. But she wasn't seeing the heel at all. She was seeing Conlon standing in front of her, asking her to help him, even though she'd made it clear that her loyalty was to John Barcroft. And that she was glad Pecos was finally getting what was due him.

"Oh, this shouldn't take long to fix."

"He's got a long ride down-county day after to-morrow," Ellie said. "He'd like to wear these boots. Is that possible?"

Inez forced a smile. "More than possible, Ellie. I'll have these ready about the middle of tomorrow morning. How's that?"

"Oh, that'll be just great."

Inez, like most people in town, knew that there were two Ellies. There was the gentle, sweet girl who stood before her now. And there was the icy, bossy girl who treated her husband the way she would a bad dog. She was always ordering him around in public, always disapproving of things he said aloud, always criticizing the way he dressed, behaved, spoke. There were a lot of jokes about Ellie and Bill Stockton. Most of them cruel.

An old prospector came in. "You got them boots o'mine ready?"

"You lived alone too long up in the hills, Lem," Inez said. "Here I am talkin' to this nice lady and you come in and interrupt us."

"All I said was I wanted my boots," Lem said. His face was so leathery, he'd started to resemble some of the desert lizards he'd spent so much time with the last thirty years or so. "Didn't mean no offense, Inez."

"Well, then, you should just wait your turn."

"I have to go, anyway," Ellie said, obviously embarrassed by the turn the discussion had taken.

"About ten in the morning, Ellie," Inez said.

"I really appreciate it, Inez."

"My pleasure. And say hello to that husband of yours."

"I will, Inez. And thanks again."

"How about my boots now?" the lizard-man said. "I'm in kind've a hurry."

"So you can wash down some more beer, no

doubt," Inez said. Five, six times a year Lem came in
from the desert and got good and drunk. He stayed
for a week or so and then went back to the desert.

Inez lifted the boot Ellie'd left and looked at the
heel. No doubt about it. No doubt at all. This was the
boot Conlon had been looking for.

So Bill Stockton had killed the Widow Gaines, Inez
thought. And then she thought of pretty little Ellie
and the kids and how terrible it was going to be for
them if the truth ever became public.

She couldn't let that happen. For one thing, it'd
mean betraying her friend John Barcroft, who badly
wanted to see Billy Pecos hang. And for another, it
would destroy the lives of the Stockton children.

No, she couldn't let that happen at all.

77

RONNIE WAS SITTING up, all right. His eyes were
open, too. In fact, if you didn't look too closely, he
looked like a person well on his way to recovery.

"Shit," the young doc said.

"What?"

"I was wrong."

The doc preceded Conlon into the room. Conlon
didn't know what the doc was talking about. Ronnie
was sitting up, wasn't he? He looked alert, didn't he?

"I want out of here," Ronnie said.

And Conlon felt greatly heartened. He wanted out

of here already. That had to be a good sign, didn't it?

"Shit," the doc said again.

"What?"

"He's delirious."

"Meaning what?"

"Meaning he doesn't know what he's talking about. He's probably having some kind of dream or something."

"Then he couldn't understand me if I asked him some questions?"

"You can try. But I want him to lie back down first."

The young doc went over and took Ronnie gently by the shoulders and pressed him back down in bed.

Ronnie said, "I seen the dog eat your pie, Mom. *I* didn't eat it. Honest."

"Just take it easy, Ronnie."

Ronnie laughed. "You shoulda seen him, Mom. He had apple pie all over his face."

The doc got Ronnie lying down again. Ronnie gleamed with sweat. His eyes were huge, crazed.

The doc turned back to Conlon. "He's all yours, Marshal."

78

"How many men you think you killed?" Mae said. "All the newspapers say you killed a man for every year of your age."

"I ain't talkin' to you, lady."

"I bet it was more than that."

"Well, I'll tell you one thing, lady. Every man I killed, I killed clean. I didn't make him suffer and bleed to death."

"You ever killed a woman?"

"No," Billy said hotly, "I ain't ever killed a woman. What kind've man you think I am?"

"Scum is what I think you are."

"Well, now, isn't that nice? I'm lyin' here dyin' and you're still insultin' me. I'd make an exception in your case, you know that? You'd be the first woman I'd kill."

"I loved him."

Billy grimaced every half minute or so. The blood was now seeping through his shirt. There was a layer of grease beneath the blood, some kind of secretion. "Loved who?" he groaned. "Who you talkin' about, lady?"

"My dad."

"Sure, you loved your dad." Another grimace. "*Most* people love their dads. That don't mean nothin'."

"He worked so hard."

Billy wasn't paying much attention. The pain was becoming too much. He was starting to shift in and out of reality. He said, "Lady, just shut up. I'm sick of your voice."

But she was wounded just as much as Billy was. Only her wounds didn't show on the surface the way his did. "His company, they made him go to Texas to open up a new territory."

Billy said nothing.

"And one day the stage was robbed, and he was killed." Tears shook her voice.

She tilted her head back against the earthen wall. Closed her eyes. Imagined her daddy dressed up the way he always was on Sunday morning for church.

A stout, strong man. A man who took pride, though
not unduly so, in both his appearance and his speaking voice. He had a strong grip, too. He was always
playing a special game with Mae. If she could wriggle
her hand out of his, he'd give her a nickel. She'd
finally been able to pull herself free about two weeks
before he left for Texas, and died.

She was six and he was giving her a piggyback
ride. She was eight and standing next to him along
the riverbank, her very first fishing pole in her hands.
She was ten and he was giving her her very first own
saddle, no more hand-me-downs, her very own. She
was eleven and he took her along on a trip to Des
Moines. She was thirteen and he caught Richard Tyler
giving her a kiss just at dusky dinnertime one Indian
summer October night—and he wasn't mad at her or
anything, looked sort of amused in fact, though he
did tell her she should wait a few more years before
she tried anything like that. She was fourteen, and her
mother was dead of consumption, and after the funeral she heard him in the little bedroom, sobbing so
hard she thought he was going to vomit. And then
she was sixteen and waiting for him to get back from
that business trip to Texas. And then came the word
that he, too, was dead.

She said, "You remember a man named Harry Roberts?"

"Who?"

"Harry Roberts."

"Just leave me alone, lady."

But she couldn't leave him alone. Not now. The
rage was on her again.

She jumped up and hurried over to him and then
did something she wouldn't have thought herself capable of. She stepped down on his wounded shoulder.
Stepped down hard.

His cry filled the small cellar. And scared her. She wasn't sure she'd ever heard a human being make the sound Billy just had—part rage, part terror, part pain.

"You robbed a stagecoach," she said, after he went back to simple moaning. "Texas. And shot and killed a businessman."

"I never shot no businessman, lady."

She stood over him. "Several people say you did."

"Well, if I did," he said, "I didn't mean to."

Her boot toe found his ribs again. This time the sound he made was simple: misery. "Oh, God, lady. Oh, God."

"Harry Roberts was my father, and you killed him. And you don't even remember him, do you?"

He had taken to crying again. "I'm *tryin'* to remember him, lady. I'm *tryin'* but I hurt so much—"

She went over and sat down where she'd been and shook her head back and forth and said, to herself, "He doesn't even remember the people he killed. He's killed so many, he can't remember them all."

"Lady, I'm just sure I didn't kill your father. I'm just sure of it. I really am."

She put her face in her hands. There was something almost funny about it. Not being able to remember all the men you killed. There was a good one for you.

"Please don't gut-shoot me, lady. I'm beggin' you, lady. And I don't even care no more if people *know* I was beggin' you. Don't care at all. I just don't want you to gut-shoot me. I'm beggin' you not to."

Then, after a time of mutual silence, he said again, "I'm beggin' you."

She looked up finally and smiled at him. That really spooky, cold smile. "All right, then, Billy. I won't gut-shoot you. I'll put two bullets in your groin. How'd you like that?"

He said nothing. Just moaned with pain, moaned with fear.

"You hear me, Billy?" Mae said. "How'd you like that?"

79

CONLON LEFT THE doc's and walked back to his own office. The day was slipping away quickly. He wondered how the posses were doing. He wondered how Mae was doing. He wondered how he himself was doing. Mae just kept making him crazier.

The office was empty. It smelled of burned coffee grounds and old tobacco smoke. There were no messages on his desk.

He sat down and stuck his unlit pipe in his mouth. He had an infantile need for the thing. He put his boots up on the desk and leaned back in the wooden swivel chair with the nice cushion on the seat.

He started thinking about Mae again, and what he thought was awful. If Billy didn't somehow get hold of her gun and kill her with it, Conlon would have to arrest her next time he saw her.

The headache came on quickly. Worry headaches. Oh, it was great good fun being in love with Mae, it was. What was next, a good case of the trots?

It was a funny thing, when the door opened he knew, even without looking up, who was coming in. The smells. Leather wax and polish. Inez, the cobbler.

"You got a nice job here, Marshal," she said. "Feet

up on the desk. Pipe in your mouth. You better be careful, you might give yourself a heart attack working this hard."

"Barcroft tell you to say that, did he?"

"I don't take orders from Barcroft."

"That isn't the way you made it sound yesterday."

"You know what I ought to do?"

He probably did present a picture of sloth, he decided. Feet up and all. Taxpayers didn't like to think of their lawmen that way. Taxpayers liked to think of their lawmen working twenty-three hours a day. He took his legs down and sat up straight. "Now what ought you to do?"

"I ought to turn around and walk right back out that door."

"I upset you, did I?"

"I don't like you."

"Well, then we're even up, Inez, because I sure as hell don't like you, either."

"You stupid sonofabitch," she said, "now you'll never know why I came here, will you?"

She gave him no time to respond.

She was out the door, slamming it behind her.

He gave her thirty seconds. She took forty-five.

Then she came back through the door. "You want to hear this or not?"

"Sure, I want to hear it. But I don't want to get my head bitten off while you're telling me."

"You started it," she said.

"All right, let's just say I *did* start it. But I'm not starting anything now. I'm just waiting for you to talk."

"I know who killed the Widow Gaines. There, how do you like that?"

"My God. Are you sure?"

"She brought the boot in herself. The one with the heel cap missing."

"Who did?"

"Ellie Stockton."

Conlon got up from behind his desk and walked over for a closer look at Inez. She wore a man's denim shirt and butternuts. The shirt collar was sweated some and needed washing. Her big, capable hands were streaked with the stain of various polishes.

"You could at least say thanks, Marshal."

He sat on the edge of the desk and said, "I'm going to make you mad again."

"I come in and do you a nice turn and—"

"Did Barcroft put you up to this?"

"Barcroft? Barcroft doesn't have anything to do with this. Besides, Stockton's his own man."

"You want to get rid of somebody, that'd be a good way to do it. Implicate him in a murder."

She sighed. "You're about the dumbest bastard that ever passed through this town, you know that?"

"So Barcroft didn't put you up to this?"

"No, he didn't, Marshal." Patient. Calm.

He watched her face. It was Indian brown from the sun, prairie flat and hard, maybe a hint of Navajo around the eyes and cheeks.

"I believe you, I guess."

"Oh, thank you so much, Marshal. You don't know how good I feel, some dumb bastard like you believing me."

He laughed. "I guess I had that one coming. But you *are* going to be in trouble when Barcroft finds out that you came to me."

She shrugged. "I don't countenance murder, Marshal. Even if John Barcroft or one of his cronies might be involved."

He put out his hand. "Thanks, Inez."

She took it and they shook.

She said, "I guess you're not *the* dumbest bastard who ever came through town here."

"Oh. There've been a few dumber than me?"

She smiled. "One or two." Then, "I better get back to my shop. I'm way behind as usual."

When she reached the door, he said, "I really do appreciate this, Inez."

She looked back at him, nodded silently, and left.

80

"DOC?"

It was funny, the way he came to. Ronnie didn't know where he was, and it scared him. His first thought was that he'd died. He wasn't sure what death was exactly, but he knew that it was something dead. He'd see a possum or a coon run over by a stage-coach, and people would say it was dead. And he'd see people—like his Uncle Bill—laid inside a coffin, and people would say he was dead. Dead meant you didn't move. Dead meant you didn't speak when you were spoken to. Dead meant people stood over your body and cried, even grown men sometimes. It was his father who always spoke about what happened *after* you died. It seemed that just about everybody on this sad old earth was going to spend alleternity (his father always said it like it was one word, alle-ternity) being flogged, whipped, bit, kicked, burned, slapped, slugged, cut, punched, slammed, bammed, and otherwise tortured by all the demons you had not chased away in your temporal life up top the planet. Alleternity.

The first thing he thought of was, *maybe I'm down below in hell. Maybe the demons are right outside my door.*

But then he heard laughter from the street outside, and he heard the neigh of horses and the distant player piano of a saloon, and closer by he heard voices, human voices, and he looked down at his shoulder and saw the wound and said, "Doc! Doc!"

Because he knew now where he was. Because of the medicinal smell. He hated the doc's office. The docs always done things to hurt you. That was why God put them on this earth, it seemed. To hurt people like Ronnie.

Then the doc was there in the door. "By God, Ronnie. You're awake."

"I got sweat all over me, Doc."

"You cold?"

"Uh-huh."

"You need some dry clothes. Your fever must've broken. I'll get you some clothes and some blankets. How's that?"

"You gonna hurt me, Doc?"

The young doc smiled. "I sure hope not."

"You hurt me that one time."

"I just gave you salve for your ringworm, Ronnie."

"It hurt. It was like pourin' real hot water on my head."

"Well, I'll try not to hurt you this time, Ronnie. I promise. Now, you just lay there and have yourself some rest, and I'll be right back. I need to ask you some questions."

Ronnie said, "I'm not real smart, Doc. Sometimes, I have a real hard time with questions."

The doc smiled. "Oh, I think you'll be able to answer these questions all right, Ronnie. I really do."

Then he hurried off to get Ronnie some dry clothes and some heavy blankets.

81

GOVERNOR LEW ADAIR, a good Christian man, was devoutly pissed off. He'd been expecting an easy morning. Tidy up some official business and then get down to some writing. Some *real* writing. Maybe three, four uninterrupted hours.

But he'd had so many interruptions by this time that every noise in the house distracted him. If he heard footsteps, he assumed they were headed to his office. If he heard conversation, he assumed they were discussing something that would ultimately involve him. And if he heard nothing at all, he wondered if his staff was keeping things from him.

But Lew Adair was a dogged man. He started writing anyway, and two pages in, he decided that he was having a good day with his novel. The nicest thing of all was that he'd hit a stretch that didn't require any research at all. He'd described Roman Legion's uniforms earlier, just as he had their steeds and their weapons and the political infighting that went on among their ranks. So all he had to do was to write the scene—dialogue and action, no backstory about Imperial Rome, no laborious detail about the Christian underground. Dialogue and action. He wrote two pages in an hour, which was fast by his standards. Very fast. His fingers and wrist didn't even threaten writer's cramp. He was sailing, he was wailing, he was Lew Adair, author, instead of Lew Adair, governor. And it was great.

He was so lost in his work, he didn't hear the conversation at the end of the hall. Didn't hear the approaching footsteps. Didn't even hear the first two knocks on the door.

Dialogue and action. Lew Adair, author, was in a world of his own.

The fourth knock, which was accompanied with a loud theatrical cough, finally got his attention.

"Yes?"

Fava, his favorite of the servants, opened the door and said, "The Marshal man is here to see you."

"Conlon?"

She nodded.

Adair sighed. "All right. Send him in."

He was done. He had been at such a peak of invention—impossible now to recapture it. Maybe later tonight, after dinner with his wife.

Conlon came in quickly, Stetson in his hand, and said, "I'm sure you're busy, Governor. But I need to talk to you about something."

"Any word on Mae or Billy yet?"

"No, unfortunately."

"Then—"

"This is about Bill Stockton."

"Bill? You look upset."

"I am."

He explained the significance of the heel cap and how Ellie Stockton had brought the boot in this morning.

"That isn't exactly incontestable evidence, you know."

"No, it isn't. But I've asked around. There are a number of witnesses willing to testify to the fact that they've seen Bill Stockton at the widow's house late at night."

"I see." He felt real disappointment. Stockton and he were often ushers together at their church. Last Christmas, they'd both had solos at services. To think of him as a philanderer was bad enough, but as a killer . . .

"Somebody could always plant a boot like that," Adair said.

"A boot, yes. A heel cap, I don't think so. It's not something you'd think to do."

"I guess you're right."

He felt himself shrinking. He'd done this ever since the war. He'd have sudden memory flashes of battle, a boy with his nose and eye blown away, a sobbing corporal looking at the bloody stump where his hand had been, a major lying by the roadside, dead long enough for the birds and wild dogs to have had at him, and he'd shrink down inside himself, his earthly body nothing more than a shell in which he could hide. He felt that way now. Bill Stockton. A church-going man, a *family* man . . . and now this lurid, sordid mess of adultery and capital murder . . .

"And you propose to do what?"

"Arrest him."

"At his office?"

"He'll be getting home in an hour or so."

Adair nodded. "Better to do it there. Home, I mean." He made a face. "Of course, Ellie and the kids'll be there." He felt drained. "My Lord, I hope you're wrong about this, Conlon."

"I just thought I'd let you know before I did anything. I knew you were friendly with him."

"Would you mind if I sat in on the questioning?"

"Not at all."

"He might feel more comfortable if I was there."

"I'll let you know when I bring him in."

"Thank you."

Conlon looked as if he was about to leave, but then said, "I've been thinking about Mae."

"Oh?"

"What if she took Billy to prevent his being lynched?"

Adair smiled sadly. "You're sweet on her, aren't you, Conlon?"

"It's a possibility."

"You're afraid you'll have to arrest her and put her in jail." Adair didn't speak harshly. He spoke gently. "But if she took him to avoid lynching, why hasn't she brought him back?"

"Maybe he overpowered her."

Adair sat back in his tall, leather chair. "Love is the most beautiful and dangerous feeling the good Lord has given us, Conlon. You're about to arrest a man you believe betrayed his family and his principles for love. And yet you're going to betray your own principles when you finally catch up with Mae. You'e going to find some excuse to set her free."

"She *must* have a good reason."

"The law's the law, Conlon. Bill Stockton has to understand that. And so do you." He stared straight at Conlon. "Don't mean to be unkind, Conlon."

"No," Conlon said, "I know you don't."

And that was the end of their conversation.

82

BILLY SAID, "I'M losin' a lot of blood here, Mae. A lot of it."

"Yes," she said, "I know you are."

And smiled again.

83

STOCKTON WASN'T IN his office. His secretary explained that he had yet to come back from lunch. He usually, she said, took lunch at home.

Conlon rode out to the edge of town where the Stocktons lived in a two-story board-and-batten house that New Englanders called a hall-and-parlor house. Two little girls in crisp yellow dresses played in the large front yard. They weren't twins, but it was obvious, with matching yellow hair ribbons and all, that their mother was trying to give the impression that they just might be. The eastern magazines had been obsessed with twins lately, and apparently that obsession had found its way out here.

The girls didn't pay much attention to him when he opened the gate of the picket fence and walked up to the front door. They were playing with dolls. He could hardly compete against dolls. He was just a worn and dusty lawman.

Through the screen door, he could see that the interior of the house lay in cool shadow. He knocked. No response at first. He listened carefully. Somewhere deep inside he could hear the rumble of voices. He couldn't make out what they were saying. But they did not sound like happy voices.

"Are you looking for my mom?" the oldest girl said. Conlon guessed her age at five.

"Yes, honey. Is she home?"

The other girl, who looked to be four or so, said, "I think they're upstairs."

"Thanks, girls. I'll try again."

He'd turned around to talk to them. When he turned around to face the door again, Stockton was there. "What're you doing here, Conlon?"

"I need to talk to you."

"I need to get back to work."

"This is important, Stockton."

Stockton, three-piece-suited as usual, looked agitated, distracted. The mesh of the screen blanched him of the little color he usually had. He pushed the door open. "Come in."

New England was the motif inside as well, the furnishings running to heavy, dark pieces that had a feeling of permanence if not downright immortality. On their way to the rear of the house, they passed a parlor filled with bookcases, a piano, and paintings of the New England countryside. The other rooms he glimpsed contained a Boston rocker, a genuine Deacon's bench—the kind of things his mother had brought from her family home.

"This is making me sentimental," Conlon said.

"Oh?"

"All the New England things in here."

"Yes. My wife."

The kitchen was the most western room in the house, the cast-iron stove, outsize kettles, a single cupboard, and a small counter packed with items including a coffee grinder, a lard bucket, and a candle mold. The kitchen smelled of spices and freshly churned butter.

There was a small, unvarnished table and four chairs around it.

"I really am in a hurry," Stockton said, as they sat down.

As a former homicide detective, Conlon had learned the value of shock. He said, "I think there's a good chance you killed the Widow Gaines."

"My God," Stockton said, "what are you talking about?"

"I found a heel cap belonging to you at the Widow's house the night she was murdered."

"This is ridiculous."

"Your wife brought the boot to the cobbler's."

"That damned Inez. She's never liked me."

Stockton was babbling. People reacted to accusations in different ways. Some got defensive and gave you speeches about their sterling virtue. Some were outraged and pounded the table with thundering fists of denial. And some babbled. Sometimes, the defensive ones were telling the truth; they just weren't stating it too well, as yet. And a lot of times the thunderous deniers were telling the truth, too; you'd falsely accused them, and they were damned mad. But the babblers . . . in Conlon's experience, the babblers were guilty more often than not.

Stockton said, "I can't believe you're sitting in *my* own house making this kind of charge."

"You were there that night."

"No, I wasn't."

"You were there a lot of nights, in fact."

"I heard the gossip, too. But it was a damned lie. I barely knew the woman."

"But the other night, you obviously had some kind of argument. She ask you to leave your wife?"

"I want you to leave, Conlon. And right now." As if he could no longer endure any of this, Stockton rose and flung a theatrical arm in the direction of the front door. "Get out right now."

"Sit down, Stockton."

"Barcroft is right about you. You're nothing but a damned rabble-rouser. You want to get back at him, and you're using me to do it."

He was still on his feet, speaking with such passion that spittle streaked both sides of his petulant mouth, and his celluloid collar had begun to chafe his neck. You could see the red mark it made.

"I said sit down, Stockton. Or I'll take you to jail right now. Right in front of your children."

"I can't believe I'm being treated like this. I'm the goddamned county attorney. Or hadn't you noticed?"

But he sat down.

"I can't believe I'm being treated like this," he said again, this time to himself. But the fight was gone from him. He looked weary and confused. He put a small, pale hand on the table. It trembled faintly, not quite a twitch.

"This isn't pleasant for me, Stockton."

"Oh, yes. I imagine you really hate it."

"Why don't you tell me the truth and let's just get it over with."

"Over with for you, maybe. Not for me." He looked as if he'd soon start crying.

"How long were you seeing her?" Conlon said softly.

At first, Stockton didn't say anything. Then, "A little over a year." He looked up at Conlon. "She was a very nice woman. I'm sure you think she was a whore, but she wasn't. She was very intelligent and very refined."

"And lonely."

"Yes, lonely."

"And you were lonely, too."

Stockton looked surprised. "You're not being sarcastic?"

"No."

Another technique Conlon had learned. Befriend the man you're interrogating.

"I'm married. Why would you think I was lonely?"

"I was married once, too, Bill. I wasn't a very good husband. My wife always told me how lonely she was."

"My wife doesn't run around on me."

"No, but from what I'm told, you don't have a very pleasant relationship."

Stockton shook his head. "God, how people in this town love to gossip." He looked out the window. The sky was bright soft blue. He said, "Do you ever wish you were a little boy again?"

"Sometimes."

"I think about it all the time these days. I was one of those kids who just couldn't wait to get older. Do all the things I saw the older kids do. Get a job and smoke and drink and meet a woman." He sighed and drew his gaze back to Conlon. "I really would like to be a little boy again. And never change. Always stay that way. Have that innocence and that sense of fun. When you're a little kid like that, it doesn't take very much to make you happy. Even poor kids are happy. You just need a stick to pretend you have a gun, and you can daydream all the time about all the little girls you like and—" He paused. Cleared his throat. Looked directly at Conlon. "I didn't mean to kill her."

"I believe that."

"Something just . . . came over me. It was like I was somebody else watching myself do this terrible thing. I couldn't stop myself. I wanted to. There was a part of me—inside my head—that kept screaming to stop. But somehow I didn't until she was on the ground and I was standing over her and it was too late to bring her back."

"What did you argue about?" Conlon asked, not thoroughly convinced.

"She wanted to move back east. That's where she was from. New Hampshire. She wanted me to leave everything and move with her. I kept stalling. And then the other night, I had a little too much to drink and—"

"You're usually a better actor than that, dear."

Ellie Stockton stood in the kitchen doorway. In her yellow gingham dress, her hair up, her prettiness had a prim, troubled quality that Conlon found curiously erotic. It would be fun to see a woman like this let go sometime. "I don't know if you've ever seen him in court, Marshal. But he's very good. Particularly in his final arguments. He was first in his class in law school in final arguments."

"Barcroft wouldn't have wanted him if he wasn't good," Conlon said.

"Barcroft," she said. "Bill here thinks Barcroft is God."

"Why don't you go back upstairs?" Stockton said. "We're talking here."

Ellie looked at him with gentle brown eyes. The harshness Conlon associated with her—especially the way she henpecked her husband—was gone. There was a loving quality he hadn't ever seen before.

She paid no attention to her husband's words. Instead of leaving, she crossed to Stockton, stood behind him, and then leaned over and spread her arms over his shoulders. "I didn't think he loved me."

"I'm sure he does, Mrs. Stockton." Conlon wondered what this was all about.

"Please, Ellie," Stockton said. "Just go back upstairs."

She leaned down and kissed her husband on the ear. "I can't let you do it, Bill."

"The girls, Ellie," Stockton said, half-whispering, as if Conlon might not hear if he dropped his voice. "Think of the girls."

She started crying then, the tears soft as her eyes, soft as her wan smile. "Oh, God, Bill, none of this would've happened if I'd treated you better. It was just . . . I was so afraid that we'd be broke and poor again—"

Conlon said, gently, "I take it you killed the Widow, Mrs. Stockton?"

She didn't say anything, her throat was too full of tears to speak; she just nodded, just nodded, and didn't say anything at all.

Stockton was up from his chair and holding her, holding her with a love and passion and concern he hadn't felt for her in many long years.

"I'll just wait in the front room," Conlon said softly. "You come out when you're ready."

The moment he left the kitchen, she started sobbing, clinging to her weak husband for strength. But he couldn't afford to be weak any longer. Now the girls would be his responsibility.

84

"YOU DON'T LOOK very good, Marshal," the young doc said as he fell into step beside Conlon.

"Just had kind of a shock, I guess," Conlon said. While he was happy that the murder was solved, he wasn't happy with what he'd learned. A young mother like that, spending the rest of her life in prison. Not something Conlon wanted to contemplate for long, especially where the girls were concerned. He had doubts that Stockton could handle the responsibilities. His wife had done everything but spoonfeed him for the whole of their married life. Then she'd become more mother than wife, and a harsh mother at that, and Stockton strayed. Nothing new there. Conlon had handled two or three murders just like it back in his New York days. Still, he kept thinking of the little girls.

They walked the baking afternoon streets. In the shadows of buildings, you could see men sleeping. The horses that had come far looked worn and hot as their owners led them to water troughs. Even the approaching stage seemed to be traveling at a pathetic rate of speed, as if the wheels refused to turn any faster.

"She killed the Widow." He had to say it out loud. He wasn't sure why. Some kind of expiation.

"Who did?"

"Ellie Stockton."

"Oh, my Lord."

"Stockton wanted me to believe it was him."

"Then she knew about the Widow."

"She knew, and was tired of it. I'm sure she gave him several warnings."

"Those poor little girls."

"Yeah, that's what I was thinking."

"I don't know if he can take care of them."

"I don't, either."

"And Barcroft won't want him now."

"Oh?"

"Barcroft's in the middle of a range war. He won't want his handpicked county attorney distracted this way. His wife on trial, and him taking over the family. He'll find a new boy right away. You wait and see."

Then the doc said, "I came looking for you to tell you Ronnie woke up for a few minutes. You know where the old Flannery ranch is?"

"Not exactly. Heard a few people mention it is all."

The doc described where the ranch was. He also told Conlon the shortest way there. Then he said, "Ronnie said that there's a trap door in the barn. Some kind of root cellar down there. He said he took Mae down there sometimes. It's worth a look. You want to round up some men?"

They had reached the doc's office. "You really think it's worth riding out there?"

"Seemed to be the only place he could think of."

Conlon shrugged. "Well, I guess I better get at it."

"You taking some men?"

Conlon shook his head. "I appreciate you talking to Ronnie for me, Doc. But I don't have a lot of hope for this place. I don't want to waste a lot of men on a job like this. I'll wait till something comes up where I'll really need them."

The doc looked disappointed. Like a kid. "I just thought you'd want to know."

"I *do* want to know, Doc. And I appreciate it. I really do."

A baby could be heard crying inside. "Sounds like I've got a customer. I'd better get on inside."

"Thanks again, Doc."

"Yeah," the doc said. But the air of disappointment was plain on him. He'd been excited to tell Conlon what Ronnie said. And Conlon hadn't reciprocated by acting excited. You do a favor for somebody, you expect a little appreciation in return.

The doc went up the stairs. When he opened the front door, the baby's bawling got much louder on the hot, still afternoon.

85

R. C. GREAVES AND Jimmy had followed Conlon from the sheriff's office to Bill Stockton's place. Now they were following him back to the sheriff's office.

Greaves sipped on his pint bottle of rotgut. Couldn't keep it out of his hand for more than five, six minutes. Never took a lot. But enough. Jimmy had heard of cocaine addicts and opium addicts, and he suspected that this was what they were like. Just couldn't leave it alone, just couldn't get enough, needed to stay at a certain level of intoxication or whatever you called it. And would do *anything* necessary to stay there.

Jimmy was tired, and he really disliked R. C., and lying down on his cot in the bunkhouse sounded real good to him about now, reading a yellowback and drifting into sleep before dinner, and then the dinner bell and the smells of the good meal awaiting him . . . Maybe this was all crazy bullshit. Sure, Billy oughtn't to have done what he done to Sam's girl and all, but maybe Sam hadn't ought to've been with such a girl anyway. She wasn't, when you came right down to it, a very *nice* girl. Not a *truly* nice girl. She wasn't a whore, but she wasn't quite respectable, either. Not the way Jimmy's wife, God love her, had been respectable. So maybe he should give it up. Say *adios* to R. C. and head back to the ranch.

"Wonder what the hell he's up to now," said R. C. Greaves.

"Just going in his office is all."

"Wonder why."

Jimmy sighed, irritated all over again at the bounty hunter. "Because that's where he works, R. C. Why *wouldn't* he go to his office?"

"What the hell's eatin' you, Jimmy?"

"You and that pint bottle. That's one of the things, eatin' me, R. C."

"The bottle's my business."

"Maybe so. But that don't mean I have to like it."

"You're like draggin' a little kid along. Always complainin' about somethin'. We're gonna find Billy, Jimmy. And then we're gonna kill him and then we're gonna get the reward money."

They watched Conlon go inside the sheriff's office. The door closed.

"I'll go around back," R. C. Greaves said. "You stay here and watch the front door."

"I'd just as soon go around back," Jimmy said. "It's got more shade back there."

"I'll take care of the back," R. C. said. And to make sure there would be no further discussion, he broke into a trot, running into the alley that ran alongside the sheriff's office.

Sure would be nice to be back in that bunkhouse, Jimmy thought, and wondered why he'd ever joined up with R. C. in the first place. Sure would be nice to be back in that bunkhouse.

IT JUST DIDN'T feel right, Conlon thought, as he pointed his horse in the direction the doc had suggested. Conlon, like most trained law officers, believed in three things—God, country, and intuition, the last being a fancy word for hunch. And this hunch, the root cellar thing, just didn't feel right to Conlon. No offense, doc, but it sounds like you took the first answer he gave you. Maybe you could've pressed him a little harder, had him come up with a few more suggestions. That way, we'd have a fall-back position. That was a military term the captain at Conlon's precinct always used in the course of a murder investigation: Say he ain't the right fella, then what? What's our fall-back position? *Then* who do we go after?

He was riding out to nowhere in the baking sun at the close of a long and frustrating day, and he wasn't happy about it. He wished the doc had let *him* question Ronnie.

The root cellar. It just felt wrong.

R. C. GREAVES HAD seen it before.

A man got all het up to kill somebody, but then his fervor started to wear thin once the actual stalking started.

People thought tracking fugitives was so easy. That's because they read all those yellowbacks. In a yellowback, tracking a man warn't nothin' much at all. Even when he had a four-, five-day head start. The bounty hunter just got hisself a good horse and set off. And sure as hell, six, seven hours later he was havin' himself a regular merry old shoot-out with the fugitive. Nobody much liked bounty hunters, so the fugitive—who was frequently the hero of the novel— usually ended up killing the bounty man and then riding off into the sunset, on his way to defile the sweet trembling virgin who'd made several appearances earlier in the book.

The yellowbacks never told you about men like Jimmy.

They started getting a little scared—a shoot-out with Billy was likely to leave a few bodies for the carrion-eaters—and then they started getting a little bored. They'd spent most of the day hanging out waiting for Conlon to lead them to Billy. And it *was* boring. And it *was* dangerous when the confrontation finally came. But it was also, at least to R. C. Greaves, an enjoyable way to earn a living.

But Jimmy was starting to fade. Last couple hours, all he could talk about was how sweet the life was back in the bunkhouse, how layin' on his bed and readin' was such a great pleasure. This said to R. C. that Jimmy was just about done. This said to R. C. that Jimmy had had second thoughts about defending the death of his friend. This said to R. C. that Jimmy was just excess baggage now, and that in a shoot-out he might even be a hindrance.

They were on a winding, sandy trail that was little more than a path. The ground was rising as the sun was starting to move slowly downward. About a quarter mile ahead, R. C. could see Conlon. Neither Jimmy nor R. C. had any idea where Conlon was leading them.

R. C. said, "Sam was quite a guy."

"You didn't know him."

"No, but everything you told me about him—quite a guy."

"Yeah, I guess he was."

Oh, no doubt about it, Jimmy was having second thoughts now. His initial anger had carried him three, four days, but now it was depleted. He was probably even thinking that Sam might not have been all that special a guy, after all. Just one more silly cowpoke who trusted somebody he shouldn't have. Hell, maybe Jimmy was thinking that Sam's girl *wanted* Billy to screw her.

Jimmy had just rendered himself totally useless to R. C., and if there was one thing R. C. couldn't stand, it was uselessness.

"You're scared of him, ain't ya?" R. C. said.

"Of who?"

"Billy."

Jimmy hesitated. "Well . . . yeah."

"You didn't seem scared of him yesterday."

"I guess I was still pretty mad yesterday."

"And today?"

Jimmy hesitated again. "I guess I been thinkin' about Sam."

"Yeah?"

Jimmy shrugged. "I don't think he'd do this for me."

"No, huh?"

"Sam looked out for hisself, you come right down to it."

He wouldn't do this for me. Looked out for hisself.

Oh, yes, Jimmy had wavered and waned until he was completely useless to R. C. And there was another problem: even though Jimmy had been no real help to R. C., even though he pretty obviously wanted to give up now, when the reward money came in, there'd be ole Jimmy, putting his hand out for his half of the reward. Now was that fair? Was that just? Was that right? And of the three things R. C. Greaves was concerned about—being a good American; a more-than-dutiful Christian; and being fair, just, and right—the last was the most important.

He gave it a little longer, an eighth of a mile across some flat but rocky land, and then he let Jimmy pull a little bit ahead of him. A gun would make too much noise. Conlon'd hear it and get suspicious for sure. Maybe he'd even drop back to check it out.

So R. C. used a knife, and he drove it deep into Jimmy's back, just about mid-spine. Then, as Jimmy cried out and slumped in his saddle, R. C. grabbed him by the hair, jerked his head back, and drew the edge of the Bowie's blade straight across Jimmy's throat. The blood started slow but then increased quickly as Jimmy clamped his hands on the wound, his eyes stunned with disbelief and terror. The carrion-eaters would be having themselves a barn dance by nightfall.

R. C. gave Jimmy a slight push. Jimmy went over

backwards, colliding with the ground hard enough to raise some serious dust.

R. C. lifted Jimmy's Winchester from its scabbard— it was a nice one—and rode on after Conlon.

88

"YOU KNOW WHAT his favorite meal was?"

"Oh, lady, don't do this to me no more. Please don't."

"His favorite meal was beef stew."

"That's nice, lady. That's real nice. Beef stew."

"And you know what book he had me read to him over and over?"

"Aw, shit, lady, can't you stop now?"

"I asked you what book he had me read him over and over."

"I don't know, lady. I'm in so much pain, and I'm losin' so much blood, I can't tell up from down no more. I really can't, lady. I really can't."

"His favorite part is where Ivanhoe wins the girl at the end."

"That's nice. That's real nice. And meanwhile, lady, I'm bleeding to death over here."

"He was a real romantic. He was very courtly to my mother. Very courtly."

"Good. Good for him."

"He was also an usher at our little Lutheran church. And he was a member of the Odd Fellows Lodge.

And his biggest hope was to live long enough to see me give him a grandchild."

"Aw, lady, please. Please. No more of this, all right? I'm sure he was a nice man, lady. I mean, you've convinced me of that. And I'm purely sorry I shot him that day. I purely am. And if I'd've known all this stuff about him—how he used to sleep out in the barn with the yearlings when they were sick, and how he used to play the accordion and all that—I never woulda killed him, lady. I really wouldn'ta. And I wish there was some way I could make it up to you. But I can't. I'm real sorry, lady. But I can't."

"You don't give a damn about any of what I'm saying, do you?"

"Sure, I do. Absolutely, I do."

"He was just somebody else you killed. Just some hard-working middle-aged man. Just somebody in your way. What'd he do, refuse to give you his gold railroad watch? He won that as a prize at the Odd Fellows one night. It was his favorite possession. He was like a little kid about it. He used to set the watch on the kitchen table and just stare at it. Just sit there and stare at it. Used to make me laugh and feel so good inside, him that happy after my mom died and all. You took his watch, didn't you?"

"The pain's gettin' real bad again, lady. I think I'm gonna pass out again."

"You took his watch, didn't you?"

"Maybe. Maybe I did. Lady, that was a long time ago."

"I can still see him there at the kitchen table. He was just so happy."

She started crying then. All the time she was crying, she was reaching out to fill her slender right hand with her six-shooter.

"Aw, shit, lady," he said, seeing what was going to happen, knowing that she was actually going to do it, actually going to gut-shoot him and leave him to die, the way the Apaches did white men sometimes.

"Please, lady. Please."

She stood up and said, "He wouldn't've liked you, Billy. He would've seen you for what you are. He would've been afraid of you—he wasn't a particularly brave man—but he wouldn't have respected you or liked you. And you probably saw that in his face when you were robbing the stagecoach. You probably saw how little he thought of you and that's why you killed him. So you wouldn't have to see that face any more. Because his face would've told you just what a cowardly little punk you really are, Billy."

He couldn't stop looking at her. At her hand. And the gun in it. Her words had begun to run together. Always about her father. He could only dimly remember such a man, only dimly remember killing him. She'd even told him what the old bastard's favorite pudding had been. And about a pair of socks she'd bought him from the Sears catalog when she was only six. Trying to make him feel guilty about some old two-bit drummer he could hardly remember.

The thing was, she was going to gut-shoot him. He was trying hard to make his peace with the pain in his shoulder. But there was no way he could make his peace with being gut-shot. No way at all . . .

Then she was crossing the cellar.

Then she was standing over him . . .

89

THE RANCH CAME into view, house and barn skeletal charred remains. A family had lived here once, a family probably much like the one Conlon had left behind in New York. You could almost hear the children and the farm animals and see the warm and friendly light of the lanterns as night captured the day.

There was just wind now, and the dust the wind raised as it whistled in whipping circles around the farmhouse.

He dismounted and ground-tied his horse.

He didn't see any horses. But then, Mac would be smart enough to hide them.

He didn't hear any voices, either. But if Ronnie's tale about the root cellar was true, he wouldn't be *able* to hear voices.

He walked toward the barn, down a sloping hump of land. There would have been chickens here, and at least a couple dozen head of cattle. The wife would have tried to grow a garden, and the kids would've done the milking in the morning.

Quite a bit of the barn remained. The fire had mostly taken the sides of the barn. The front and back were largely intact, though a lot of the front had suffered large areas of char, like cancers on red wood.

He stood in the barn, listening. Just the wild wind again. The sun was losing some of its warmth. The birds flew in melancholy arcs against the air currents. The shadows were long inside the barn.

He looked around. For fifteen minutes he looked

around and didn't find a damned thing. The young doc had meant well, but Conlon had been suspicious right off. Ronnie was not what you'd call a reliable witness. He needed to be questioned and re-questioned before you'd even *consider* believing what he said. The doc had taken Ronnie's first word. Burned-down ranch. The root cellar.

Well, here was the burned-down ranch, and there was no root cellar. All he could find were remnants of the ranch that had once been. A harness hanging from a nail. A horse stall, a Navajo blanket spread out in the corner, rodent turds brown and hard as rocks covering it. Pitchfork and till and saddle.

Nothing useful to him.

He was ready to head back to town when he heard it. At first, he wasn't even sure what it was. A range animal, maybe. But close by. The wind whipped most of the substance of the sound away.

He listened for the sound to be repeated. But just silence. Wind and silence.

He was just turning to go when he heard it again. Oddly, the sound was fainter but clearer as to its source. Not a range animal. A human animal.

The root cellar.

The sound had come from the right. He walked over and began searching this section of earthen floor.

He found it easily this time. He'd been looking for a clearly marked square in the dust. But tumbleweed and dirt had covered up the shape of the trap door, and he'd missed it.

He haunched down, found a dirt-buried ring.

He pulled up.

The gunshot was crisp and clean, forcing him to throw himself to the left of the trap door.

"You got to help me, Marshal! She's gonna kill me!"

Billy.

"Just go back to town, Marshal," Mae shouted up from the root cellar. "This isn't your business. It's mine, mine and Billy's. We'll handle this in our own way."

"You're wrong about that, Miss," said a voice behind Conlon. Conlon had been so busy with Mae and Billy that he hadn't heard R. C. Greaves sneak up behind him.

Greaves said, "Drop your gun, Marshal."

Conlon started to roll over on his backside, to squeeze off a few rounds and surprise Greaves. But Greaves was a pro and knew just how to handle it. He fired two quick shots to the left of Conlon, in the direction Conlon was rolling. The bullets thwanged off the rocky ground and filled Conlon's face with bitter dust.

"Now toss your gun over there on the ground, Marshal." R. C. Greaves smiled. "You just be a good little boy."

Greaves kept his eyes fixed on Conlon as he went over and kicked Conlon's gun even further away. Then he bent slightly so he could yell down into the root cellar.

"I'm afraid there's been a slight change in plans, Miss," Greaves said. "If you don't bring Billy up, I'm gonna be forced to kill the marshal here. And I'm only gonna give you five minutes to think it over. Then I shoot your friend."

R. C. Greaves looked down at Conlon and smiled with his black teeth. "Nothing personal, you understand, Marshal."

90

GOVERNOR LEW ADAIR said, "And you think that's where he went?"

"I assume so," the doc said. "I told him what Ronnie said—about the root cellar and all—and he rode out of town right away. I think he was going to check out some other places, too."

"I see."

"I'm not sure he put much stock in it."

"Oh?"

"Ronnie's a little slow, I guess you'd say."

"Nothing to be ashamed of," Adair said. "We've got a couple of 'slow' people in my family. They can be very useful citizens. I think we pamper them too much."

The man had just made the young doc very happy. "I used to get into arguments about that in medical school. I had a cousin who was a couple years older than me, and he was slow and everybody treated him like a little child."

Governor Adair was used to ending discussions by simply turning toward the door he'd come in through. He did that now.

The doc trailed him to the door, still talking. "I gave my cousin his head, and he was able to play baseball and climb trees and he even helped me paint my bicycle, too. And he did a darned good job."

"So who's running the sheriff's office?" Adair said.

The doc looked as if somebody had stabbed him in the chest. Here he'd assumed that Adair, even though he was walking toward the door, had been listening. But now it was clear he was not.

"I guess I don't know," the doc said.

"We'll have to beef this office up when Conlon leaves."

"Yessir."

"A sheriff and two deputies."

"Yessir."

"Maybe *three* deputies."

"Yessir."

"This is getting to be a big town."

"Yessir," the doc said, though coming from the East as he did, Furner still wasn't much more than a wide mud hole to him.

And then they heard the chanting.

Adair drew back the curtain on the glass inset of the doctor's front door and gaped out.

"Damn," Adair said.

"What is it, sir?"

"Oh, those ninnies and their placards."

"The anti-amnesty people, sir?"

Adair nodded and made a sour face. "Everywhere I go, they're there waiting for me. I thought maybe my luck had changed today. I didn't see any of them around. I figured they didn't know I was in town. But I guess they have their own ways of finding me, don't they?"

"Yessir. Apparently, they do."

Adair shrugged. "If I can get through that crowd out there, I'm going to ride out to that ranch and see if I can give Conlon a hand."

"I'm sure he'd appreciate that, sir."

There was something so professorial about Lew Adair that it was easy to forget that he'd been a man of action and a war hero in his younger days.

Adair said, "Wish me luck."

He stepped outside. The air was several degrees

cooler now. The rich colors of New Mexico were growing somber now as the day faded and died. He should be home working on his novel or simply enjoying the day. He should not have to be facing a crowd of zealots like these.

There were maybe fifteen of them, and they formed a tight semicircle around the front of the doc's house. There were a few more women than men. They were all dressed respectably, and most of them carried placards that read NO AMNESTY.

"Good afternoon, my friends," Adair said, remaining on the top step. "My day wouldn't be complete without seeing you people." He smiled. "I'm even starting to *enjoy* our little meetings."

"No amnesty for killers!" one of the bonneted women shouted.

He started down the steps. He wanted to get to Conlon, to help him. He had to move fast.

The crowd didn't move. He didn't want to force his way through them. He stopped just before reaching them. "I hope you're not going to be foolish enough to block my way. That could land you in jail."

"No amnesty for killers!" This time, it was a man who shouted.

Adair looked at each face, one by one. "The federal government asked me to stop this range war out here. And that means sending the gunnies back to where they came from—anywhere but here in Furner Township, or even New Mexico, for that matter. Let some other place worry about them. But how can I get rid of them if I don't give them amnesty!"

"Kill 'em!" another man shouted.

The crowd rumbled agreement. Kill them.

Adair checked out the faces again. "You know, that'd be a pretty dumb thing to do. Because if I kill one gunnie, then his friend is going to want revenge.

And if I kill his friend, then a new friend'll come along. And the range war'll never end."

"Billy don't deserve no amnesty," a woman said. "Not after all the people he's killed. Especially the widow."

The governor gave them the news about Ellie Stockton being the real killer.

"But I'm beginning to think you're right," Adair said to the crowd. "I'm not going to give Billy amnesty. He's killed way too many people for that."

They didn't know how to react at first. They looked at each other, and then they looked at Lew Adair.

And while they were looking and absorbing the information he'd just given them, he eased through the middle of the crowd and headed to the hitching rail where his pinto was tied.

91

MAE KNEW SHE had no choice.

R. C. Greaves would kill Conlon if she didn't hand Billy over to him. No doubt about it.

Billy was shaking his head and smiling bitterly. "I got me some choice, don't I? Either you gut-shoot me and leave me here to die, or R. C. executes me soon as I get up top."

"Maybe that's how some of your victims felt, Billy," she said "Trapped like that."

"You don't give up, do you?"

"You killed my father."

"Oh, God, I wish I could take it back, lady. I really do."

"I wish you could take it back, too." Tears tugged at her voice. "There's nothing I'd rather do than sit down across a table from my father right now."

"You gonna hand me over to R. C.?"

She shrugged. "What choice do I have? I care about Conlon. And Greaves'll kill him for sure."

"He'll kill me, too."

She stared at Billy. "There's something between you two, isn't there? You and Greaves?"

"Why you say that?" But he looked away from her, and there was deceit in the tone of his voice.

"You ever tell the truth, Billy?"

"Please don't send me up there, lady. He'll kill me for sure."

She walked over to where he was slumped against the wall. Blood had soaked and leaked down the entire front of his shirt by this time. In the jumping light of the lantern, he looked sallow and tired. Blood loss, she figured.

"Get up."

"I can't."

"Sure you can."

"You're a hard one, lady."

Seeing he had no choice, he sighed. He put out an arm and hand to use as a lever. He then began the laborious and painful business of getting to his feet. He'd make a little progress and then slump back down. Little progress, slump back down.

"Help me," he said.

"My father didn't have any help."

"God, I wish you'd forget about that, lady. It's over and done with."

"Not with me, it isn't. Now move."

He started in again. This time, he was able to rise to his feet. It wasn't pretty, but it was successful.

Once he was on his feet, he wove left and right violently. He put a steadying hand on the earthen wall. He looked as if he might crash to the floor at any moment.

"Now walk over there and start climbing that ladder."

"Lady, I plumb don't think I've got the strength."

"You've got the strength. Move."

He looked at her. "It was all gonna be so easy. The Governor, he was gonna grant me amnesty, and I was gonna move to Missouri and be a farmer and start my whole life over again."

"Too bad the people you killed can't start *their* lives over again."

He started to say something but then stopped. What was the use? She hated him so much; she didn't even hear what he said. The funny thing was—and Lord, she'd never understand this—he hadn't had anything personal against her father. That was the hardest thing to explain to people. That it wasn't anything personal. It wasn't because Billy considered the person bad or hateful or anything like that. It was just because, for one reason or another, the person had to die. More often than not it was simply because the person was in the way somehow. Would run for help and bring the law too quick. Or somehow got a clean glimpse of Billy and would testify against him later. Or wouldn't hand over something Billy wanted. Truth was, Billy couldn't even *remember* her father. That's how impersonal it had been. If Billy had hated him or something, he would have remembered him for sure. He always remembered the ones he hated. Always.

Billy started up the ladder. He had two good legs and one good arm. The other arm sent out shocking pain every few moments, sometimes so shocking that he thought he'd black out.

He got three rungs up the ladder and stopped.

"I don't think I can make it."

"You can make it."

"R. C.'s gonna kill me soon as I get up top."

"If you don't keep going, I'll kill you right here."

He started to climb again and then stopped. "I ain't bad like they say, lady. They say I'm this cold-blooded killer and everything. But inside, I ain't like that at all. I mean, I think about it a lot. I really do. And I know I ain't like that inside. I even pray, lady. I get right down on my knees and pray. I really do."

"Get moving, Billy."

"I just want you to know that. It's *important* for you to know that, lady."

"Move."

"You try to be nice and look what you get."

She waved her gun at him.

"That was really the truth, lady. It really was. About how I feel inside."

He looked down at her over his shoulder. He looked young and weak and stupid. He started moving.

She supposed it *was* tough for him. Pulling himself up the ladder, wounded and all. But she didn't give a damn, of course. He deserved pain, and she was happy to give him some.

A couple of times he made whimpering sounds as he completed his climb. He started to say something once and then stopped himself. His words were lost on her.

92

"I SHOULD SHOOT the sumbitch right off," R. C. Greaves said.

"You always make your bounty hunting this personal?" Conlon said.

Greaves smirked. "Oh, it's personal, all right, Billy and me. Real personal."

"He kill somebody you know?"

"You just never mind what he done. You just never mind at all."

The day was fading fast. The mountains were losing detail, and the sky was becoming turquoise. You could hear dusk in the horses, too. Conlon fancied *he* could, anyway. He'd always thought, ever since fleeing here from the East, that a horse sounded different after sundown. He'd expressed this a few times to cowboys. The polite ones only stared at him; the rude ones laughed. Them damned easterners. They was a hoot.

Billy said, as he climbed unseen up the ladder, "He's gonna kill me, Conlon. He's gonna kill me soon as he sees me. He thinks I still got the money."

"What's he talking about?" Conlon said. "What money?"

R. C. Greaves said, "Since I'm the one holdin' the gun on you, I'll be the one askin' the questions."

Billy said, "Conlon, you got to help me. I'm caught betwixt and between. The lady down in the cellar, she wants to kill me, and now R. C. wants to kill me. You got to help me. You're sworn to; you're the law."

"There's nothin' I can do, Billy."

"Oh, isn't that just great?" Billy said miserably. "A badge-wearin' lawman and he tells me there's nothin' he can do."

"You tell me where the money is, Billy, and I promise you I won't kill you."

There was just the wind for a time; that lonely eternal wind that ran down the sky and stirred up the desert floor.

"Billy," R. C. Greaves said. "You heard what I said?"

"I heard." Then, "I'm comin' up, R. C. You gonna shoot me?"

"You tell that gal down there I want her up here, too. And if she tries anything funny, I kill Conlon here right on the spot."

Billy shouted down the cellar. "You hear that, lady?"

"I heard."

"He ain't kiddin', lady. He'll kill Conlon for sure." Then, "You never answered my question, R. C. I asked if you were gonna shoot me?"

"I guess there's only one way to find out, Billy."

"You sonofabitch."

"Get up here, Billy. And right now."

They saw Billy's hand first, wrapped around the top ladder rung. It looked small and pale, almost childlike. Then the top of Billy's head, mussed blond hair. Then Billy's face, his expression almost comical, all big-eyed like a blackfaced minstrel on a showboat stage.

"Don't shoot me, R. C.," Billy said. "Don't shoot me."

"Where's the gal?"

Billy glanced back down the ladder. "She blew out the lamp. I can't see her."

"I'm on my way up," Mae said.

Billy climbed higher on the ladder. "I'm gonna need help, R. C. My shoulder's real bad."

Greaves pushed Conlon toward the ladder. "Help him up."

Conlon didn't like being pushed. He'd been a man of authority most of his adult life, first a cop and then a U.S. Marshal. If there was pushing to be done, he was the one to do it. This was difficult for his ego to accept. Some sagebrush greaseball sonofabitch like R. C. Greaves pushing him around.

"Don't push me," he said over his shoulder.

Greaves laughed. "Ain't showin' you the proper respect, is that it, lawman?"

"Just don't push me. You understand?"

"Just help him up, Marshal. Like a good boy."

Conlon's face felt seared with anger. The punk in him came up. He wanted to turn around and run back to R. C. and push his smirking ugly face in.

He walked to the ladder. Like a good boy. Got down on his haunches. Shoved an arm under Billy's good arm and pulled upward. He didn't even try to be gentle. Billy groaned. He also smelled. Sweating out poisons was a smelly process. Billy's shirt was soaked with sweat. The blood had started to dry. Billy groaned as Conlon started to haul him up. Conlon looked down into the cellar. Nothing. Darkness. No sign of Mae. It was stupid, how he ached to see her. Positively *ached*.

Billy did a kind of folk dance. Got his feet on the ground and then started doing this wide, wild dance step. He looked crazed or drunk or both.

"What the hell's wrong with him?" R. C. said.

"Fever," Conlon said. "Fever dance. Fever dreams."

"He looks crazy."

Conlon went over and grabbed Billy, who was now arcing down like some vast mountain bird riding the winds, and put a stop to the performance. "Stay here, Billy."

"She shot me, Marshal."

Conlon laughed. "You got a line of shit a mile long, Billy. And the worst thing is, you believe it yourself. Nothin' personal." He shook his head.

"I got my gun on Billy," R. C. said. "You go get the gal. She's up to somethin'."

Conlon went back over to the trap door and haunched down again. "Mae."

Nothing.

"Mae."

Nothing.

R. C. was right. She *was* up to something.

"You listen to me, little gal. I'm gonna shoot your friend here in ten seconds if you don't come up. And I'm startin' to count right now."

He counted backwards, loudly.

When he got to five, he said, "You think I'm shittin' you, Mae? You think I won't kill him?"

Then he said, "Four, three, two—"

"I'm coming up," Mae said from the darkness below.

She came up squinting. The last of daylight was sufficient to partially blind her for the moment.

Conlon helped her up. When he touched her, he felt dizzy. Good dizzy. He loved her. He didn't know how the hell such a thing could ever have happened to him, but it had. And even though R. C. had the gun and was likely going to kill all three of them right on the spot—use Billy's gun to kill Conlon and Mae, and his own gun to kill Billy—Conlon was temporarily ecstatic. Mae was here.

"Good thing you came up," R. C. said.

She stood next to Conlon. She glanced up at him only once. She knew what was going to happen, too. R. C.'d get the reward for Billy, and he could kill off the two witnesses and blame Billy for it. That R. C. Greaves was a mastermind, all right.

Billy stood a little ways from them. He was trying to stand up straight. He wasn't doing so good. He said, "He's gonna kill us."

"We know," Mae said.

"He thinks I've got the bank money."

"Well, if you don't got the bank money," R. C. said, "then I bet you know where it is."

"Me and R. C. and another fella robbed us a bank about a year ago," Billy said. He was shellacked with sweat. His fever had broken. He didn't sound or act delirious now. He just sounded weak, even near collapse. "R. C. shot him in the back. Said that way we only had to split it two ways. But I'd already hid the money. If I didn't, R. C. would have backshot me, too. Then I knocked R. C. out and took off."

"And I been chasin' him ever since." Then, "Where's the money, Billy?"

"I give it to Tunstall."

"Sure you did."

"I did," Billy said. "Fightin' Barcroft cost him a lot of money. He was runnin' low. I give him the bank money."

He was telling the truth. Conlon was sure of it.

"He was the most decent man I ever knowed," Billy said. "He took me serious. He was gonna help me finish my eighth grade test and everything. Once the war with Barcroft died down and all. And he was gonna show me how to dress proper and act proper and all that so I could get me a good wife for when I headed to Missouri to set up a farm."

Conlon watched R. C.'s face. R. C. was also coming to the reluctant—and angry—conclusion that Billy was indeed telling the truth.

"My money," R. C. said.

"Our money," Billy said.

"You didn't have no call to give him my money."

"Our money," Billy said.

And that's when R. C. raised his Winchester higher and sighted down it so he'd hit Billy right in the heart.

"You sonofabitch," R. C. said. Then, "You two get away from him."

"There's no need to kill him," Conlon said. "You'll get your reward money just by bringing him to Texas."

"He thinks he's such a big man," R. C. said. "All the time I knew him. Always struttin' around. Actin' like he could do anything he wanted." His eyes were whiskey mad. There was anger in his voice, too, but also a curious sorrow. Knowing Billy didn't sound like much fun.

"Put the gun down," Conlon said. "There's no reason to shoot any of us."

"Stand aside, like I said, Conlon, or I'll kill you and the girl right now."

Billy was having trouble standing. His knees were sagging, and every few seconds he'd weave sharply forward and then catch himself from falling face down.

Conlon and Mae moved a few feet away from Billy.

"You just gonna let him kill me?" Billy said.

"Not much they can do about it," Greaves said.

He got close enough to Billy to hit him hard in the ribs with the butt of his Winchester. Billy folded, collapsed to the ground.

Greaves said, "I'm sick of you, Billy. All the time pushin' me around, givin' me orders."

He lifted a dusty boot and stepped right on Billy's shoulder wound. Billy cried out.

"Oh, God," Mae said.

Conlon looked at her.

"I was no better than him," Mae said.

But Greaves not only stepped on him—he kicked him hard in the leg and then brought the butt of his repeater down against Billy's ear. The ear began to bleed. Greaves lifted a boot and was about to stomp on Billy's face.

"Stop!" Mae said. And she lunged at Greaves.

Greaves swung around, holding the rifle on her. "By the looks of things, you worked him over pretty good yourself. What're you bitchin' about?"

Conlon took Mae by the arm and tugged her back, away from Greaves. He could see that Mae was seeing herself in Greaves—and Greaves wasn't anybody you wanted to be like. "Like I told you one time, Mae. Revenge is never pretty."

"I guess I never knew what you meant, Conlon."

This time, when Greaves raised his foot, he kicked Billy in the ribs. Billy moaned, rolled from side to side.

"I guess it's my turn," Conlon said. And he started forward.

But Greaves spun around and said, "You two stay right where you're at. Soon as I kill Billy here, I'm gonna start in on you two."

Greaves turned back to his business. He pressed the barrel of his Winchester into Billy's left eye. It's gonna make a big hole, Billy."

"Please don't kill me, R. C." Billy, weak from his wound and all his pain, could barely speak. "Please don't."

"Sure are a lot of people who'd like to be in my place right now, Billy, all the people you pushed around and cheated and bullied and lied to."

"Please, R. C. I'll help you rob another bank and I'll let you keep it all. I promise I will. I promise."

Conlon was so caught up watching Greaves that he didn't see Mae take the Colt from where she'd stuck it in the back of her jeans. But then there it was, aimed directly at Greaves. She said, "Throw your Winchester over here, R. C."

Greaves didn't know what she was talking about, obviously. He was the one with the gun. Why should she be giving orders? But then he glanced over his shoulder and saw where she was aiming the Colt. "Shit."

Greaves's repeater was still jammed against Billy's eye. "All I need to do is pull the trigger."

"That's all I need to do, too, R. C. He'll be dead but so will you."

"I thought you hated him so much."

"I do—but I'm going to turn him over to the law."

"You won't have the same satisfaction."

"Maybe not. But I saw you kicking him." She shook her head. "I don't want to be the same kind of animal you two are."

"Listen to her, R. C.," Billy said, even weaker now. "Listen to her. Please."

"All the shit he done to people," Greaves said.

"I know that," Mae said. "But the law's the one to deal with him. Not us."

Greaves looked down at Billy. "You ever think she'd be stickin' up for you this way? Kinda strange, don't you think?" He made a sour face. "But I guess maybe she's right. Maybe the law's the best way to handle things."

He waited only a moment. It was plain to see that he thought he'd taken her in with his conciliatory talk. Set her off guard.

He crouched and feinted to the left and raised his Winchester and squeezed off two quick shots.

But she'd been expecting it—R. C. being one hell of a bad actor—and her bullets were there first, three of them in the chest. Enough to lift him several inches off the ground and slam him into the jagged, charred remnants of the wall behind him.

No dying declarations from R. C. Greaves. He crossed over quickly.

Billy was crying. The sound irritated Conlon. A punk who inflicted all the pain on people that Billy had—all his misery was of his own making.

Mae walked over to Billy. Stood above him. "Maybe I should've killed you and done us both a favor."

"I got to see a doc," Billy said. "God, I got to."

She looked down at him. "You killed a good man, Billy. My father was a decent soul. He really was."

She turned to search for Conlon. He was outside the burned frame of the barn. A lone rider was approaching.

Billy went back to his blubbering.

Mae went to stand next to Conlon. The wind was cool and felt good. "Who is it?"

"Maybe Adair. You all right?"

"I guess. Sort of, anyway."

"Wish you'd killed him?"

"Every time I look him right in the face, I do. He's pretty disgusting. Especially when he cries the way he is now." Then, "Adair'll want you to arrest me."

"I suppose."

"I broke the law."

"Yeah, you did."

He angled himself toward her and took her by the shoulders. "I can't stop thinking about you, Mae."

She waited before she spoke. "This kind of thing scares the hell out of me, Conlon."

"What kind of thing are we talking about."

"You know."

"Yeah, I know. But I want to hear you say it."

"Oh, hell, Conlon. Don't do this."

"It'll be good for you to say it out loud. Then it won't scare you so much."

"Oh, it'll still scare me."

"Say it anyway."

She sighed. "That I love you?"

"Yeah. That you love me."

She was just about to say something—maybe even what Conlon wanted her to—when the rider shouted, "Conlon! It's me, Adair!"

Conlon and Mae stood next to each other watching him ground-tie his horse and then walk over to them. He smelled of sweat and heat and dust. But he still looked proper in his suit and expensive white Stetson.

"Where's Billy?" he said.

"In the barn there," Conlon said. "He's wounded pretty bad. We had to kill R. C. Greaves."

"That's not exactly a loss."

He nodded to Mae. "You just made things worse, young lady."

Conlon had already thought through an argument. "If she hadn't abducted him, the mob would probably have lynched him."

"She took him to kill him," Adair said. "And you've got to arrest her. I'm sorry, but if you don't obey the law, who will? I'm sorry, young woman."

93

THEN HE WALKED away, upslope into the barn.

Soon enough, they could hear him talking to Billy.

"In some ways, I think he's as taken in by Billy as the yellowback writers," Conlon said.

"I think so, too." Then, "You have to arrest me, Conlon."

"No, I don't."

"It's your job."

Adair came back. "We have to get him to a doc right away."

"That's up to you, Governor," Conlon said.

"What're you talking about?"

Conlon had already slipped his badge off his shirt. He handed it to Lew Adair. "Here. You take it."

Adair smiled. "Is this so you don't have to arrest Mae?"

"I suppose it could be."

"She really should be charged. You know that."

Conlon shrugged. "A lot of people should be charged with a lot of things."

"So if I said that you *didn't* have to arrest Mae—"

"—or ever charge her—"

" or ever charge her "

94

FIVE MINUTES LATER, Billy slumped against Adair's back atop the big pinto Adair was riding; the three of them left the burned-out farmhouse.

By the time they reached town, a light rain had begun to fall. But Conlon hardly noticed; hardly noticed at all.

No one knows the American West better.

JACK BALLAS

❏ *THE HARD LAND*   0-425-15519-6/$4.99

❏ *BANDIDO CABALLERO*

0-425-15956-6/$5.99

❏ *GRANGER'S CLAIM*

0-425-16453-5/$5.99

The Old West in all its raw glory.

PENGUIN PUTNAM INC.
Online

Your Internet gateway to a virtual environment with
hundreds of entertaining and enlightening books from
Penguin Putnam Inc.

*While you're there, get the latest buzz on
the best authors and books around—*

Tom Clancy, Patricia Cornwell, W.E.B. Griffin,
Nora Roberts, William Gibson, Robin Cook,
Brian Jacques, Catherine Coulter, Stephen King,
Jacquelyn Mitchard, and many more!

Penguin Putnam Online is located at
http://www.penguinputnam.com

PENGUIN PUTNAM NEWS

Every month you'll get an inside look at our upcoming
books and new features on our site. This is an ongoing
effort to provide you with the most up-to-date
information about our books and authors.

Subscribe to Penguin Putnam News at
http://www.penguinputnam.com/ClubPPI